T0286838

The Jewel
& the Ember

Forget not to be bountiful,
One toward another.
Surely God sees the things you do.

—Qur'an, Surah II

Three things I marvel at,
four I cannot fathom:
the way of an eagle in the sky,
the way of a snake on a rock,
the way of a ship in the heart of the sea,
the way of a man with a woman.

—Proverbs 30:18-19

With a sweet string at hand, play a sweet song, my friend,
so we can clap and sing a song and lose our heads in dancing.

—Hafiz (Ghani-Qazvini, no. 374)

Love Stories from the Ancient Middle East

Retellings by

Jennifer Heath

INTERLINK BOOKS
An imprint of Interlink Publishing Group, Inc.
interlinkbooks.com @interlinkbooks

First published in 2024 by Interlink Books
An imprint of Interlink Publishing Group, Inc.
46 Crosby Street, Northampton, Massachusetts 01060
www.interlinkbooks.com

Text copyright © Jennifer Heath, 2024
Illustrations copyright © Alexandra Zeigler
Design copyright © Interlink Publishing, 2024

All rights reserved; no part of this publication may be reproduced, stored in a retrieval system, or transmitted, in any form or by any means, electronic, mechanical, photocopying, recording or otherwise, without the prior written permission of the publisher.

Library of Congress Cataloging-in-Publication Data available

ISBN-13: 978-1-62371-753-7 (hardback)

Publisher: Michel Moushabeck
Editor: David Klein
Cover design, interior design, and illustrations: Alexandra Zeigler

Printed and bound in Korea

10 9 8 7 6 5 4 3 2 1

Table of Contents

for

Soraya and Wahid Omar

In memory of Jack Collom

and for

true lovers everywhere

Introduction

My affair with love stories of the ancient Middle East probably began in Bolivia at the Sez de Agosto theater with a movie called *Flame of Araby,* in which Maureen O'Hara plays Tanya, a fiery, redheaded faux-Tunisian princess, to Jeff Chandler's Tamerlane, a bronco-busting Bedouin who defeats his enemies with a slingshot.

Flame's bad guys include two corsairs from the "House of Barbarossa," who, despite solemn oaths sworn "by the beard of the Prophet," appear to have galumphed fully costumed across Universal Studios from a Viking picture into this one. Their turncoat ally is an evil, goateed prince named after one of Islam's holiest cities, Medina. Time and place are as limitless as cultural sensitivity and vocabulary are finite ("By the beard of the Prophet, we will capture the mighty stallion and return to the mighty black tents of the mighty Bedouin," etc., and reprise).

Flame is a love story, sort of, and a horse story, mostly, with Chandler as a muscular Semitic stand-in for John Wayne. Chandler's manly, ho-hum-ish romancing is as Wayne-ian as it gets, focused more on the stallion than the gal.

In late-1950s La Paz, what did I know about Arabia? *Flame of Araby* invented the ancient Middle East and so did I. O'Hara/Tanya was my kind of princess, feisty-but-feminine, unafraid to battle her way out of a jam. Just the role model for a tomboy of six, seven, or eight, whose life was built on fantasy. Tanya could ride and think with equal agility, the sort of female protagonist who shows up in several stories in this book, such as Saljan and Mayasa and even the Queen of Sheba, who, though not a ride-'em-up, shoot-'em-down fighter, was her own brainy woman who absolutely knew her way around diplomacy, cross-examination, and governance.

A few years later, like any adolescent, I fell in love with love. By then we had moved to Afghanistan, where I climbed down from the trees, put away my sabers and scimitars, moored my pirate galleons, and let my mother dress me in skirts.

(I should mention that we were in Bolivia and Afghanistan because my father was a United States diplomat. As a "dip-brat," constantly on the move, I relied heavily on my uncontrollable imagination for entertainment.)

Somewhere along the line, my mother gave me a copy of the King James version of the Bible. I was appalled and frightened by Genesis, so I didn't get much past Sodom and Gomorrah, what with all that smoting and smiting. My father suggested I read *The Song of Songs*. Gorgeous. And I could relate to the sexual awakening of a young woman. Yet it seemed not to belong in the Bible. In *The Song of Songs: A New Translation*, Ariel and Chana Bloch write:

> A poem about erotic love would seem out of place in Holy Scripture, particularly if one's point of reference is the antipathy to sexuality in the New Testament. ... sex is no sin in the Old Testament. ...But sex is sanctioned only in marriage; on this point the Old Testament laws are unequivocal. Outside the pale of marriage there are crimes and punishments, catalogued in exhaustive detail.

Among other examples are the death of King David's and Bathsheba's first son, conceived in adultery, and David's eliminating the competition by murdering Bathsheba's first husband, Uriah the Hittite.

David and his son Solomon were said to each have a thousand wives and/or concubines. They were hardly unusual. The stories in this book occasionally mention large harems and multiple partners, courtesans notwithstanding, yet remarkably—happily—nearly every tale here focuses on one, very special, sought-after love that usually results in often-hard-won marriage.

Love and desire are the binding strengths of matrimony. Celibacy is frowned upon by all Abrahamic faiths, as well as by other religions. We are all called upon to go forth and multiply in the belief that marriage fulfills the dual nature of the divine by unifying masculine and feminine. While it can be difficult for Westerners in the twenty-first century to fathom, even arranged marriages can result in warm, doting relationships.

In her essay "The Deep Meaning of the Torah's First Great Love Story," Rabbi Shana Chandler Leon tells us that the "Torah's first reference to love between adult partners" is that between Isaac (Abraham's second son) and Rebecca. "The acceptability," she writes, "of arranged marriages was strengthened by an ancient belief that marriages were truly 'made in heaven.' It is *kiddushin*, holiness, a sacred partnership." Rebecca is not forced into marriage, but "is asked, 'Will you go with this man?'…and she accepts the call to 'go forth' into history."

Indeed, arranged marriages can be far less tumultuous, confusing, and unhappy than "love" marriages, which were not invented even in Euro-America until relatively modern times. Marriages were—and still are in myriad cultures and faiths—contracted between families to create close economic and political ties. Girls are not the only ones whose choices are limited. Boys haven't many options either. Yet it is possible for love to burst clean through rules, deals, or clan customs.

"A common denominator of most successful marriages, arranged or not" Leon writes, "is a quality called *tzimtzum*, the ability to withdraw one's ego to make space for the other partner's needs."

The greatest love story in Islam is that of the Prophet Muhammad and his first

wife, Khadija. Their twenty-five-year marriage was fruitful and faithful, and Khadija, the first convert to Islam, gave unwavering support—tzimtzum—to her husband and his mission. And this was kiddushin, a sacred partnership. Khadija's love, Muhammad said, was God's greatest gift to him.

As a widow of means, Khadija was freer than most to choose her own mate. In pre-Islamic Arabia and elsewhere, everywhere, marriages were not—and are not—uncommonly made by purchase, capture, or contract. Most women had or have no legal rights, no access to any bride price or financial freedom. They could, and can, be discarded at men's will. Men could take as many wives as they wanted. Divorce was unconstrained, and conjugal violence and sexual abuse were rampant (rape is an expression of unleashed power, employed individually and domestically in peacetime, as well as under official orders as a weapon of war).

Islam changed that. Muhammad decreed that men were allowed only four wives; it ensured women's inheritances and property rights and assured that the *mahar*—the bride price—was her own to be used as she pleased and that it would be returned to her in the event of divorce or her husband's death. This was made law in the Qur'an, yet, as with so many evenhanded religious rulings worldwide, the spiritual lawgiver is hardly cold in the grave than the laws are ignored and older, tribal customs revived or integrated into the new.

"No man may come upon his wife like an animal," the Prophet said. "And let there be an emissary between them." When asked to describe this emissary, he replied, "The kiss and sweet words."

I could always count on the Sez de Agosto for my Biblical (mis)education. There, too, I saw Yul Brynner and Gina Lollobrigida in *Solomon and Sheba*. Eventually, I thumbed through the King

James seeking their "real" story, only to find it unfulfilling, unsatisfactory, unfinished. I put the Bible away and did not open it again until I began this book. At first, it occurred to me that, having seen Victor Mature and Hedy Lamar in Samson and Delilah— at, of course, the Sez—that story might be good to include here. Alas, it was hardly love, what with Delilah's Philistine betrayal of poor Samson by chopping off his long, lovely locks. At some point, I considered Rebecca and Isaac, but could not wrap my dizzy romantic head around it. Most intriguing—more so than Solomon and Sheba—was the love triangle between Sarah and Abraham (Isaac's parents) and Hagar, the mother of Abraham's first son, Ishmael. Yet the story's labyrinthine complexities seemed far too demanding for this book. Sarah, then Sarai (before God renames her), is old and cannot conceive. Hagar is her Egyptian maidservant, a mere object she bestows on her husband, Abraham (then Abram), in order that she give birth to the child Sarah cannot have.

"Sarah," Temina Goldberg Shulman writes in "A Love Triangle for the Ages," "does not take into account that Abraham and Hagar might develop feelings for one another, that Hagar could turn the straight line between Sarah and Abraham into a triangle, changing the dimensions of Abraham's heart, especially if Hagar is carrying Abraham's heirloom child."

Once Hagar is well and truly pregnant, then gives birth to a son, Sarah's jealousy rises to a boiling point, and she expels Hagar from their home. And here, Shulman says, she "demonstrates that she continues to underestimate the power of the love that her husband had for the other woman."

Sarah banishes Hagar into the desert and the poor thing frantically searches for water for herself and her child, Ishmael. Here the story takes two paths. Shulman reminds us that in Genesis, after Sarah dies, Isaac "seems to understand that his father cannot be whole without Hagar's love."

(Hagar is now renamed Keturah.) "In this way, Isaac guarantees that Abraham will find comfort in his final years."

The second path, however, is the Islamic tradition. All three Abrahamic religions trace their roots to the covenant between God and Abraham, or Ibrahim. But in Islam, it is Ishmael, not Isaac, who Abraham/Ibrahim tries to sacrifice to show his loyalty to God/Allah. Through all this and more, Muslims trace their descent to Abraham through Hagar and Ishmael. Jews and Muslims are, "at least in a metaphorical sense," Frederick Denny writes in *Jews, Christians, Muslims: A Comparative Introduction to Monotheistic Religions,* "half-brothers, having the same father but different mothers." And here, as elsewhere, the story of Abraham, Sarah, and Hagar becomes intricate and knotty, out of the purview of this book's humbler goals.

(Despite my runaway imagination, I could not fathom a nonagenarian woman giving birth, though I understand all those mega-aged icons—at the Biblical beginning of time—to be agents for building Judaic tribes and houses and thus required excessively long lives. Yet, after all that smoting and smiting, the jealousies and in-fighting, separations, and reconciliations, I did rather enjoy that Sarah guffawed at God for suggesting she give birth in her tenth decade. But as always, God—not renowned for his sense of humor—had the last laugh.)

Across recent decades, much of the space on our collective bookshelves and in our collective Western minds has been occupied by conflict: religious and cultural battles, wars, unspeakable injustices, fear, loathing, cruelty, racism, and environmental degradation. Brutality everywhere has deepened our prejudices and defenses, alienated communities, and stripped us of civility, love, and beauty.

In "Notes on Beauty," from his marvelous *Columns & Catalogues*, Peter Schjeldahl writes that "insensibility to beauty may be an index of misery." Beauty—and, I would add, love—is "not luxury but is a necessity ... reconciliation with life."

For Jews, beauty provides an occasion to love God, to love one's neighbors, and to help heal the world. Jews are encouraged to create and increase the beauty in the world through the good deeds they are called on to perform.

"Beauty is indeed a good gift of God," St. Augustine wrote in *City of God*. Without beauty, the liturgy and the faithful are removed from the divine presence.

In the Hadith—the sayings of the Prophet Muhammad—it is written that "God is beautiful and loves beauty."

One summer, amid global ugliness, despair, and indignity, I turned to these fables for comfort, writing at a table in my garden. I hungered after plain storytelling for its own sake, but also for the sake of tolerance and understanding. For the sake of love and beauty. By climbing into these tales, I could be transported. In the process, I tried to consider many kinds of love, from mother/father love to friendship to fascination to adoration to lust. I tried to give back beauty where I found it. I tried to shape moments of stillness against the chaos and dread we now live with every day.

The stories here are based on retellings and poetry from pre-Islamic sources, narratives in the Hebrew and Christian bibles, as well as a touch of enchanting poetry, including some written during a golden age called *la Convivencia* in Moorish Spain, when Jews, Christians, and Muslims coexisted in harmony, sharing rich cultural interactions in literature, science, philosophy, art, medicine, and mysticism—though not entirely without controversy. La Convivencia lasted from the late eighth century until the late fifteenth century, which brought the *Reconquista* (reconquest), when the Christian rulers Ferdinand and Isabela succeeded in ridding Spain of all Muslims and most Jews, then introduced the oppressive centuries of Inquisition.

In *A Miniature Anthology of Medieval Hebrew Love Poems*, Raymond P. Scheindlin writes that these poets' "themes and rhetorical figures are drawn from a common fund of literary material that the Jewish literati acquired through their education in Arabic poetry, used, and recycled." So it is with artistic endeavors always and everywhere: continual swapping, borrowing, adoption, and adaption to make it new.

María Rosa Menocal, in *The Ornament of the World*, quotes the mid-ninth-century Christian luminary Paul Alvarus of Cordoba:

> The Christians love to read the poems and romances of the Arabs: they study the Arab theologians and philosophers, not to refute them but to form a correct and elegant Arabic. ... Alas! All talented young Christians read and study with enthusiasm the Arab books ... they despise the Christian literature as unworthy of attention. They have forgotten their own language. For everyone who can write a letter in Latin to a friend, there are a thousand who can express themselves in Arabic with elegance and write better poems in this language than the Arabs themselves.

Scheindlin adds that "the courtier-rabbis of the Golden Age used poetry to a large extent as a ritual way of giving expression to an ideal shared by their social class as a whole. ...They valued poetry for its power to articulate the devotion to beauty as a cardinal value of the spatial life."

It is primarily through *The Book of the Thousand Nights and a Night*—also called *The Arabian Nights*—that most Westerners are acquainted with secular stories of Arabia and Persia. Notwithstanding the courage and ingenuity of the storyteller

Scheherazade, Sir Richard Francis Burton's nineteenth-century translations repeatedly describe women as enslaved, coquettish, oversexed, wily, manipulative, acquisitive, amoral simperers and schemers or as bitter, vengeful hags. The men don't fare much better, generally coming off as lustful, greedy, bloodthirsty, passive, or stupid. Burton's characters are not unlike stock figures in any folklore or pulp fiction, but they are filtered through Victorian Orientalist eyes and given a lurid, voyeuristic, colonialist overlay that's misleading and distasteful.

In heroines such as Shirin, Vis, Saljan, or the Queen of Sheba, to name but four, readers of *The Jewel and the Ember* will come to know women who are more than greedy, obnoxious sex objects and shrouded creatures at the mercy of male oppressors, but who are eloquent, wise, clever, educated, and good sportswomen and warriors to boot. In Majnun, Miqdad, Antar, or Ramin, readers will meet men who are complex, vulnerable, loyal, and loving, full participants in life's sufferings and joys.

I hope this book fills a few gaps and offers an alternative to Western renderings beginning with Antoine Galland's eighteenth-century *Les Mille et Une Nuits: Contes Arabe* marching right through to the Disney film *Aladdin* in the twentieth. None of the stories in *The Jewel and the Ember* are derived from *The Arabian Nights*. I dug elsewhere for treasure, into vaults where scholars preserve and study tales rarely popularized in the West. Stories in this book come from Zoroastrian Persia, Judea, pre-Islamic Arabia, archaic Turkic lands, and Afghanistan. Nor did I borrow from essential collections like Inea Bushnaq's *Arab Folktales,* Nathan Ausubel's *A Treasury of Jewish Folklore,* or Aisha Ahmad's and Roger Boase's *Pashtun Tales*, though they were tempting to raid. And, via many marvelous Midrash—ancient commentary about Hebrew scriptures in biblical texts—and Aggadah—legends,

parables, or anecdotes used to illustrate points of Law in the Talmud—as well as other interpretations, oral traditions, and sacred speculations, I was provided with larger narratives and could therefore piece together, for myself, an account of the relationship between King Solomon and the mysterious Queen of Sheba.

Collecting stories is like eating potato chips—it takes a determined will to stop.

Refining and putting to paper (or papyrus) some of the tales I've explored in this book seems to have begun in earnest during the Abbasid dynasty in Baghdad (750 to 1258 CE). Among the pioneers of Arabic prose was Abdulla Ibn al-Muqaffa (ca. 725 to 760 CE), a major influence in the development of *adab*, or belles-lettres. Adab also refers to courtesy, respect, and appropriateness. According to Kabir Helminski, writing in the magazine *Crescent Life*, "Adab is not formality; it helps to create the context in which we develop our humanness. Every situation and relationship have their proper adab."

The stories and poems included here are of course mere samples of the hundreds of epics, legends, myths, folktales, and religious lore originating from the Middle East. I decided against seeking Mesopotamian, Sumerian, Babylonian, or Assyrian tales. While I am completely enchanted by the *Epic of Gilgamesh*, particularly Stephen Mitchell's version, and Samuel Noah Kramer's *History Begins at Sumer*, among others, I simply don't have the knowledge, the connective tissue, to pursue those ancient-ancient spectacular literary accomplishments, let alone tamper with them.

Many of the stories in this volume can be found as court romances, by which I mean they were lifted from folk tellings and recreated during post-Islamic periods—the early centuries after Islam was established in 610 CE—on behalf of the upper classes. Their protagonists tended to be (or were transformed into) princes and princesses, prophets, nobles, and the children of chieftains—characters that pleased the 1 percent. The Hebrew Bible, however, was traditionally held to have originated in the sixth century BCE, but shards of Hebrew writing have been discovered showing that it may be much older. The Torah comprises the first five books of the Hebrew Bible: Genesis, Exodus, Leviticus, Numbers, and Deuteronomy. The Hebrew Bible, called the Tanakh (and called the Old Testament by Christians) collects Jewish sacred writings containing the Torah, the *Nevi'im*, which contains the writings of the prophets, and the *Ketuvim*, consisting of Ruth, Psalms, Job, Proverbs, Ecclesiastes, Song of Solomon, Lamentations, Daniel, Esther, Ezra, and I and II Chronicles. The Midrash and Aggadah come later, emerging across time. Without the kind of literary patronage afforded to romantic Islamic writers, it seems to have taken much longer to elaborate the powerful stories of the Bible into novels and poetry (not to say movies like those that packed the Sez de Agosto).

Some tales here—such as "Antar and Abla" or "Miqdad and Mayasa"—started life as oral tradition that originated long before the Abrahamic eras. Pre-Islamic travelers and traders from North Africa to Southeast Asia, including Jews and Christians, exchanged legends and songs. They met in *caravanserai* (rest houses), at *wadi* (oases), or in pilgrim houses, journeying on foot, by camel, horse, or donkey. Thus, the accounts of Yusuf, or Joseph, of Solomon and Sheba, of Abraham, Sarah, and Hagar, as well as others were refashioned from their initial shapes in the Hebrew Bible to resurface in the Qur'an, the Muslim holy book.

Stories like "The Seven Princesses," which apparently began as a commission to court poets to entertain the royal and the rich, have drifted from the page into oral tradition, to take on new lives of their own. They continue to be transmitted by word of mouth. The adventures of the treasured hero Antar still enthrall audiences in cafés or other gathering

places performed by storytellers constantly adding to them so that by now they comprise hundreds of pages and thousands of stanzas.

Galland introduced his *Les Mille et Une Nuits: Contes Arabe* (The Thousand and One Nights) to Europe in 1704. He translated the Arabic into French, reconstructing tales told by *hakawati*, public storytellers, and *rawl*, professional poetry reciters, into a cohesive, Europeanized text. Some of the folk- and fairy tales written by European noblewomen to entertain one another in their salons or collected by the Brothers Grimm may have been birthed from Galland's popular book. Indeed, so-called Oriental stories had already been floating around Europe for centuries, brought back by Christian pilgrims to Jerusalem, merchants, and Crusaders. Dante's *The Divine Comedy* (written from 1308 to 1321 CE) was inspired at least in part by the work of the Persian philosopher and theologian Abu Hamid al-Ghazali (1058 to 1111 CE), who expanded one of the two versions of Paradise as presented in the Qur'an. The Arthurian romance *Tristan and Isolde* is almost a dead ringer for the far older Zoroastrian epic, *Vis and Ramin*. This is not to deny coincidence or the collective unconscious, which can generate similar stories from dissimilar peoples worldwide. (Therefore, we have, for instance, multitudes of multicultural Cinderellas.)

The flow and exchange of literature is hardly one-sided. In the eighth century, al-Muqaffa translated the Sanskrit *Panchatantra* into Arabic. It already had a long history in India, Mongolia, and Tibet and is believed to have been the prototype for the Greek *Fables of Aesop*, somewhat sappy morality tales—quite unlike the *Panchatantra*—repositories for, if not human wisdom, then the goal toward goodness as told through the actions of animals. Al-Muqaffa's *Kalila wa Dimna* features two shrewd jackals, who exchange brutal parables reflecting the savagery of human behavior. In the great love story *Layla and Majnun*, retold most famously by the Persian poet Nizami Ganjavi (1141 to 1209 CE), the wild animals that surround the mad, lost poet-lover are vessels for primal insight, guides to the sweet and sour truths of the natural world and who are closest to the Divine.

The famous troubadours of the Middle Ages are thought to have originated in Arabia and to have perfected their art in Moorish Spain. Troubadours often sang of courtly love, sensual romances usually outside of marriage, sometimes platonic, sometimes not. "Troubadour" has its root in the Arabic *taraba*, "to sing." I like to think that my alterations and abridgements are somewhat in the venerated tradition of troubadours, poets, and taletellers everywhere. Stories inevitably change and change again, shifting slowly and subtly with each recitation. I've altered nothing of context or plot. And except for "Solomon and the Queen," I did not reinvent. Naturally, in the retellings, I made these sagas my own and brought them into my own vernacular. Unfortunately, I do not have sufficient Arabic, Hebrew, or Farsi, so none of these tales are direct translations.

I do not claim this is a scholarly presentation. I tried to make these stories accessible to the public without distorting them. This was challenging, especially when boiling, say, three-hundred-page texts down to, say, thirty. I found the intensity of repetition addictive and engaging, and I tried to maintain what I imagined were the stories' fundamental rhythms. I arranged these tales and poems mostly by tone and tempo. I tried to mix them up but did not always succeed in avoiding cultural traffic jams.

To give readers a bit of ballast, the notes at the end of this book provide each tale with a brief history of its roots, as well as short descriptions of the accompanying poems.

The Jewel and the Ember opens with a segment from *Mantiq al-Tayr*, or *Conference of the Birds*, by the celebrated Persian Sufi poet Farid Ud-Din Attar (1142 to 1221 CE). "The Moth and the Candle" illustrates how desire can be irresistible and all-consuming, passion-ravaging, hazardous, fulfilling, absolutely life-changing.

Conference of the Birds, after which Chaucer allegedly modeled his *Parliament of the Birds*, consists of 4,600 couplets, and traces the journey of a flock of birds to the home of their leader, the Simurgh, whom they have never met. When they arrive after an arduous voyage, the surviving birds discover their leader is not another individual, but themselves as a cohesive group. Although *Conference of the Birds* is a meditation on the Sufi pursuit of unity with God, and not on an individual lover, the quest, with its yearning, obstacles, torments, ecstasies, and revelations, is similar.

Many of us have been, like me and some of the characters in this book, in love with love, insisting that it is so transformative, so enlightened, that between lovers there can be no misunderstandings, no restlessness, no turbulence, no roiling doubts. *Tra la*! Trip lightly into the sunset, hand-in-hand, happily ever after, each one the other's savior. (Is it any surprise that lovesickness was once considered by physicians, East and West, to be an actual, sometimes incurable disease?)

Sooner or later, *true* love itself comes along, and like the moths to the flames, we rush to catch it, to grasp hold of it with every fiber. And we discover this: Love *is* transformative. It *is* enlightening. Love's turbulence, misunderstandings, missed connections, roiling doubts, and discontents are the wildly rough trail that leads to partnership with the Self, with Another and finally with the World.

Love brings us to wisdom, often with scraped hands and bruised knees, breathless yet victorious. Love breaks through the strongest social fortresses to unsettle souls, rattle spirits, disrupt hearts, and distract minds.

With this book, I not only hope readers will embrace the Other—who and whatever they perceive the Other to be. It is my fervent wish that these stories, like love stories worldwide, will remind us in their assorted and wondrous ways, that love is tough, love is delicate, love is exquisite, love gives us meaning, love is potent creative force, love is worth it, because love is beauty and love is all we've got ... if only we don't weaken.

The Moth and the Candle

One night,
The moths met
tormented by a desire
to be united to the candle.

They said:
"We must send someone
who will bring us information
about the object of our longing."

One of them set off and came to a castle.
Inside he saw the light of a candle.

He returned and reported what he had seen.

But the wise moth who presided over the gathering
thought he had understood nothing about the candle.

So another moth went.

He touched the flame with the tip of his wings.

The heat drove him off.
His report was no more satisfying,
and a third moth ventured out.

At the sight of the candle
the third moth became intoxicated with love.

He threw himself on the flame.
He grasped the flame with his forelegs
and united joyously with her.
He embraced her completely
and his body became red as flame.

The flame and moth appeared to be one.

The wise moth, watching from afar, said:
"He has learned what he wished to know.
But only he understands."

—From *The Conference of the Birds*, Farid Ud-Din Attar, 1142–1220

Yusuf and Zulaykha

Yaqoub of Canaan had in his garden eleven branches that celebrated the birth of each of his sons by growing into trees. Eleven sons, eleven branches, eleven trees. But when the twelfth son, Yusuf, was born, the branch put forth only a little stump.

When Yusuf grew, he asked his father why he had no tree. Yaqoub prayed that the boy should be given a fertile branch. No sooner was the prayer finished than an angel descended carrying a flowering branch from Paradise, proof that Yusuf was destined to be a great prophet. And Yaqoub presented Yusuf with a special garment, a coat of many colors. His brothers were envious.

Yusuf planted his branch, and it took root. Then he dreamed that, while his brothers' branches, too, had grown into trees, his was bigger and stronger and spread across the firmament to embrace the world. When a wind came, Yusuf's tree stopped it, but his brothers' trees were all ripped from the earth. And his brothers hated him.

Then Yusuf dreamed the moon and eleven stars prostrated themselves before him.

Yusuf's brothers grew more jealous, afraid he would have dominion over them. They conspired to kill him. But his brother Yahudi stopped the others. "Do not kill Yusuf," he pleaded, "for he is our brother in blood."

The brothers threw Yusuf into a pit. As he tumbled, a female djinn caught him and guided him gently to the bottom. There, Yusuf languished, quiet and lonely and naked, for his brothers had stolen his colorful coat and spread upon it the blood of a slaughtered goat. They took it to Yaqoub and told him a jackal had eaten Yusuf. The old man mourned and wept for his beautiful, disappeared boy.

Yusuf lay at the bottom of the pit until

his brothers brought him up to sell him into slavery. The shaykh who bought him took him by caravan to Egypt, where he was again sold for his weight in musk and silk to the Pharoah, who gave Yusuf to serve his queen, Zulaykha.

Yusuf was a beautiful boy, and when Queen Zulaykha laid eyes on him she was overcome. Her heart melted to water, while at the same moment it burst into flame.

"Come forward," she said, and locked the doors. She pulled him toward her bed. She opened her arms to him.

Yusuf refused, saying, "I seek the Lord's refuge."

He escaped the queen's embrace that day, yet she still made advances.

"I am your servant," Yusuf said. "Order me instead to sweep or fetch water."

Zulaykha ordered Yusuf to sleep with her.

"Your husband has favored me with the keys to the house," Yusuf said. "I cannot betray his confidence."

"You are so beautiful," Zulaykha said. "I cannot stop looking at you."

"What is beauty?" said Yusuf. "In old age, you wither. In your grave, you rot. God gives beauty, then takes it away."

Zulaykha continued her advances.

"Satisfy my need," said Zulaykha. She lay upon the silken sheets. She, too, was beautiful.

Yusuf backed away. "I will not go into your bed and forfeit my chance of Paradise," he said.

"Who will know?" Zulaykha said. "I have closed the curtains. No one will see us. Do not make it hard for me. Cure me. I suffer so."

Yusuf, too, was suffering and could have been cured by her, but he said, "Let your husband cure you. Tell him what you want and he will do it for you."

"O Yusuf," Zulaykha moaned. "You are cutting my insides. Come into the alcove. I'll give you money beyond comparison. You will have rich food and many servants, rubies, emeralds, silver, and gold to give alms and please God. Is that not what you want?"

"God would never accept it, for it is not lawfully earned," he answered, but all this time Yusuf's will to resist was weakening. Love had also entered his heart and love pushed him toward her. He closed his eyes. He leaned into her. His lips were moist and puckered. She wrapped her arms around him, smiling.

Suddenly, his father Yaqoub appeared in Yusuf's mind and admonished him, saying, "You are on the verge of perdition. You, who possess the light to prophethood, do not stray."

And Yusuf jumped away in fear.

"It is only that you are young and inexperienced. It is only that you are shy," Zulaykha pleaded.

He did not hear her. He scrambled for the door. Zulaykha followed him and seized his shirt from behind, tearing it open.

Just then her husband appeared. "What is the punishment, if not imprisonment or painful chastisement," she demanded of him, "for he who intends evil to your wife?"

There were two babies in the room, and when Pharoah questioned them, God gave them speech. "If his shirt is rent from front, she speaks the truth. And if his shirt is rent from behind, she tells a lie."

"This is the guile of you women," Pharoah lamented. "Your guile is too great. Yusuf! Turn aside from this. Zulaykha! Ask forgiveness for your wrongdoing."

Zulaykha watched Yusuf go about his duties day by day, and her love for him increased minute by minute. News of the queen's desire for her slave spread around the city. "Pharoah's wife desires her slave to yield to her," the gossips whispered. "He has affected her deeply. She is in manifest error."

When Zulaykha heard of their sly talk, she sent for them and prepared a feast.

She called for a banquet and ordered her servants to hang silk curtains and

banners of many colors along the walls. She seated all the women along the walls on cushions soft as petals. The women ate and ate. They ate cheeses and grape leaves stuffed with the meat of lambs. They ate yogurt and raisins and rice and cool cucumbers. They sipped sweet tea, and, with the presentation of each delicious new delicacy, they dipped their fingers in rosewater, until the last offering when the slaves brought oranges bright as golden balls and a newly whetted peeling knife for each woman.

When every woman was served and slicing into her orange, Zulaykha made a signal, and Yusuf, who was standing behind a silken curtain, passed by, parading slowly from one end of the hall to the other, then back again.

The women's gazes stuck fast to Yusuf's dazzling beauty. Young and old, they forgot what they were doing. Blood spurted and flowed upon the orange peels. "This is not a mortal! This is a noble angel," they cried. Some cut off their thumbs and some even tried to slit their vital arteries.

"This is he, about whom you blamed me," Zulaykha admonished them. "Certainly, I wanted him, but he abstained. You have cut yourselves for the sake of this man whom you suspected I had slept with."

Now, through their cries of pain, they understood why she desired her slave and they begged forgiveness.

The next day Zulaykha called Yusuf into her chambers again. This time when he refused her, she told her husband that she was afraid of walking freely in the streets because of people's tongues: "I am shamed because of that young man," she said.

Pharoah called his soldiers. They seized Yusuf and threw him into the dungeons.

Two youths entered the prison with Yusuf. They were the royal cupbearer and the royal breadkeeper accused of trying to poison the Pharoah. As the days and weeks passed in that damp, dark place, the three became friends.

One morning, the breadkeeper told Yusuf of a dream: "I wore a loaf of bread upon my head, which the birds were eating."

"Breadkeeper," said Yusuf, "the bread on your head signifies that your brain will be eaten by birds."

Hardly had he spoken when a guard appeared and took the breadkeeper away, chopped off his head, and left it lying in a field where the birds came and ate the brain, cawing and rejoicing.

The next morning, the cupbearer told Yusuf of his dream: he was cutting grapes from a vine, squeezing them into Pharoah's cup. The juice was sweet and refreshing.

"Cupbearer," said Yusuf, "you will return home."

Three days later, the cupbearer was released. Yusuf begged to be remembered to Pharoah and the cupbearer promised he would intercede for Yusuf.

Twelve years passed. The cupbearer had forgotten his promise to Yusuf, until Pharoah dreamed that seven fat cows rose out of a dry riverbed followed by seven lean cows, and these were weak and unhealthy.

Then he dreamed of seven full fields of grain. But quickly the seven fields became desiccated and fallow.

Pharoah called his priests. None could interpret his dreams. He called his scribes and musicians. None understood the dreams. At last, Pharoah's cupbearer remembered his friend and said, "Bring Yusuf the Hebrew up from the dungeons and he will disclose it for you."

Yusuf was cleaned and given a new robe. He warned Pharoah of a coming famine and warned him to guard the grain store and to keep it full. Then Yusuf told Pharoah that he knew numbers, as well as dreams, and asked to be appointed keeper of the grain and accountant of the royal treasure. Pharoah also gave Yusuf Asenath, the priest's daughter, in marriage. They had two sons, Manasseh and Ephraim, who grew to inherit portions of the Land of Israel.

Yusuf increased Pharoah's wealth thousandfold. Pharoah retired from the capital, taking Queen Zulaykha with him. Yusuf, now vizier of the land, sat on a golden divan on plush cushions of many colors. He wore a gold crown with emeralds and rubies, and his beautiful face shone like the moon.

And just as Yusuf had forecast, in seven years, a period of famine came upon the land and the people ate all their provisions. Yusuf was prepared for the hunger and doled out grain to the people, bushel after bushel.

The famine spread from Egypt to Syria and to Canaan, where Yaqoub, now blind, felt the hunger entering his camp and sent his sons in search of stores.

Yusuf's eleven brothers went to Egypt to ask for grain and were fooled by Yusuf in his vizier's garb. When they sold him, he was a whiskerless boy, and now he wore a king's beard. Yusuf recognized his brothers and made them squirm when they lied to him, saying they once had a brother who had disappeared in the desert. Yusuf smiled and finally revealed himself to his brothers, who wept for forgiveness, fearful he would execute them. But he forgave them, saying, "Do not be sad, and let it not trouble you that you sold me here, for it was to preserve life that the Lord sent me before you. You did not send me here. God did."

Then he bade his brothers to bring their father Yaqoub from Canaan with all the animals and people of his household: slaves, maidens, wives, and children. In Egypt, they saw Yusuf crowned Pharoah, for the old ruler had died. They watched Yusuf take his seat on a golden throne surrounded by hundreds of servants and guards, his wives and children, each holding a shining lamp. Yaqoub and his eleven sons prostrated themselves before Yusuf.

At that moment, Yusuf remembered

the dream in which the moon and eleven stars had bowed before him and exclaimed, "This is the significance of my vision; the Lord has indeed made it true."

Yusuf ruled as Pharoah of Egypt for eighty years. He healed Yaqoub's blindness and Yaqoub lived to be one hundred and seventy-four.

Each year Yusuf traveled his country bringing relief to his people where they needed it. One year, he came to a village where there lived an old hungry woman.

She was withered and emaciated. She trembled from starvation. She lurched toward the Pharoah. She kneeled before him. She raised her stiff hands begging for a morsel. Yusuf ordered that food be given. His clerk asked her name.

"Zulaykha," she said in a voice like dried leaves underfoot. "I am called Zulaykha."

Yusuf stared in awe at this hunched and twisted hag. Time had not touched Yusuf, but Zulaykha was wrinkled as ancient leather and frail as a cloud.

"Do you know who I am?" Yusuf asked.

"Of course," Zulaykha answered. "You are king of us all, your subjects."

"I am also your former slave, Yusuf."

Zulaykha gasped. Love had never left her heart. Now it was rekindled. She began to sob. She was old, but he had not aged. She could never have him, though now she was free of her husband. As tears rolled from her dim eyes, an angel descended from Paradise. Touching the ground, he said, "Whosoever endures patiently and perseveres, good will come in the end. Whosoever loves fervently, peace will come in the end."

The angel turned to Yusuf. "The Lord sent me to tell you that He has given you this woman for your wife."

"But she is old," Yusuf protested. "She is too ugly to lie with and too aged to bear children."

"What is beauty?" the angel reminded Yusuf. "God gives beauty then takes it away."

Zulaykha fell to her knees. She

begged Yusuf and the angel to pray to God to restore her youth.

All at once, Zulaykha looked again like a girl, even lovelier than before.

On the night that Zulaykha and Yusuf married, he tenderly inclined toward her and met her kiss, like salt tantalizing the tongue before a meal. The fire of love intoxicated them, and the world was forgotten, engulfed in passion. Yusuf clasped Zulaykha in his arms, and below her navel he found the virgin's jewel.

Yusuf and Zulaykha were at last cured, satisfied and at peace. They lived happily. Zulaykha gave Yusuf three more children: two sons they named Furathima and Misha and a daughter they called Rehema, which means "mercy."

A Flight to Egypt

Incite our camels to be swift.
The dawn unfolds upon the desert like a rose.
Zulaykha's voice,
lamenting in the dark
through Egypt like a weary river flows.

—Shiri, India, d. 1586

Drink water from your own cistern,
clean, flowing water from your own well.
Should your streams be scattered,
gushing water into the streets?
Let that water be for you alone.

Let your fountain be blessed,
take pleasure in the wife of your youth,
a graceful doe, an agile gazelle.
Let her affection fill you always with
delight.
Be enraptured by her love.
Do not be lost in the arms of adventure
and infatuation.
For the Lord watches your path and sees
your sins.
Let your wife's breasts fill you with
pleasure.
Always be entranced by her love alone.

—Proverbs 5:15 18–19

Khan Turali and Saljan

Dede Korkut reclines on the rugs of the Sultan. His bones squeak, for Grandfather Korkut is three hundred years old. Wherever he walks, a gravedigger awaits him and wherever he sits, a crowd demands his stories. He clears his throat: "O my Sultan, on your white forehead I invoke blessings, may they be accepted. May Allah grant you increase and preserve you in strength and forgive your sins for the sake of Muhammad of Beautiful Name—peace be upon him."

Then Dede Korkut begins:

In the days of the Oghuz, there was a doughty warrior, Khanli Khoja, who had a son, Khan Turali. And what a son! Khan Turali was a braggart and a daredevil, and still up to his boyish antics, though he was now a grown man. Khanli Khoja determined that Khan Turali must marry, for a boy who is a man but will not settle down can hardly be called a man at all.

So Khanli Khoja summoned Khan Turali and said, "My son, you must get married while my eyes can still see."

"Father," Khan Turali replied indignantly, "how can there be a girl fit for me? The girl I love will have to rise to her feet before I do, and before I mount my horse, she must already be on horseback. Before I reach the infidel lands, she must already have got there and won the battle."

"I see," Khanli Khoja said, stroking his beard. "You don't want a girl, you want a hothead, a hero who will also look after you."

"Indeed," Khan Turali said. "And no doubt you'll find me some sheep-herding doll whose belly will split as soon as I fall on her."

Khanli Khoja rose from his couch sighing. "Son, I will see that you are fed and provided for. Finding the girl is up to you."

Khan Turali, hero of heroes, especially in his own mind, took his forty young men and went searching for a bride. They galloped around Inner Oghuz and went home that night having not so much as glanced at a suitable maiden. The next day, they cantered around Outer Oghuz and again returned brideless.

"Father, what did I tell you? There is no girl to suit me."

"This is not the way to go looking for wives," said Khanli Khoja.

"Oh no?" his son replied. "Then how does one go?"

"Son, look after the property. I'll find a girl for you."

Khanli Khoja rode with his forty graybeards into Inner Oghuz and Outer Oghuz but could find no girl who might suit his son, so he wandered on until he came to the land of Trebizond.

The infidel king of Trebizond had a daughter he treasured above all. Besides being beautiful, Saljan could draw two bows at once, to her right and to her left, and shoot arrows so high they never fell to earth. She could outrun any of the king's warriors and outride any of his horsemen. The king adored her but provided only three beasts for her dowry: a green bull, a red lion, and a blue camel, monsters one and all. Whoever could subdue these beasts, conquer and kill them, might have Saljan for a wife.

"But!" the king pronounced, "Those who fail to kill them will be beheaded."

So far, the heads of thirty-two suitors hung on the battlements of Trebizond, tongues and eyes pecked out by vultures, skin molting and peeling, while Saljan awaited her perfect mate. Those she'd most favored looked, with every gory passing day, less and less attractive.

Khanli Khoja and his graybeards noted the dwindling virility of the princes hanging from the battlements. Indeed, the sight of these rotting noggins and the three monstrous beasts contained in cages below them caused the lice on Khanli Khoja's trembling head to leap off and run away.

Yet he turned to his companions and said, "Let us go straight home to my son and tell him that if he's clever enough he can come and take her. Otherwise, he'll have to be satisfied with the girls at home."

O my Sultan, the horse's hoof is swift as the wind and the minstrel's tongue is swift as a bird. Khanli Khoja made his way back to his own tents and sent word to Khan Turali.

Khan Turali went with his forty young men to meet Khanli Khoja and his father's forty old companions.

"Have you found a suitable girl for me?" he asked, kissing his patriarch's hand.

"I have, son. If you are clever enough."

Khan Turali puffed out his chest.

"I surely have gold and silver, mules and camels enough."

"Son, it is cleverness that's wanted. C-l-e-v-e-r-n-e-s-s."

"I shall saddle my black-maned Kazilik mare and raid the bloody infidel land! I'll cut off heads and spill blood! I'll make the infidel vomit guts! I'll bring back slaves and slave girls!" Khan Turali shouted.

"Son. My dear son, what did I just say?" Khanli Khoja groaned. Then he told of Trebizond's twisted and tortuous roads, its swamps that suck down horsemen who never reappear, its forests so thick even the serpent cannot find a path, its fortresses that rub shoulders with the sky and soldiers who dance on their shields on the backs of the easily defeated. And he carefully detailed the green bull, the red lion, and the blue camel. He told Khan Turali of the executioners who whisk heads off in seconds and the gruesome skulls clinging to the turrets of Trebizond.

"I'm off!" Khan Turali shouted. "If I don't go, I bring disgrace on my head and shame on my face."

Khan Turali and his faithful forty galloped seven days and seven nights to Trebizond.

Saljan was a confident maiden, and she had built her own palace on the square.

All the maidens who surrounded her wore red, but she alone wore yellow. And this was gilding the lily, for Princess Saljan was already dazzling as the sun.

Khan Turali strutted around and around the square, avoiding eye contact with the thirty-two dripping heads encircling the battlements. Saljan watched him and fell in love, for Khan Turali, while not without his faults, was a handsome man and a skilled warrior.

After seven revolutions around the square, Khan Turali and his men came to rest before the king.

"Where do you come from?" the king demanded.

"I come to climb your mountain," Khan Turali replied. "I come to cross your eddying river. I come to seek refuge in your narrow skirts, your broad embrace. By God's command and at the word of the Prophet—peace be upon him—I come to marry your daughter!"

"Strip this ready-tongued boy mother-naked!" the king ordered, and they did.

Saljan went weak at the knees. Her cat meowed. She slavered like a sick calf. "If only God Most High would put mercy into my father's heart," she said. "If only he would fix a bride price and give me this man! Alas that such a man might perish at the hands of the monster beasts."

"Bring on the green bull!" the king ordered, and his minions dragged the creature to the square with a chain of iron. The bull knelt, kneaded a marble paving stone with his horns, and shredded it like cheese. The executioner whetted his beheading axe.

Khan Turali looked to his left and then to his right and saw his forty warriors weeping.

"What's this? Stop crying and sing my praises!"

Let us see, my Sultan, how they praised him.

Which gallant hero never quails before the enemy?
Khan Turali!

Which fearless warrior has inflamed the
princess with love?
Khan Turali!
Glory to the girl in yellow!
Glory to her gallant hero!

"Turn loose your bull and let him come!" Khan Turali bellowed.

Khan Turali flayed the green bull. He carried the skin before the king and said, "First thing in the morning, give me your daughter."

"Bring on the red lion!" the king roared.

"Don't just stand there!" Khan Turali ordered his companions. "Sing my praises!"

Let us see, my Sultan, how they praised him.

Who never turns from the pure dark
steel sword?
Khan Turali!
Who pierces the quarry's vein and sucks
its blood?
Khan Turali!
Who fears not the white-thonged bow?
Khan Turali!
Glory to the girl in yellow!
Glory to her gallant hero!

"You there! King!" Khan Turali bawled, "Bring on the red lion!"

O my Sultan, shall I tell you how Khan Turali spoke a blessing on Muhammad of Beautiful Face—peace be upon him—and snatched the cloak of a nearby shepherd and held it out to the lion's paw? Shall I describe how he grabbed the red lion around the neck and how the lion, choking and strangling, grew redder still, so that it was as if the sun were blinding Khan Turali? Yet that hero broke the lion in the middle and picked him up and threw him down, and the lion was shivered to pieces.

"Tomorrow, you will give me your daughter," Khan Turali said.

"Bring on the blue camel!" the king ordered.

"Shall I turn aside from a camel?"

Khan Turali asked his companions. "Sing my praises!"

Let us see, my Sultan, how they praised him.

By night you entered the infidels' lands.
When the green bull came you smashed him to pieces.
When the red lion came you broke him in the middle.
Now comes the blue camel.
News will climb mountains.
News will cross rivers.
News will reach Oghuz.
Glory to the girl in yellow!
Glory to her gallant hero!

Princess Saljan stood on her balcony, punching at her nose as if to say, "The camel's weak spot is his nose. Hit the camel's nose!"

Khan Turali glowered. "If I punch the camel's nose, they'll say I did so because the girl told me to. Tomorrow news will reach Oghuz that I was at the camel's mercy and the girl saved me."

O my Sultan, shall I tell you how Khan Turali spoke a blessing on Muhammad of Beautiful Name—peace be upon him—and gave the blue camel a kick, then kicked it again until it screamed? How he jumped on it and cut its throat? How the blue blood of the camel stained the marble square as Khan Turali drew two sinews from the monster's back?

"These may come in handy for sewing," Khan Turali said, presenting the sinews to the king.

"By God, the moment my eye saw this young man, my soul loved him," the king said. And he ordered a white tent and red bridal bower to be pitched. Khan Turali and the girl were led to the bower as minstrels played nuptial music.

Khan Turali stopped cold before the tent. "May I be sliced by my own sword and spitted on my own arrow if I enter this bridal bower before I see the faces of my Lord Father and my Lady Mother!"

He swung Princess Saljan onto a stallion. He mounted his black-maned

Kazilik mare and summoned his faithful forty. They galloped for seven days and seven nights until they arrived at the border of Oghuz, where they made camp. Then Khan Turali sent his forty comrades ahead to ask his father and mother to meet him.

Princess Saljan was happy in the place where they camped. Swans and cranes and pheasants and partridges fluttered and flew about on rivers and flowered meadows and lawns. The couple ate and drank until Khan Turali began to snore.

Saljan looked lovingly at her sleeping warrior. "I have had many suitors and my father was not pleased to lose me," she thought. "The chances are there will be a cavalcade coming to kill my young lord and take me back to my parents' house. This must not be."

She quietly dressed in war gear, saddled her horse, took up a spear, and rode to high ground to watch for her father's warriors.

Lo, my Sultan, Princess Saljan knew her father well. For indeed, he had repented and said to his companions, "Just because Khan Turali killed three beasts, he thinks he is entitled to take my only daughter." And the king dispatched six hundred of his black-clad, blue-armored warriors.

The princess was ready for them. No sooner had she gotten to high ground than she saw the raiding party coming upon them. She spurred her horse to where Khan Turali lay, and found him snoring, his mouth stained red with wine.

"Wake up!" she cried. "Raise your dark head, warrior! Open your eyes before your hands and arms are tied and your forehead trodden to the ground, your head cut off, your red blood spilled! Wake up! They are upon you."

Khan Turali sputtered awake. "What are you saying, my lovely one?"

"I am saying, my dear, that the enemy are upon you. My part was to rouse you. Yours is to fight!"

Khan Turali rubbed his eyes. He unglued his eyelids, leaped to his feet, and noticed then that his bride was dressed for battle, spear in hand, and that she had arrived in this state long before he.

Khan Turali dropped to his knees and kissed the ground. "My wish has been granted! You are the girl of my dreams!"

He mounted his horse, spoke a blessing on Muhammad of Beautiful Name—peace be upon him—and drove at the black-garbed, blue-armored warriors. Princess Saljan followed, then sped ahead of Khan Turali.

"Hey, my lovely one," he called. "What are you doing? Where are you going?"

"My lordly warrior, like head and cap, we are inseparable! We fight together!"

O my Sultan, the battle raged fiercely, and Khan Turali and Princess Saljan were separated in the melee. Shall I tell you how bravely each fought? How heads rolled and the enemy's blood stained the green valley? Princess Saljan routed the infidel, but she did not pursue those of her countrymen who fled, nor kill those who asked for mercy.

Assuming her enemies were defeated, with sword still bloody, Saljan turned her horse back to camp, back to Khan Turali. But instead of her beloved, she found his mother and father.

"Who are you?" Khanli Khoja asked. His Lady Wife pointed her finger and shrieked. "Have you let my boy be captured? Have you carelessly let them cut off his perfect head? Here you are, but my one son is not to be seen!"

Saljan pointed at the rugs folded by the campfire. "Sit down," she said, and turned her mount toward the valley, where dust gathered in clouds. As she approached, she saw Khan Turali's horse shot dead by an enemy and Khan Turali himself wounded by an arrow over the eye. Blood masked his face. The infidels closed in for the kill while he flailed blindly with his sword.

Princess Saljan smashed into the infidel circle, shrieking and chanting a war cry. She thrust her sword now here, now there, now at this throat, now at that heart. She drove the enemy off. Khan Turali wiped the blood from his eyes and saw that someone was chasing the warriors away.

"Warrior!" he bawled. "You there! What warrior are you? Hey, warrior, nonchalantly cutting off heads, attacking my enemy without so much as a by-your-leave! Who are you? Be off with you! This is *my* enemy, *my* fight! Get back, I say, *get back*!"

"My darling," Saljan called, swinging her sword at the last of the fleeing infidels. "Do heroic warriors slaughter their beautiful wives?"

Khan Turali climbed to his feet and charged at the infidels. "One wing of this enemy for you and one for me!" Saljan whooped. They brandished their swords and pressed on. The enemy was crushed; the foe was routed. Princess Saljan and Khan Turali rode from the battlefield victorious.

My Sultan, a thought began to tease, then torment, our valiant prince.

"Princess," he said, "when the women of Oghuz tell their stories, you will boast. You will say that Khan Turali was helpless. That you led the way and that he followed after."

Khan Turali glowered at Saljan. "It must not be! Anger consumes me, Princess. The heart has gone out of me. I shall have to kill you!"

"Warrior prince," Saljan replied. "If man will boast, let him boast. He is a lion. For a woman to boast is unnatural. I am yours. Your friend. Your lover. Spare me!"

"No," said Khan Turali. "You will shame me. I must kill you."

"Quickly you fell in love and quickly you wearied," Saljan said, spurring her horse to high ground. "You are nothing but a pimp and the son of a pimp."

She poured ninety-nine arrows onto the earth.

She pointed her hundredth arrow at Khan Turali. "Go ahead, warrior, shoot!"

"Girls first," he said. "You shoot!"

"All right!" She squinted and aimed.

Her arrow lanced the lice on Khan Turali's head like shish kabob.

"My bright flame, my waving cypress, royal maiden, daughter of lions," he said tenderly, when at last he found words. "Could I bring myself to kill you? I was only testing you."

"And I was only testing you, my lordly warrior." she replied.

They rushed at each other and gave their sweet mouths one to the other and when they had done with kissing, they mounted their horses and galloped until they came to the campground where Khanli Khoja and his Lady Wife waited.

Khanli Khoja gave thanks and pitched white tents on the grass. He made a wedding banquet and feasted with the chieftains of the mighty Oghuz. A gold-decked pavilion was raised, and Khan Turali and Saljan entered their red bridal bower and attained their hearts' desires.

The Sultan lies asleep smiling and Dede Korkut creaks to his three-hundred-year-old knees.

"O my Sultan, may God grant you increase and preserve you in strength and forgive your sins for the sake of Muhammad of Beautiful Name, peace be upon him."

Then Grandfather Korkut walks on, and wherever he goes he passes patient gravediggers. They have waited for him a long, long time.

I woke, opened my eyes, raised my head:
There, with bright face
Like a full moon, he was standing, upright.
Was it my lucky star? A blessing? Divine power?
I met Jupiter ascending.
His clothing was pagan.
From his face—I saw clearly—light streamed.
I blinked. He vanished.
A celestial angel.
Mihri will never die.
She's found the elixir of life.
She saw Yskander beaming in the darkness.

—Mihri Khatun, Turkey, d. 1506 CE

If I made shrouds
No one would die.
If I sold lamps
Then in the sky
The Sun for spite
Would shine at night.

—Abraham Ibn Ezra, Spain, 1089–1167 CE

Layla and Majnun

When Qays is born, his father opens the treasury in celebration. All the Banu Amir share their chieftain's happiness. The boy is handsome and beaming. His face is round as the moon, his namesake.

As Qays grows, he becomes comelier. He opens his mouth, and each word is a pearl spilling from his tongue. His wit is sharp as a scimitar. "No man on Earth is more fortunate than I," his father exclaims. "I have been given a poet for a son."

Qays is sent from the camp to school in the village. One morning, a little girl appears, slender as a cypress and graceful as a skylark, with skin the color of ripe olives, lips like rosy clay and the piercing black eyes of a gazelle. Her black hair is lustrous as satin and she is called Layla, Night.

Layla enters the school tent and love awakens in Qays' heart. He can't read or write or recite his lessons. He can only stare at her.

"Layla!" he whispers as if in prayer. "Layla! I will love you all my life."

They are still children, but Layla loves Qays in return. They have no need to speak. Their souls are perfectly attuned. Each morning, they hurry joyfully to school, but they can concentrate only on each other. In the evening, when they are apart and the sky darkens, they rush eagerly to their beds, the sooner to dream of one another.

The other children tease and taunt: "See how Qays stares at Layla like a sheep. He is a madman, chanting her name all day."

"Layla! Layla!" Qays shouts, running from the school tent. He runs into the bazaars. He runs around the women stirring their cauldrons. He leaps over babies in their cradles. He runs through corrals and past shepherds and camel drivers, crying, "Layla! Layla!" He dashes around in circles. People shake their heads and cluck: "Indeed, he is a madman. He is *majnun*."

And Qays comes to be called Majnun. Word reaches Layla's father. He is outraged: "Who is this Majnun shouting Layla's name in the bazaars and among the people, insulting my daughter and my tribe?"

He removes Layla from the school. He takes her to his desert camp, where she sheds lonely, secret tears for Qays.

Majnun sits listless before his open books. He stares forlornly at Layla's empty place. He has lost his beloved and he has lost himself. He closes his books. He flees to the bazaar. He wanders among the stalls, murmuring her name. "Layla!"

His ravings become poems. His wild talk becomes love songs. The wind carries his tunes into the wilderness. He follows them, crying "Layla! Layla! May my songs fall at your feet."

At night he sneaks to Layla's camp and like a shadow kisses the threshold of her tent.

And Layla, alone in her tent, feels the gentle billow and shudder of Majnun's yearning. It drifts onto her shoulders. It kisses her cheeks and lips. It tumbles all around her. She walks on words of love, supple as clouds beneath her soles.
One night, Layla sits restless and sleepless outside her tent. Majnun appears on a moonbeam. They gape at each other. Each is mirrored in the other. Mouths refuse to open. Tongues and lips refuse to shape sounds. Neither can move. They are alone for the first time.

They stare at each other until dawn. Then Majnun hurries back to his own camp.

Passion devours him. He has lost his heart; now he is losing his reason. He wanders away from his camp. He roams the desert. He stumbles through the mountains. He tears his robes. "Layla! Layla!" One song after another flutters from his mouth.

His father gathers the elders and wise men of the Banu Amir to a council circle: "My son has lost his heart. His senses are confused. Without Layla he lives as if he was blind. If he could win her, surely he will find his light."

Majnun's father sends a search party to find him and sets out for Layla's camp. His camels are laden with precious gifts; his hopes are high.

"My daughter will not marry a madman!" Layla's father shouts. "Who has not heard of Majnun's lunacy? See first that your son is cured, then come to me again. For if I grant your wish, as surely as the sun beats upon the desert sand, Layla's name will be heard again in the bazaars and every man in Arabia will laugh at me."

Majnun's father is a tender man. "Why must you worship only Layla?" he asks his son. "Among our tribe there are a hundred lovely maidens. Choose one as your wife and forget Layla. Then you will be happy, your ardor satisfied."

Majnun gasps and flees once again into the wild lands. He plunges across burning sand. Thorns catch in his robe. "Layla!" He tears his hair. "Layla!" Each grain of sand resounds with his songs.

In village after village the people marvel at his eloquence. Some pity him; some turn their backs in shame at this outcast who brings disgrace upon his family.

In the desert, a group of shepherds find Majnun lying on the sand. They take him back to his father's camp. He lies in his father's tent, chanting Layla's name. His good father laments. "I no longer have a son."

He takes Majnun to Mecca to ask God's blessing. He carries Majnun in a litter like an infant in a cradle. He showers alms upon the poor. He brings Majnun before the Ka'aba, the holy house that Ibrahim built. "My son, ask God, all-Merciful, all-Compassionate, to save you from your passion. Pray to Him to end your madness. Certainly, you will be cured."

Majnun laughs. His laughter grows wild, until it turns to sobs. "I pray to you, almighty God, let me not be cured of my love, but let my passion grow! Take what is left of my life and give it to Layla, yet let me never demand from her so much as a single hair! Let me love her for love's sake and make my love a hundred times greater than it is this very day!"

His father bows his head in sorrow. He turns to his kinsmen. "Majnun will never be cured, for he has blessed Layla before the holy Ka'aba and cursed himself."

Word of Majnun's prayer reaches Layla's father, who vows to kill Majnun, but Majnun has fled again to the desert. Again, Majnun's father goes in search of him. He finds Majnun in a desolate gorge, writhing like a snake, moaning and sighing, talking to himself, weeping and swooning. His father wraps Majnun in his arms. His father begs Majnun to be patient and prudent, to give up despair.

"There is no creature on Earth who is not ruled by destiny," Majnun mumbles. "To love Layla is my fate and I can never throw off my burden."

His father carries him from the rocky gorge back to camp. His kinswomen bring him food and water. His mother sings lullabies to him. Majnun stares blankly into nothing and does not know her.

When Majnun's strength returns, he runs again into the desert. He strays under the blistering sun until his face is black. His feet bleed.

He stumbles into the towns. He rambles through the bazaars muttering, "Let Layla's father threaten. I'm not afraid. What lover fears a sword?"

People from far and near come to listen. They memorize his poems. When they find love themselves, it is Majnun's words they sing to the stirrings in their own hearts. Layla is growing into the most beautiful maiden in Arabia. But she can't outgrow the sorrow she has felt since she and Majnun watched each other in the moonlight. No night passes that she does not stand outside her tent, listening for his step, watching for his shadow. No one visits but the wind and the silhouettes of clouds above the sand.

She hears his songs on everyone's lips. Children and travelers alike. She falls asleep repeating them. Layla creates her own songs for Majnun and writes them on little scraps of paper. She scatters them on the sand for the wind to carry away. The wind carries her songs into the villages. The people come upon the little scraps of paper as if encountering precious jewels. Soon Layla's songs reach Majnun. He sings replies, and the words are carried back and forth across the desert on the lips of the people.

They are answering each other's cry. There is a *wadi* near Layla's tent, and every day she visits it with her companions. Her friends dance and play among the palm trees, but Layla sits apart thinking of Majnun.

Tears fall from her black eyes. Layla weeps and her mother consoles her, embraces her, rocks her. Layla has never spoken a word to her mother about Majnun, yet her mother knows. Her heart cracks to see her child's suffering.

One day, a young man named Ibn Salam passes by the palm grove and catches a glimpse of Layla. He falls in love. He is from a rich and noble clan, and he goes at once to ask Layla's father for her hand. The chieftain is pleased and readily agrees. But Layla is too young. "Be patient," Layla's father tells Ibn Salam. "In a few months, the bud will blossom into a full-blown rose. Then the wedding feast will be set."

"Layla! Layla!" Majnun takes shelter among bleak and barren rocks. A Bedouin prince, Nowfal rides by and stops, shocked at the boy dressed in rags, staring into the sky and shouting.

The prince is kind and brave in battle. He pities Majnun. He sets a banquet before him. He takes Majnun's hand: "My friend, listen to me. I've heard your story and want to help you rebuild your heart, stone by stone. Trust me, and you will find Layla and have her for your own to love all your life. You will have Layla, even if I must do battle!"

Majnun goes with Nowfal to his camp. He dons fine robes and a silk turban. He rides each morning with Nowfal. They ride all day. He feasts with the prince. He calls for wine and listens to the songs of minstrels. Months pass, and the cheerful youth who was Qays is restored.

One afternoon, the two friends sit in the shade of a tree. "Nowfal, good prince," Qays says, "my patience has come to its end. I beg you, help me unite with Layla as you promised. If I must wait even a minute longer, I will die."

The prince leaps to his feet. He takes up his sword and summons his men to arms. The two friends ride across the desert and reach the pasturelands of Layla's tribe. They pitch their tents. Nowfal sends a messenger to Layla's father: "Tell him we come in Qays' name, that he is restored and that he must have Layla. Tell him if he refuses, I will attack."

The chieftain replies with curses: "I will die rather than give my daughter to this madman!"

Nowfal sets upon Layla's people. The desert resonates with the clash and screams of war. Qays, so anxious to claim Layla by any means, transforms again into Majnun and huddles away from the battle, sobbing, ashamed, praying for peace. He cannot fight. He cannot raise his sword. Every injury to Layla's tribesmen is a wound to himself.

At dusk, a truce is called. Nowfal sends a messenger to the chieftain. He offers many jewels and precious gifts for Layla. The chieftain scornfully repudiates the prince. He has mustered tribesmen from surrounding pastures and hunting grounds, until his army outnumbers Nowfal's. Then Majnun's father sends his warriors and the warriors of his allies to join Nowfal. Layla's father is defeated.

He kneels at Nowfal's feet: "I am a weak old man. I have no strength. My men are all dispersed. Do what you will with me, but there is only one thing I ask. Do not give Layla to Majnun, for he is a fool and a demon. He has disgraced his name and hers!"

Compassion for the chieftain overtakes Nowfal. Hadn't he gone to battle for Majnun's sake? And hadn't Majnun then refused to fight? Instead of fighting, he weeps over the bodies of Layla's dead kinsmen. He is not only a madman, Nowfal thinks, Majnun is also a traitor.

Nowfal grants the chieftain's request and bids him farewell. He gives the order to break camp. Majnun takes his few possessions and rides into the desert. Nowfal never sees Majnun again.

"Layla! Layla!" echoes across the yellow dunes.

Layla listens in silence when her father tells her that she will be married to Ibn Salam. Never, not for a moment, has her love for Majnun faltered.

Majun rides slowly through the wilderness and comes upon two gazelles in a trap. A hunter stands over them, dagger raised. Majnun looks into the gentle black eyes of the gazelles and remembers Layla's eyes. "I beg you, good hunter, do not kill these beautiful creatures!"

"I am a poor man with a wife and family to feed," the hunter says. "I've waited two months for this catch. What will you give me in exchange for the gazelles?"

Majnun dismounts his horse and places the reins in the hunter's hands. He frees the gazelles, and they lope away. He walks in the desert, chanting, "Layla! Layla! Our loving souls combine in absence."

He comes upon a stag caught in a net and wounded in the neck. A hunter stands over the stag, knife drawn.

"I beg of you, good hunter, release this stag. Think of the pain of those whose suffering you cause."

"I don't want to kill the stag," the hunter says, "but how will I survive? What will you give me if I let the stag go free?"

Majnun gives the hunter all that remain of his possessions. He frees the stag. He continues on his way to nowhere: "Layla! Layla!"

On the third day, the sun glares so fiercely, the sand shimmers like embers. Majnun sits in the shade of a date-palm tree. A crow perches above him. "Why are you dressed in black as black as Layla's hair?" Majnun asks the crow. "Do you share my sorrow? Help me in my loneliness."

Ibn Salam comes to claim Layla as his bride. He arrives with caravans full of gifts. He showers silks and gold upon the chieftain. Carpets are spread and a wedding feast is set. For seven days and seven nights, there is celebration. Fires are lit. Incense of aloe is burned. Silver coins are tossed into the air. Then Ibn Salam departs with his bride. When the caravan reaches his own lands, the happy bridegroom tells Layla: "Everything you see is yours, my love."

He reaches to embrace her. She recoils. He tries again to take her in his arms. She strikes him hard across the face: "Don't come within an arm's length of me! I have vowed never to give myself to you. Take your sword and kill me, but I will not submit, not in a hundred years!"

Ibn Salam falls to his knees: "I would rather be allowed to look upon your face than lose you forever."

Thus, a year passes and Layla lives only in thoughts of Majnun, hoping for a message.

Majnun lies hungry and exhausted on the sand. A stranger passes and tells him: "Have you not heard? Layla is married. Her husband is rich and noble. At this very moment, he squeezes her in his bed. Better to turn your back on Layla than to scorn the world, my friend."

Majnun collapses. The stranger is overcome with regret. When Majnun opens his eyes, the stranger begs pardon. "I have been wicked and spoken falsely. Layla is married, but she loves you still and will not share her husband's bed. She is chaste in longing for you."

Majnun scrapes on. "Layla, I love the night for you are in it."

In the next breath, he reproaches her for betraying him.

In the following breath he sings, "Layla, you are my sun, my lamplight."

Majnun's father grieves greatly for his son. He seeks him in the desert once more. Leaning heavily on his walking stick, he sets out with two companions. He is feeble with age. It is many days before he finds Majnun wasted and withered in a cave. "I beg you, Qays, my son, come home. I am close to death. As I die, I want you by my side. When I am dead, you must take my place."

Majnun hears his father's words but does not at first understand them. Who is Qays? Who is this old man standing before him?

At last, a glimmer of memory and Majnun says, "Father, I am lost to you and can never return. I live like the wild animals who are my companions. I am a stranger to my tribe."

His father returns home and dies. A kinsman visits Majnun to tell him the news: "Wicked son of a good father, pray for exoneration from your sins."

Majnun visits his father's grave and prays without ceasing for a day and a night. The lion, the stag, the antelope, the wolf, and the fox come to Majnun. The wild ass, the hare, the timid gazelle befriend him. No place is more forsaken than the wilderness where Majnun and the animals reside, but Majnun calls it paradise and lives in peace with his new tribe. He sings his songs to Layla. The beasts bow their heads in sympathy. The fox sweeps clean Majnun's sleeping place with his bushy tail. The wild ass is Majnun's pillow. His knees rest on the haunches of the antelope. The gazelle caresses his feet. The wolf keeps watch through the night: "Now that I am among my true clan, I have tamed the beast of my soul."

An old man approaches Majnun's cave. He has flowing white hair and a face so kind the lion ceases growling, the wolf does not bare her teeth.

"I have seen Layla," the old man tells him. "One day I came upon her grieving in a garden. Her sorrow was so strong, I begged her to speak. She wept and said: 'I am a thousand times madder than Majnun. He is free to wander as he pleases, while I'm a prisoner in this camp. My torments are a thousand times greater than Majnun's. I hunger for news of him. Where does he go? What does he say? Has he companions? I beg of you, find him and tell me how he is!'

"And when I promised to search for you, she gave me this for you."

The old man hands Majnun a letter. His heart quickens as he reads it. He asks for paper and pen: "Please take this to Layla with my love."

His mother is old and yearns for her son. She is brought to Majnun and her heart shrinks when she sees him. With her tears, she washes the dust from Majnun's body. She plucks the thorns from his feet. She combs his matted hair. She pleads with him to return. Majnun is adamant: "Your people, Mother, are no longer mine. I know only the desert and my animals." He throws himself at her feet. He begs her forgiveness.

The old woman, bent with melancholy, returns home and breathes her last. Majnun visits her tomb to pray. His kinsmen reprimand him, calling him a cruel, neglectful son. He flees from their blame and anger. He returns to his friends, the wild beasts.

Layla eagerly awaits an answer to her letter. Each night she slips from her tent to stand at the village crossroads, watching and listening for the kind old man. At last he arrives, and when she reads Majnun's letter, she rewards the gentle graybeard with jewels and a sack of coins and asks him to bring Majnun to a nearby grove: "The trees there are thick as a wall. We won't be seen. Tell my beloved that I long to hear him sing his songs."

The old man leads Majnun to the

grove. The faithful animals follow and stand patiently outside. Layla waits, keeping her distance from Majnun. She fears she will disappear in the warmth of his nearness. She sits beneath a tree and listens. For long, long minutes, there is no sound. Majnun has fainted.

When he awakens, he sings, "Layla! I am yours. I will live forever with you!" The lovers gaze at each other with bliss and wonder, as when they were children.

When the song ends, Majnun runs from the grove. Layla runs back to her tent, terrified of her own passion.

Layla's husband, Ibn Salam, takes ill and dies. Layla weeps without restraint. All who look upon her believe she weeps for her young husband, but in truth she mourns for Majnun, free at last to give way to her grief in the presence of others. She dutifully retreats to her tent to seclude herself for two years, as is the custom. She welcomes solitude. She thinks every minute of Majnun.

In autumn, the trees blaze red and gold. The wind blows. Layla is so frail, she can no longer rise from her bed. A fever overcomes her. She calls to her mother: "Grant me one wish. When I die, dress me in bridal robes. Thus I shall wait for my beloved, for Majnun will come to my grave. Comfort him as you would comfort me."

On the day that Layla dies, scarlet leaves float to the ground. Her mother dresses her in bridal robes.

Majnun lies on Layla's grave, weeping his heart's blood. The ground turns crimson. Majnun's animal clan guards him closely. He sings his songs. His voice is weak with sobbing. "Layla! Layla!"

The beasts defend his body so that no one can touch him until at last Majnun crumbles to dust.

His tribesmen come forth to bury his bones beside the bones of his beloved Layla.

Song of Majnun

And who am I, so far from you, yet near?
A singing beggar! Layla, do you hear?
My soul is yours and yours is mine.
Our two souls combine.
We are two riddles to the world,
Answering each other's deep lament.
Our parting cannot sever us,
One radiant light envelops us,
Though our despairing bodies separate,
Our souls wander freely and
communicate.

I'll live forever.
Mortal Fear, decay, and death
Have ceased to hold their sway.
Sharing your life through eternity
I'll live if only you remain with me.

—Nizami, Persia, 1149 to 1209 CE

Yes, I am Layla.
My heart beats wildly like ferocious Majnun.
I want to plunge into the desert,
naked and singing,
but modesty is like thick mud on my feet.

A nightingale came to the rose garden.
He is my pupil.
I am an expert in the decoration of love.
Even the moth is my disciple.

—Zeb-un-Nissa, India, 1638 to 1702 CE

The Seven Princesses

Yazdegerd, the king of Persia, had a son he named Bahram. The royal astrologers searched their charts, and when they finished their calculations, they went before the king. "Magnificence," they announced, "all the stars concur: your son will have good fortune. But if he is to fulfill his happy future, he must be brought up in Yemen."

And so it was that Bahram grew to manhood in the court of Yemen, in a residence especially built for him by magicians. He was schooled in mathematics and astronomy, riding and polo, and the arts of war and hunting. Indeed, he was so skilled with a bow, and had once so unerringly killed a wild ass and a lion with one arrow, that he became a legend and was called Bahram Gur, after the *gur*, the wild ass.

One day, the prince came upon a locked door to a room he had never encountered. He bade his chamberlain to unlock it, then walked across the threshold into a splendid treasure house. On the walls were seven portraits of seven princesses from seven regions on Earth. Dark and fair, slender, and full, sober, and smiling, each one's beauty was so perfect as to make diamonds seem dim, rubies seem drab, and emeralds cheap as gravel. The prince's heart was captured. And to his amazement, he also came upon a likeness of himself, beneath which was an inscription within a triangle within a rectangle: "The stars have ordained that Bahram Gur will wed these seven princesses when he is king."

The prince was filled with joy. He went often to the room to contemplate the seven princesses. Seven is the first perfect number—the seven seas, the Seven Sleepers awaiting God's enlightenment, the seven notes of the spheres, the seven planets that are the agents of God, the seven heavens, the seven climes whose

colors on Earth are illuminated by their own astral light, the seven soul birds soaring through the seven valleys, and the seventh day of rest.

When he was fully grown and his father had died, despite the pleasant auguries, Bahram Gur had to fight to gain the throne of Persia. But these battles were merely the true tests of kingship, and soon the prince triumphed. He became ruler of Persia and settled into a time of peace and plenty. He thought often of his youth in the land of Yemen and remembered the locked room and the portraits of the seven beautiful princesses and marveled at the glory foretold in those murals, so real he might have stepped right into them

Each year in winter, King Bahram Gur held a great feast. One night a craftsman named Shideh proposed to build Bahram Gur a palace of unsurpassed magnificence, with seven lofty domes to reflect the wonders of Heaven, above seven sumptuous pavilions for seven beautiful princesses. "Each dome," Shideh promised, "will be a different color, constructed according to the position in the sky of the planet that governs that color. The pavilions will be furnished with the finest carpets and silk hangings, the most precious metals and woods, the sweetest wines, and the world's most fragrant flowers."

Bahram Gur ordered Shideh to begin work at the first auspicious moment. Shideh labored for two years. The king was so delighted, he showered the craftsman with splendid gifts, and sent his most trusted companions to seek the seven princesses who would reside in each of the seven pavilions.

Then Bahram Gur prepared himself for the pleasures that had been foretold. "Even as the planets move, so shall I," he said. "Each day for a week, I will visit one pavilion."

The Black Pavilion

On Saturday, the day of Saturn, Bahram Gur dresses all in black and enters the black pavilion. The Princess Furak, youngest daughter of an Indian raja, awaits him. The air is sweet with incense of opium that rises into the dome where the planet and its rings are shaped of black pearls. The walls are painted with glossy black birds. A sundial sits within a wild garden. An onyx pool, fed from an underground spring, is lined with tiles glazed with the seven flames of Saturn, and within the pool float a pair of black, iridescent ducks.

All that day, in the dim incandescence of the pavilion, Bahram Gur enjoys the charms of Princess Furak, with her sable skin and agate eyes. When night falls and the sky turns dark, the birds mistake Furak's beauty for the radiance of the dawn and sing to her. But daybreak is still many hours away when the enchanted king makes his request.

"A story, my love," he murmurs. "I would have a story."

And with a languid smile, Princess Furak begins her tale:

Once there was a Rainbow King, whose palace shone with all the colors of the world. The king was carefree and high-spirited. Laughter reigned in his palace. Wine flowed and travelers were never turned away.

One day, a traveler arrived dressed all in black. The king asked for his story, but the stranger only shook his head. The king asked again and again, until, after a week of coaxing, the traveler gave in. "I beg you, my king, do not ask the secret of my sorrow. I can only tell you that when I was a youth, I made my way to the remote mountains of Kafiristan, where there is a place for those who dress only in black, called the City of the Stupefied."

The stranger would say no more and continued on his way. For weeks, the king brooded upon the traveler's words and finally dispatched messengers to find the man, but there was no trace of him.

Neither had anyone heard of the City of the Stupefied.

Unsatisfied, the king journeyed to Kafiristan. He traveled many days and many nights over high mountains, across wide rivers, through scorching deserts and dark forests. At last, he beheld a city rising in the cool blue dusk. The king drew nearer. Black flags fluttered on the rooftops, and in the streets, the citizens were all dressed in black from head to foot.

The king told no one who he was. For a year he sought the secret to the city's sorrow, but the townspeople would not speak, yet every morning they raised their mournful flags. After a year had passed, the king met a kind, honest man, a simple butcher by trade. The king lavished gifts on him, so, reluctantly, the butcher invited the king to his house. "Why, my friend," the good man asked, "do you give me such precious gifts? Look at my humble dwelling. Even if I were to live a hundred lives, how could I ever repay you?"

The king told the butcher who he was and begged to know the secret of the City of the Stupefied.

No moon or stars were visible as the butcher led the king out of the city to an ancient place, where amid the shards and crumbled bricks, they found a basket encircled by a rope. "Sit here, my king," the butcher said, "and you will know why all the people of the city dress in black."

No sooner was the king seated in the basket than the butcher vanished. The basket rose slowly into the air and alighted on a desolate mountain tower. Suddenly, a giant black bird landed and perched beside him. Terrified, the king clutched the bird's talons and, as dawn approached, the bird flew off, carrying the king through the dim sky. As day broke, the exhausted king looked down to see an enchanted garden, where jasmine bloomed, and rosewater flowed from a stream. He let go of the bird's claws and dropped into the perfumed paradise. All that day, he sat beside the river wondering what would happen next. As night descended and the king nodded off to sleep, a company of pretty maidens, singing and holding lighted candles, entered the garden. They were followed by another group of maidens bearing rich carpets and a throne of gold. Then a lady of perfect beauty appeared, and the king was overcome by love.

The queen of the fairies sat on a golden throne, signaling the maidens to dance. They danced in circles and lines, and as they danced, they passed by the king. They took his hand and led him to the queen, who nodded her head in welcome. The king gasped with pleasure.

"Come sit upon the throne with me," the queen said, and all night they feasted on sweet dainties and fruits and drank wine from silver goblets. The king had never been so happy and passionate. He tried to embrace her, but she drew back and gave him instead to one of her handmaidens.

And so it happened that each night, an exquisite maiden awaited the king and at daybreak bathed him, then departed. All day, the king slept. At night, he begged the queen for her love, but she scolded him, saying, "Impatience does not become a king. Content yourself with my handmaidens and ask for nothing more."

For thirty long nights, the king ached for her, until he could bear his yearning no longer. Under the full moon, his passion overtook him and he forced himself on the fairy queen. When he was done and holding her to his heart, she whispered, "Close your eyes, my king." From what seemed like a very long distance, he heard her say, "Now open your eyes, my king, to what must be."

The garden was gone. The maidens, the golden throne, and the fairy queen had disappeared. The king found himself sitting in the basket among the ancient ruins with the faithful butcher by his side.

"Now you see, my king," the butcher said sadly, "why all the people of the city dress in black. We were all enchanted by the fairy queen, her maidens, and her garden. We were all impatient and presumptuous, then punished for taking what does not belong to us and was not offered. We are all in mourning at the absence of beauty."

Back in his own land, the king retired from his court in guilt and shame. He gave away his brilliant robes and jewels and dressed himself from head to foot only in black.

So ends the tale of the Indian princess. Embracing, Furak and Bahram Gur drift into sleep. All too soon, the sky turns golden with the dawn. Bahram Gur arises and returns to his own chamber. It is Sunday. The day of the sun.

The Yellow Pavilion

Bahram Gur dresses all in gold. On his shoulders he places a golden cloak, and on his head a golden crown to visit the yellow pavilion.

"So sweet was my first bride, can the second be even sweeter?" he wonders.

The Princess Humay of Byzantium awaits him. She is as fair as the sun that gleams through the mica panels fitted into the golden dome above. Her hair is yellow, her eyes are flecked with amber.

The air is fragrant with saffron; the walls are lined with bricks of pyrite and ornamented with images of the divine eye peering from nets of golden threads. A simurgh flies in golden circles through tiles shaped like stars. In the garden the Tree of Life springs and is surrounded by the Trees of Knowledge and Truth.

Princess Humay offers Bahram Gur bowls of blushing peaches, crimson pomegranates, and ripe, shining mulberries. She brings him cushions of golden cloth embroidered with golden threads, and all day long he basks in her golden light. When evening comes and the sun stretches its golden fingers across the heavens, Bahram Gur makes his request.

"A story, my love," he murmurs. "I would have a story."

And with a radiant smile, Princess Humay begins her tale:

Many years ago, in the land of Iraq, there was a king twice blessed by fortune. He had innumerable riches, and he was the handsomest man in the realm. Even so, he was miserable, for he had no wife.

His loneliness weighed heavily on him until he could bear it no longer. He commanded a magnificent palace to be built and in it installed the most beautiful maidens he could find. Days and nights of pleasure passed, but one by one, he tired of the maidens and sent them away. When they were all gone, he wandered the palace gardens alone, still yearning disconsolately for a wife.

As it happened, among the king's servants was an old woman, who had for many years wished evil upon the king. When she saw him walking sorrowfully through the gardens, she was delighted.

"I can find you a woman to love," she told him. And she brought more maidens, even more beautiful than the ones the king had sent away. She enticed each one with tales of the king's great wealth, and as the king became enchanted, he gave each woman a precious gift. But no sooner were the gifts bestowed than the maidens cried for more silken robes, necklaces of pearls, silver caskets filled with rubies, and golden caskets brimming with emeralds. Such was their greed that they howled and shrieked for more until the king ordered the palace guards to carry them away. Alone again, he wandered sadly through his gardens.

One day a slave-dealer arrived, bringing with him a girl as lovely as the morning star. The king saw her, was devastated by love, and resolved to buy her at once. But to his astonishment, the slave- dealer refused.

"I beg of you, Magnificence," he said, "take any but her. In every country I have traveled, she has been bought by kings and princes and the richest merchants. But whoever buys her returns her to me at sunrise the next day. I do not know why."

The king offered the slave-dealer so many jewels, so many pieces of gold and

other precious gifts besides, the man at last reluctantly agreed.

The king took the maiden to his palace, where he gave her the finest apartments. The slave-dealer awoke at sunrise, ready for the king to bring the girl back to him. He waited for three days, and on the fourth, when the king had still not come, the slave-dealer went his way.

The king and the maiden feasted and sipped wine and sat under silken canopies or in the garden among the flowering trees. They spoke of love the whole day long. But with nightfall, the king burned with passion and readiness, the girl drew back and hid. At dawn, she showed herself again, eyes full of affection, but only smiled sadly and said nothing when the king asked her why she had fled.

Finally, the king's patience was spent. One morning, he sat the maiden down and said, "Listen, my love, for I have a story to tell.

"Long ago, when King Suleiman ruled the land, a son was born to him and Bilqis, the queen of Sheba. The infant was deformed in all his limbs. He could not walk. He could not lift even a crust of bread to his hungry lips. Suleiman and Bilqis prayed for a cure. At last, an angel appeared and told them that if only they could speak the truth to one another, their child would be made whole. Immediately Bilqis told him Suleiman that whenever she set eyes on a handsome young man, her heart ached with lust. As she spoke, the child stretched forth his hands. Suleiman then confessed that whenever one of his subjects came before him seeking wisdom, he thought only of the gift he would receive. As Suleiman spoke, the child stood up and took a step."

"If Suleiman and Bilqis spoke the truth," the king pleaded, "why can't you, my love? Don't be afraid but tell me what you must."

The king was so gentle and mournful, the maiden could not refuse. "It is the fate of every woman in my family to die in childbirth," she told him. "And I dread that I will also die in anguish if I submit to the love of any man."

At hearing the truth, the king loved her even more. "Of all the maidens I've taken to my palace, you are the only one who is not greedy for my wealth," he said. "I feared you had kept yourself from me, because I had not given you sufficient gifts."

Still, she refused to yield, and the king's joy sank to sorrow.

The old woman heard of the king's plight. "Magnificence, if you would have this girl," she advised, "you must first arouse her passion. Go to another, then she will burn with envy. She will be so jealous, she will grant you what you wish."

"Where might another girl be found?" the king sighed. "I have sent them all away."

But the old woman had saved the fairest of the maidens he'd dismissed and kept her in a secret chamber, out of the king's sight. How pleased the old woman was when the king stayed several nights with the maiden she had saved.

Meanwhile, the girl who had denied herself to the king sat in her apartments alone, terrified that she had lost the one she truly loved. Hour by hour she grew more agitated, until on the fourth night she sent a chamberlain to find the king and summon him. He rushed to see her, and she gave him what he had desired above all things.

No more is known or needs to be.

So ends the tale of the Byzantium princess. Embracing, Princess Humay and Bahram Gur drift into sleep.

When the heavens grow light, it is Monday, the day of the moon.

The Green Pavilion

Bahram Gur dresses all in green. With sprightly steps, he walks through a fresh meadow toward the green pavilion. "So sweet was my second bride, can the third be even sweeter?" he wonders.

The Princess Pari, daughter of the Tartar chieftain, awaits him. She is as graceful as the swaying willow and stately as the tall cypress that adorn the garden. Her hair is black as loam and her green eyes reflect the jade of the dome above, inlaid with silver crescents and wheels made of mother-of-pearl. The air is sweet with aloe, the walls are lined with opals and green tiles below bursting with blossoms. A fountain of milk bubbles on the wall, and koi swim languidly in a mirrored pool.

Princess Pari holds out her hand and leads Bahram Gur into the garden. There, on carpets of fragrant spring blossoms, they give themselves to pleasure all day. At evening, when the trees and flowers shimmer in the starlight, the king makes his request.

"A story, my love," he murmurs. "I would have a story."

With a smile gentle as a moonbeam, the Princess Pari begins her tale:

Once upon a time, in the country of Rum, there lived a man named Bashr, whose charity was known throughout the land. He was greatly learned, as eager for new knowledge as he was for daily bread. He meditated at sunrise and sundown every day and prayed many times in between.

Of all his virtues, the one Bashr clung to most was chastity. He took no wife. He paid not the slightest heed to any woman. He lived alone with his books, and every evening, while other men delighted in domestic comforts, Bashr studied until his eyelids grew heavy and his chin dropped. Then he shook himself awake, walked through the town, and, refreshed, resumed his studies for a few hours more.

One autumn night, when Bashr was revitalizing his mind walking in the streets, the wind rose and pushed a woman directly into his path. He moved to step aside when a sudden gust lifted her veil and Bashr saw her face.

He was dumbstruck. He shivered. He nearly fainted and tears sprang to his eyes. Alarmed, Bashr rushed home to his cherished books.

But he could not study. He could think of nothing but that woman. He had no idea who she was. He shut his books, despairing, and tried to sleep, but all night long he burned with passion. In the morning, he was weary and feverish. All day, he was distracted. He couldn't eat or drink and had no strength to read. He prayed. He burned with fever. After many days of suffering, Bashr resolved to make a solitary pilgrimage.

At last, he reached Jerusalem. As he prayed in the holy city, Bashr's anguish seemed to ease. When he felt his madness finally calm, he prepared to journey home. Along the road, he met a fellow traveler, a merchant called Malikha, also from the country of Rum. Malikha was a braggart who claimed to understand the secrets of the universe as no other mortal could.

"I have risen into the heavens, higher than any bird can fly," he shouted. "I have descended to the bottom of the sea, lower than fish can swim. I have seen it all, and at the mere snap of my fingers the wind will tell me when it will blow, and the rain when it will fall, and the sun when it will shine. That which ordains men's lives is known to me alone!"

Bashr sighed and shook his head. "These, my friend, are known only to God. Don't say such things or you will anger him."

"What do I care about your God?" Malikha yelled. "Let God be angry if he wants!"

Thus did Bashr and Malikha travel across the desert, the latter's boasts echoing for miles. The sun glared; the sand shimmered. The two men trudged on, seeking shade. The water they brought was quickly drunk and they could find no more. Bashr's mouth was parched; his cracked lips moved in silent prayer.

Just when they thought they would surely die, Bashr and Malikha came across an enormous tree, its spreading branches thick with leaves. In the tree's shade, sunk into the ground, was a large vessel filled to the brim with clear, cool water. They dropped to their knees and drank like beasts, then rested in the shade.

"Praise be to God, who has delivered us from death!" Bashr cried.

"Fool!" Malikha exclaimed, removing his robes so that he might bathe. "Do you think that God would put a vessel here to save our lives? A hunter sunk this vessel so that a wild ass might drink from it and be trapped."

"My friend," Bashr said softly, "do not speak so of God. And do not bathe, I beg you, for God's water is pure and you are covered with dust. You will leave the water dirty for other thirsty travelers."

Malikha would not be restrained. Bashr turned quietly away and walked toward the dunes. Malikha jumped gleefully into the sparkling water, only to discover that what he had thought was a hunter's vessel was actually a deep well. He could not climb out. He flailed. He kicked. He grabbed for the sides but could gain no hold.

When at last Bashr returned, there was no sign of Malikha, except for his robes by the side of the well. Bashr's heart pounded as he searched for his companion in the thick leaves of the tree and in the dunes nearby. He broke a branch and probed the water for Malikha's body. With a huge effort, he pulled the drowned man from the well. He buried him in the shade of the tree, praying for his soul. Then he packed Malikha's belongings and continued home.

It took much searching to find Malikha's house, but Bashr wished to return the dead man's clothes and possessions to his wife. At last, Bashr knocked on the door. A woman led him into the house, where he told her how her husband had died.

She sighed behind her veil and tears came to her eyes. "May God have mercy on his soul, as he has mercy on mine. I am relieved of a terrible burden, for Malikha was a wicked, unkind man."

She raised her veil to dry her tears. Bashr gasped. She was the very woman he had glimpsed that windy autumn evening. Love filled his heart. When her time of mourning was finished, he took her as his wife.

Thus did Malikha's arrogance cause his death and Bashr's goodness bring him joy.

So ends the tale of the Tartar princess. "If only every man in my kingdom was as good as Bashr," Bahram Gur says and is well pleased. Embracing, Princess Pari and Bahram Gur drift into sleep.

Dawn comes. The moon disappears. Bahram Gur rises and returns to his own chamber. It is Tuesday, the day of Mars.

The Red Pavilion

Bahram Gur dresses in his red cloak and red headdress. The morning is glorious. The sky is streaked with scarlet, as if the Heavens have been set afire. "So sweet was my third bride, can the fourth be even sweeter?" he wonders.

The Princess Nacarene, daughter of the Slavic king, awaits him in a dense garden of red roses and orange lilies. She is splendid in crimson robes and wears a headdress ablaze with rubies. Her hair is the color of fire, her lips red as garnets. She settles Bahram Gur on a maroon carpet with claret cushions under a dome inlaid with arrows made of hematite. The air is sweet with rose. The walls are replete with patterns like eggs and darts, illuminated by roaring flames from an iron fire pit.

Princess Nacarene and Bahram Gur idle the day long, drinking red wine and at last, as the sun begins its slow descent and the heavens explode into pink and orange and crimson flares, the king makes his request.

"A story, my love," he murmurs. "I would

have a story."

With a glowing smile, the Princess Nacarene begins her tale:

Once upon a time, in a far-off province of Russia, there lived a princess of surpassing beauty. Every man in the realm loved her. Yet the princess would not marry, for she could not find her equal. As if her extraordinary beauty were not enough, she excelled with a painter's brush and her learning was greater than that of most men. So also was her strength and her skill with the bow and arrow. Moreover, she could draw the sweetest songs from the strings of her lute.

One after another, suitors came to her, begging for her hand in marriage, but the princess merely shook her head and laughed scornfully. "I will never wed," she resolved, and when her father, the king, heard her, he feared for the continuation of his line. If the princess did not marry, he would have no heir to his throne. He pleaded with her to be merciful and thaw her cold, cold heart.

The princess ignored her father's entreaties and grew more disdainful every day. She built a palace high on a mountain and, with her handmaidens and guards, left her father's court to live in isolation. The palace was surrounded by thick, towering walls, with iron gates held shut by heavy locks and chains. Along the road leading to her forbidding palace, the princess placed swords devised so that anyone who approached was beheaded.

The princess painted a portrait of herself, then inscribed a poem on it declaring that she would give her hand only to the man who could satisfy four conditions: he must be the handsomest, strongest in the land; he must travel the road leading to the palace and escape her dreadful beheading swords; he must find the secret that unlocked the palace door, and guess the answers to the princess's four riddles. Those who tried and failed would be put to death.

The princess ordered her portrait

to be hung high on the palace gates. Undaunted by its dire warnings, hundreds of suitors arrived, and one by one, their heads were spiked on the palace gates. The king wept bitterly at their unhappy fate and begged his daughter to end her cruelty, but the princess laughed as more and more suitors were skewered. The hapless skulls were piled so high, they could be seen from miles away.

So it was that a prince who was riding through the country came upon the city and saw the portrait of the princess. Like the hundreds before him, his good sense was conquered by love. He beheld the skulls. He read the inscription. He determined he would break the spell and win the princess for himself.

He was young and handsome and graceful. He excelled at the hunt, and it was said he had killed a dragon with his bare hands. He could run faster than a gazelle, and in the time it took the sun to journey through the heavens, he could swim the deepest river and walk through the thickest woods.

The prince was also bright and clear of mind, so although his passion could have led him straight down the fearful road toward the princess, he went first into the wilderness to find a sage.

"The princess has no heart," the prince told the sage. "Thousands have died for her and she does not care. Tell me how I might escape her swords, unlock the palace door, and answer her four riddles. Although she is cruel, I would risk my life to win her."

In all his hundred and twenty years, the sage had never seen a youth like this prince. "Death comes to every man," he said, "but love does not. If you would have the princess, do as I advise."

The prince went forth with light spirits and a heart full of hope, carrying a stick the sage had given him and dressed in brilliant robes of blood red as a reminder of the many suitors who had died. He set out at daybreak, and as

he ascended the perilous road, he raised his stick and fended off the beheading swords. He passed through the thick fortress walls and the iron gates.

The prince now beat on the palace door in the intricate rhythms the sage had taught him. The doors opened, and he entered a desiccated garden where no flowers blossomed and no trees would grow. He sat on a rock and waited. Hours went by until a handmaiden arrived with a message: "Return to the king's court," she said. "The princess will come to you in two days to ask you her riddles."

Meanwhile, the prince removed the portrait of the princess, then bravely set about removing the ghastly heads of his competitors from the walls. The people acclaimed him with tumultuous cries. The king embraced him and showered him with gifts. A banquet was set and for two days, while they awaited the princess, the king and the prince feasted and drank the finest wines.

At dawn on the third day, the prince was taken to a chamber. The princess entered the room. For all his courage, the prince thought his heart would stop.

"Ask me your riddles and I shall answer them, even on pain of death," the prince said.

The princess smirked and removed her pearl earrings. With a lofty smile, she gave them to the prince. "What is your answer to such a gift?" she asked.

"May you live another hundred years, good sage," the prince whispered and brought forth three pearls that the old man had given him.

"If life is but two days long," the prince said, handing the three pearls to the princess, "here is your life and mine, and here is yet another life, which is our life together, when we are made one by love."

The princess said nothing but called for a mortar and pestle. She ground the pearls into a powder and added sugar to them. She poured the powder into a cup and, with a mocking smile, gave it to the prince. "What is your answer to such a gift?" she asked.

"May you flourish like a flower in the wilderness, good sage!" the prince whispered and brought forth a flask of milk the old man had given him. He poured the milk into the cup and bade the princess drink. Though she drained the cup, the powdered pearls remained at the bottom, not a grain more or less.

"Pearls will not mix with milk and sugar," the prince said. "So shall our love never be touched by anything impure."

The princess did not reply but slipped her most precious ring from her finger and gave it to the prince. "What is your answer to such a gift?" she sneered.

"May your wisdom find its reward, good sage," the prince whispered and brought forth a single pearl the old man had given him. It was as exquisite as the depths of the sea. The prince handed it to the princess.

"As we give each other treasures, so shall we give each other love," he said.

The princess said nothing but unfastened from her necklace a pearl that exactly matched the one the prince had given her. It was impossible to tell one from the other. With a scornful smile, she gave the prince this pearl. "What is your answer to such a gift?" she asked.

"May God bless you, good sage!" the prince whispered and brought forth a string and a glass bead, which he strung between the pearls.

"So shall our love guard against evil spirits, that we may always enjoy good fortune," he said.

The princess responded with a loving smile. The prince had answered her four riddles and satisfied all four of her conditions. She had at last found her equal and swore off her cruel behavior. She gave him her hand, for she had made her own choice. There was great celebration throughout the land, and the prince and princess lived happily all their days.

From that time forth, the prince dressed always in robes of red.

So ends the tale of the Slavic princess. Bahram

Gur is well pleased.

Embracing, Princess Nacarene and Bahram Gur drift into sleep.

Morning comes and Bahram Gur rises reluctantly with the sun and returns to his own chamber. It is Wednesday, the day of Mercury.

The Turquoise Pavilion

Bahram Gur dresses in indigo robes. There is not a cloud in the sky. The heavens are blue and smooth. "So sweet was my fourth bride, can the fifth be sweeter?" he wonders.

The Princess Azarene, daughter of the king of Maghreb, stands at the entrance to her sanctuary in the center of two crossed azure carpets. She greets Bahram Gur with outstretched arms and smiling eyes bluer than all the cornflowers, flax, and irises swaying in the garden. She is wonderful in cerulean robes, and slippers the color of the sea. Upon her blue-black hair she wears a crown of sapphires. Her rings and bracelets are set with turquoise and lapis to match the stones inlaid in serpentine patterns within the dome. The air is sweet with music and incense of juniper. The tiles are patterned with crescents, birds, and wheat sheaves. Water flows from a fountain in the wall.

Princess Azarene and Bahram Gur idle the day long, drinking from bright blue bowls until one by one the stars flicker into the cobalt sky and the king makes his request.

"A story, my love," he murmurs. "I would have a story."

With a lustrous smile, the Princess Azarene begins her tale:

Once upon a time, in the city of Cairo, lived a youth named Mahan. He was so handsome and cheerful there were none in the city who did not wish to be his friend. Every night, Mahan was invited to a banquet and went to one house or another, joining his companions as they feasted and sang and drank great quantities of wine.

One evening, when the moon was

full, Mahan wandered off by himself into a grove. There among the palm trees he saw a stranger who held out his hands. "I have been searching for you, my friend," said the stranger. "I have just arrived from the Orient to find the gates of the city already closed. My caravan, laden with precious goods, waits outside the city walls. I want to sneak it into the city under cover of darkness and escape the notice of the guards, so that I might avoid paying taxes. Help me, my friend, and you will be my partner and share equally in all my gains."

The merchant then took Mahan by the arm and led him deep into the grove. Mahan followed eagerly, imagining piles of gold coins before his eyes. The stranger began to run, and Mahan ran after him. He ran and ran, but Mahan could not catch up and at last slumped exhausted to the ground and slept. When he awoke he was on an arid plain, under a glaring sun. All around him, serpents writhed and hissed.

Mahan struggled on, with no idea where he was. He traveled aimlessly, driven by fear. As the light dimmed, he saw an old man and woman approaching in the distance.

"How do you happen to be in this desolate place?" they asked Mahan, and he told them his story.

"You have been deceived!" the old couple cried. "The stranger is no merchant, but a demon who has led you to a land of demons. If you want to leave this plain, travel with us, but first we will give you magic words to shield you from harm."

They whispered secret words to Mahan, though there was not a soul to hear. Then the three set out. They journeyed across the plain, until at last a village appeared. Mahan shouted with joy, but when he turned to his companions, they had disappeared and the village had also vanished, leaving Mahan alone in a bleak, rocky gorge.

Mahan ached with hunger. He dug among the rocks, devouring meager roots. As he chewed, he heard the sound of hooves. A man approached riding a stallion and leading a second horse.

"Why are you digging so fitfully among the rocks?" the man asked Mahan, and Mahan told the man his story.

"You have been deceived!" the man exclaimed. "The old couple are demons, and their magic words are worthless. The village was but a mirage. If you want to leave this gorge, take up these reins, mount this horse, and ride with me."

They rode the whole day and finally descended into an empty valley, where faint music filled the air. Mahan became uneasy and spurred his horse to gallop far ahead of his companion. The music grew louder and louder until it became a roaring din. An orchestra of monsters proceeded along the valley. Each had the trunk of an elephant, the tusks of an ox, and hides of slimy pitch. Each carried in its mouth a lighted torch. The reins slipped from Mahan's hands. His horse swayed to the rhythm of the monsters' howling, and as it swayed, it transformed into a dragon with seven heads, scaly wings, and a spiked tail. With a ferocious shriek, the beast flew from the valley, carrying Mahan aloft. At dawn, the beast threw Mahan to the ground.

Mahan lay bruised and torn alongside a rocky road. A light beckoned him. He squinted and saw a fruit-laden orchard. Starved and thirsty, he crawled among the fruit trees and plucked a juicy peach from a low branch. No sooner had he eaten it than the owner of the orchard rushed at him, shouting with rage and brandishing a stick.

"Do not beat me," Mahan begged. "Let me tell my tale." The man was amazed as Mahan related how he had escaped demons, writhing serpents, and a dragon with seven heads. He shook fruit from the branches so that Mahan might gather all he wanted. Then, because he had no son of his own, he proposed to make Mahan his heir. But first Mahan must spend the night in silence. Mahan consented and a platform was built, high in a tree.

Mahan watched as the moon rose.

In its opal light, a company of fairies entered the orchard with their queen and set up a banquet. Forgetting his promise of silence to the owner, Mahan climbed down from the tree and sat by the queen's side, nibbling dainties, sipping wine, and talking all night of love.

As the moon descended, Mahan embraced the fairy queen, but the creature he entwined in his arms transformed into a monster so hideous Mahan fainted from fright. When he came to, morning was in full glory, the demons were gone, and so was the orchard.

Mahan wept with remorse. "I have fallen prey to the temptations of the world. Had I not followed the merchant, greedy for ill-gotten gains, I would not be in this wilderness where nothing can live or grow."

As he wept, a man appeared, dressed all in green. Mahan stepped back in terror, for this was surely another demon in disguise.

"Fear not, my good Mahan," the stranger said softly. "I am Khizr, and I have been sent to you from Heaven. Close your eyes and let me take your hand."

Mahan had no choice. When he opened his eyes, the angel was gone, and he was back in the grove where he had first met the wicked merchant. He ran to his own house, and there he found his friends weeping with grief and dressed in mourning robes of blue. Tears of sorrow turned to tears of joy and there was great celebration. Mahan resolved that always, as a symbol of his salvation, he would wear mourning robes of blue. He led a life of goodness and was happy all his days.

So ends the tale of Princess Azarene. Bahram Gur is delighted.

Embracing, Princess Azarene and Bahram Gur drift into sleep.

When morning comes, Bahram Gur rises regretfully and returns to his own chamber. It is Thursday, the day of Jupiter.

The Sandalwood Pavilion

Bahram Gur dresses in brown silk robes and a turban, rich as earth. "So sweet was my fifth bride, can the sixth be even sweeter?" he wonders.

The Princess Yagme, daughter of the Chinese emperor, awaits Bahram Gur between carved oak pillars, guarded by two auburn marble lions rendered so perfectly they seem alive. Her tiny feet rest on a russet carpet with raised designs of lotuses, beneath a dome of pewter on which the rain falls like the timbrel music of the qing. She is delicate as porcelain, dressed in taupe robes, wearing a headdress of yellow butterflies. The air is sweet with sandalwood. They recline on fawn cushions of satin and gold embroideries, surrounded by mahogany screens patterned with lightning tridents, jasmine, and storm birds.

Princess Yagme and Bahram Gur take their pleasure the day long, until at last the sky turns rosy orange and the king makes his request.

"A story, my love," he murmurs. "I would have a story."

With a subtle smile, the Princess Yagme begins her tale:

Once upon a time, in a faraway country, lived two friends. All who knew them wondered at the friendship, for the youths were as different as day and night. One was gentle and kind, while the other was harsh and wicked. Even their names mirrored their natures, for they were called Kheyr and Sharr, Good and Evil.

Kheyr and Sharr decided to journey to a distant city. The desert sun beat down on them relentlessly. After a few days, Kheyr had drunk all the water he'd brought and he thirsted mightily. "Surely, we'll reach an oasis soon," he said.

"I know the desert as I know my right hand," Sharr replied. "Tomorrow we'll come to an oasis and have all the water we want. I, too, am thirsty."

But Sharr spoke falsely. The oasis was a week's journey away. That night, when Kheyr had fallen asleep, Sharr crept off by himself to drink from a waterskin he had hidden from Kheyr.

All the next day the two friends traveled, with no oasis in sight. Exhausted, Kheyr collapsed on the blistering sand. "I can no longer bear my thirst," he told Sharr. "I marvel at your strength."

Sharr laughed scornfully, drew forth his waterskin and gulped down the water. He wiped his mouth and sneered at Kheyr.

Kheyr gasped. "My friend, I must have water or I'll die. In the name of our friendship, please give me just a sip."

Sharr laughed again and again raised the waterskin to his lips. Kheyr reached for the waterskin and tried to cry out, but all he could manage was a weak, dry croak. Sharr merely shook his head grinning.

"Take these, my friend, in return for water," Kheyr begged, bringing forth the two precious rubies he had hoped to exchange in the market of the distant city.

Sharr laughed again. "What do I care for your rubies? If I took them, later you'd say that I'd stolen them. I'll exchange water only for your eyes."

Kheyr trembled with disbelief and horror. He pleaded throughout the night and kissed Sharr's feet, but all in vain. Finally, Kheyr drew his dagger and gave it to Sharr. "If I do not have water, I'll die. And if I die, what use are my eyes? May you be punished for your wickedness."

Sharr took the dagger, and when the dreadful deed was done, he drank deeply from his water skin and spat in Kheyr's face. He gathered Kheyr's possessions, as well as the two rubies, and journeyed on alone, leaving the blinded Kheyr, half dead and bleeding, in the burning sand.

A tribe of Kurds were camped not far from where Kheyr lay. That very morning, the daughter of the Kurdish chieftain happened to be walking in the dunes carrying a water jar. When she saw Kheyr, she ran to his side and gently put the jar of water to his lips. When he had drunk his fill, he told her his grievous story.

The maiden put Kheyr's eyes back into his head and bound them with tender care. She guided Kheyr to her father's tent.

"Someday your wicked friend will be punished for his treachery," the Kurdish chieftain said. "But fear not, my good Kheyr, for I know a potion that will make you whole again.

"Pick leaves from the sandalwood tree that grows outside our tent," the chieftain instructed his daughter. When she returned, he pounded the leaves into pulp and put it on Kheyr's sightless eyes. Five days later, the maiden unwrapped the poultice.

His sight was restored! His first vision was the chieftain's daughter, who was as beautiful as she was kind. Kheyr loved her then and there with all his heart. A wedding feast was set. For seven days and seven nights the camp celebrated. When the revelry was done, the chieftain showered Kheyr with gold coins, yards of silk, many animals and precious gifts, riches enough to last him all his life. And Kheyr departed with his bride to his own country.

On their way, they came to a city where, to their astonishment, all the people wept and wailed.

"What is the cause of your deep sorrow?" Kheyr asked a passerby.

"Have you not heard?" the citizen replied. "The daughter of our king has been afflicted with a trembling in her limbs and will surely die."

Kheyr went straight to the royal palace. He knelt before the king, promising to make his daughter well. The king shrugged permission, doubtful, but he was desperate.

Kheyr prepared the sandalwood leaves and bid the princess swallow the potion. She grew still and the trembling stopped. She slept for three days, then she arose, her health regained. The king wept with joy and offered his daughter's hand to Kheyr. She was as beautiful as Kheyr's first bride. A wedding feast was set, and for seven days and seven nights, they rejoiced.

Kheyr had just settled down with his two wives when a high official of the court visited him, begging for a cure for his own stricken daughter. Once again, Kheyr complied and made the girl whole again, then took her as his third wife. Once more, there was merriment in the city for seven days and seven nights. The king made Kheyr his heir, for he had no son.

Kheyr ruled with justice and kindness. The city prospered and all his subjects were content. His first wife's father, the Kurdish chieftain, lived in his court and Kheyr loved him like a father.

One day, he stood at a window looking into the street when he saw a familiar face. "Bring that man to me at once!" Kheyr ordered his attendants. The merchant entered the court, spread his carpets before the king, and set out his goods. "I came from the Orient only yesterday, Magnificence," he said. "I can show you treasures such as you have never seen before."

"What is your name, my friend?" Kheyr asked.

"Magnificence, I am called Mobashshar," the merchant replied.

"You lie!" Kheyr shouted. "Sharr is your name! You are none other than he who would not give me water in the burning desert, who put out my eyes, stole my rubies, and left me in the sand to die."

Sharr shrieked as if he'd seen a ghost. He kissed Kheyr's feet and begged for mercy. Kheyr agreed to spare his life, but ordered Sharr banished from the city, never to return.

Kheyr's father-in-law watched as Sharr pleaded for his life. He could see that Sharr had not really repented from his wickedness and told Kheyr that Sharr must be punished for his treachery. The chieftain followed Sharr as he lurched out of the palace and stumbled past the city gates. Sharr continued into the desert with the chieftain behind him, and when they reached a high dune, the chieftain confronted Sharr, drawing his dagger and killing him. In Sharr's pouch, he found the two precious rubies and brought them to the king.

Kheyr lived for many happy years. From time to time, he went into the desert to savor the scent of the sandalwood tree.

And he dressed always in robes the color of sandalwood bark.

So ends the tale of the Chinese princess.

Bahram Gur shudders. "May I never meet a man as wicked as Sharr."

Embracing, Princess Yagme and Bahram Gur drift into sleep.

Morning comes and Bahram Gur rises reluctantly with the sun and returns to his own chamber. It is Friday, the day of Venus.

The White Pavilion

Bahram Gur dresses in purest white, his turban resembles a cloud and on it he wears a white feather. "So sweet was my sixth bride, can the seventh be even sweeter?" he wonders.

The Princess Diroste, from a distant city in Persia, awaits Bahram Gur under a dome set with gold around a window shaped like a white rose made of diamonds. She is dressed all in white damask embroidered with pearls and her headdress is of the sheerest silk. At her feet are silver pots of white lilies and narcissus, reflecting the delicacy of the apple and peach blossoms that drop like snow onto a meadow of columbine. Doves coo in the trees, swallows dart above a pool of crystal lined with cowrie shells. White peacocks are woven into a plush carpet, strewn with supple oval cushions. Tiles of pure white, lightest blue, and melodious coral are set with mirrors of stars, reflected in the white wine flavored with rosemary, which the princess serves Bahram Gur in cups of carved figwood lined with abalone. The air is sweet with patchouli.

Princess Diroste and Bahram Gur bask in each other's company until, at last, the sky darkens, and the king's rapture turns to dread lest he no longer be able to see the princess's face. A white taper is lit, and the king makes his request.

"A story, my love," he murmurs. "I would have a story."

With a smile fleeting as the light of day, the Princess Diroste begins her tale:

One night, in a far-off city, there was a young man who had an exquisite garden, surrounded by four high walls. The young man sat beneath a tree, savoring the greenness all around him and the fragrance of his roses.

But one day, he arrived and found the garden door would not unlock. He heard music within and singing and laughter. He knocked loudly. No answer. He beat the door with his fists. No one came. He shouted and yelled. An hour passed and then another. Still, there was no response. Enraged, the young man took an axe and smashed a hole in the gate, but no sooner had he crawled through it than he was seized by two fierce women. His hands and feet were bound, and he was beaten and scolded for breaking in like a thief.

"I am the owner of this garden!" the young man protested. The young women untied him and soothed his wounds. "We ask for your forgiveness," they said, "but surely you will look on us with favor when we tell you that because this garden is a paradise, beautiful maidens gather here to dance and sing. When you have seen all the maidens, you may choose one for your own."

The young man watched from a secret room. In the center of his garden was a marble pool, gleaming with clear blue water, where many maidens bathed. Around the pool, among the trees and flowers, many more maidens frolicked and danced and sweetly sang to the music of a harp. He nearly swooned with desire.

He agonized for hours over which to choose, enchanted by this maiden's eyes, that maiden's hair, the slim waist of a third, and so on, until at last he made his choice. The harp player was brought to him. No sooner did the maiden eagerly stretch her hands to him, and he took her into his arms, than the floor of the secret room gave way. With a terrible crash, the lovers tumbled, unhurt, onto the grass below.

"Don't despair, my love!" the young man cried, and led the maiden to a tree. They climbed to where two branches met.

"These boughs are thick and strong and safe," he said, and the maiden opened her arms to him. But as soon as they were entwined, one of the branches cracked. The lovers were thrown, again unhurt, onto the grass below.

The young man led the maiden to a corner of the garden thick with trees and flowering vines. "Let's make our bed of these rose petals," he said. "Nothing can disturb us here, my love."

But as soon as he took her into his arms, a family of foxes came running through the vines, pursued by a ferocious wolf. This time, the lovers fled to the far end of the garden, where the young man embraced his maiden again.

"Don't despair, my love," the young man said softly. "We will have time enough to know the joys of love once we are wed, for surely the unsteady floor and the broken branch and snarling wolf are signs that I should take you not simply as a lover, but as my lawful wife."

"And surely," the maiden answered, "these obstacles are like those of marriage that must be overcome with dear embraces and patience."

A wedding feast was set in the lush garden. The maidens danced and sang before the young man and his bride. They lived happily forever after, and every week they retired to the garden to sit beneath a tree, savor the fragrance of the roses. and talk of love.

So ends the tale of the Persian princess and Bahram Gur is satisfied.

Embracing, Princess Diroste and Bahram Gur drift into sleep.

The eighth day comes, and Bahram Gur rises reluctantly with the sun to return to his own chamber. His seven brides were beautiful, each in her own pavilion, like jewels in their own settings. All day he recalls his seven pleasures, but when he looks out, each princess and her palace has vanished, leaving only their signs and images, their colors and wondrous tales dancing in Bahram Gur's head.

Caress a lovely woman's breast by night,
And kiss some beauty's lips by morning light.

Silence those who criticize you, those
Officious talkers. Take advice from me:
With Beauty's children only can we live
Kidnapped were they from Paradise to gall
The living: living men are lovers all.

Immerse your heart in pleasure and in joy
and by the bank a bottle drink of wine,
Enjoy the swallow's chirp and viol's whine,
Laugh, dance, and stamp your feet upon the floor!
Get drunk and knock at dawn on some girl's door.

This is the joy of life, so take your due.
You too deserve a portion of the Ram
Of Consecration, like your people's chiefs.
To suck the juice of lips do not be shy,
But take what's rightly yours—the breast and thigh.

—Moses Ibn Ezra, Al-Andalus, ca. 1055–1158 CE

I am a lioness.
I will never let my body
be anybody's stopping place.
But if I should decide to,
I would not listen to a dog—
Indeed, how many lions
Have I turned down!

—Ashra bint Ahmad, Al-Andalus, tenth century CE

Bahram Gur and Fitnah

One day, Bahram Gur went hunting. Fitnah rode with him, his love, a girl as fair as the moon and quick as silver. She was not only beautiful, but skilled in music and dancing. When she played, the birds left the trees to join her in song. Her instrument was the harp, and the king's instrument was the arrow.

They rode to the plain toward a herd of swift deer. Bahram Gur raised his bow and let loose his arrow. His aim was true. He looked proudly at Fitnah, but though she laughed with delight, she did not praise him. Instead, she said, "I wonder, Majesty, can you turn a stag into a doe?"

Bahram Gur grinned, drew his arrow, and shot through the rack of a buck. The rack clattered to the ground. Bahram Gur turned to Fitnah, expecting praise. She nodded and smiled. "I wonder, Majesty, can you turn a doe into a stag?"

Bahram Gur drew two arrows and planted them on the head of a doe. He turned to Fitnah. She merely smiled. "I wonder, Majesty, can you pin a deer's hind hoof to its ear?"

Bahram Gur drew his shaft and grazed the ear of a passing deer. It stopped, and as it raised its hoof to scratch the itch, the king shot again, and this time the arrow pinned the hoof to the ear.

"See now," he said, "you cannot deny my strength and cleverness."

"This was not accomplished with strength and cleverness," she said. "Anyone could do it with enough practice, day by day, year by year."

Bahram Gur turned away. "Brave heroes cannot slaughter women. Minutes ago, I loved her, but no longer," he said to himself. Then he turned to one of his officers: "Get this girl out of my way. Take her! Go."

The officer bound Fitnah and hauled her away from the monarch. He would not kill her there but strike off her head

out of the king's sight. When they had gone a mile, the officer raised his sword. Fitnah's eyes filled with tears.

"Do not kill me, I'm guilty of nothing. I am the king's favorite, the one most chosen of all his slaves. He did not order you to kill me, and by the time he hears that you have spilled my blood, he may have a change of heart and miss me. Do not take the chance," Fitnah said.

"What must I do?" the officer asked.

"Wait awhile. Then go to the king and tell him you have killed me. If he rejoices, then return and do so. But if he is saddened by my death and threatens you, you will be safe." Then Fitnah offered her necklace of seven rubies to the officer, who took them as a promise and told her to pretend to be a servant in his house.

A week later, the officer went before the king. "What news of Fitnah?" Bahram Gur asked the officer, who lowered his chin and replied, "I have killed her."

Tears sprang to Bahram Gur's eyes, and he wept for love of Fitnah.

And then he went to war, and the war went on for six years.

The officer's home was far away in the country. It was a fine and flourishing farming estate near the sea. The large house had a terrace at the top of sixty steps, and it was here that Fitnah had her quarters. She played her harp, gazing at the sea. She wandered the farm in loneliness, singing her songs and making friends with the beasts.

One day, a cow gave birth, and Fitnah took the gentle calf each morning on her back up the sixty steps from the barn to the terrace. She carried the calf up the stairs, day after day at feeding time, and the calf grew into a fine and sturdy bull. And though the bull was huge, Fitnah did not feel the load, for her strength had grown in proportion to the animal.

On a lovely evening, as the sea lapped against the shore, the officer sat with

Fitnah while she played a sad song on her harp, grieved and heavy of heart, for he had told her that the king, returned at last from the wars, planned to hunt near his estate. Fitnah played on quietly, then stopped, removed her pearl earrings, and gave them to the officer.

"I beg you, take these and buy sheep, rosewater, incense, fruit, and wine. When the king comes, make a banquet for him, here on this lovely terrace above the sea. Bahram Gur has a gentle temperament," she said wistfully. "He has a noble and indulgent mind. When he receives your invitation, he will come."

The terrace was laid with plush carpets and piled with exquisite foods on golden cloths and platters, with fragrances of myrrh, under a blue canopy. When the hunt was over, the king arrived and climbed the sixty steps and was seated, panting and perspiring, on a throne that faced the sea. He wiped his brow with a silk handkerchief and, catching his breath, said to his host, "What a pleasant place you have, but how can you climb to it every day? And when you are old, when you have sixty years, how will you walk these sixty steps at all?"

"This is no problem for me. I'm a man," the officer said. "How should I ever be wearied by such steps? And there is a woman, a soft, dainty, moon-like woman who bears a bull up these stairs on her back each day, without resting, without stopping, at feeding time."

"How can this be?" Bahram Gur demanded. "A woman? Carry a bull? Up these stairs? Oh, come now! Surely this is sorcery. I won't believe it unless I see it with my own eyes. Prove this claim!"

The officer signaled Fitnah. Adorned with pearls, which fastened a diaphanous veil across her face, Fitnah lowered her head and raised the bull, then ran up the sixty steps to the foot of Bahram's throne. The king was dumbfounded at the sight of this small creature bearing the giant beast upon her back.

Fitnah put the bull down and said to the king, "Here is a gift I now submit, unaided, all alone, by my own strength."

Bahram Gur scoffed. "This is not from your strength, but from your having practiced little by little, day by day, across many years."

Fitnah bowed low to him. "I, who can carry a bull up sixty steep steps, am credited only with practice, but why, when you hit a little deer, should no one use the word 'practice,' too?"

Bahram Gur gasped and leaped from his throne. He lifted Fitnah's veil. He embraced her and begged her forgiveness. Then he called forth his priests, and they were married and lived together in sport and pleasure and luxurious ease from that time forward.

Occasionally, Fitnah spoke a truth that shook the king from his contentment. But he never punished her, never retaliated, for this was her way. She was, after all, Fitnah, true to her name: fitnah, which means disturbance.

Bahram Gur rode into the desert to hunt.
He rode so swiftly,
he left his companions far behind.
Suddenly, a wild ass appeared before him.
"The gur, my namesake, has come to me as a sign," he thought,
and followed it into the dark depths of a cave.
When the king's companions arrived at the mouth of the cave,
there was no sign of Bahram Gur.
They searched and searched
Within the cave and all around it.
They searched for days.
They searched for weeks,
and those who loved him,
soldiers, slaves, and beauties
waited and wept.
Never again did they see Bahram Gur –
that day or ever more.

—Nizami, Persia, 1149 to 1209 CE

Solomon and the Queen

King David was old and decrepit. No matter how his servants stoked the palace fires or how many blankets they piled upon him, he could not stop shivering. The healers met and decided to give him a beautiful maiden that she might cure or comfort him. They searched the land and found Abishag the Shulamite to nurse David and lie on his chest to provide fresh, virginal heat that had not been diluted by bearing and nurturing children. And with this arrangement, David and Abishag became friends, though not lovers.

Perhaps she was a virgin, as the healers hoped. Perhaps she was a childless widow. But Abishag had a paramour, unknown to any but her brothers. Late at night, when the king finally slept in peace, and before the early morning chill overcame him, she stepped into the dark and called:

Kiss me.
Your love is sweeter than wine.
Your fragrance, myrrh, and oil
call all the young women toward you
Hurry! Draw me to you.
The king has brought me into his chambers
Let us be glad. Let us rejoice. Let us laugh.
I exult your love, yet rightly do we love him.

David briefly opened his heavy eyelids. He heard her. He smiled.

David confided to Abishag that, of all his four sons, the youngest, Solomon, son of Bathsheba, would follow him onto the throne as was foretold by Nathan the Prophet. But Solomon's brother, Adonijah, son of Haggith, had already claimed the kingship, even riding the king's mule in procession. Hearing this, David summoned Nathan, Solomon's mother, and the few others he trusted. Bathsheba wondered why he had allowed her to convince him that her son be chosen. Was it because Nathan predicted his rise before the boy was born? Was it because she and

David had loved each other long ago and when she became pregnant, David sent her husband, Uriah the Hittite, one of his best Mighty Men, to the most dangerous front in a futile war and ordered that he be abandoned by his troops? Then Bathsheba had married David. Was his decision guilt about their adultery and Uriah's murder, then their punishment with the death of their first child?

Nathan told David that Solomon would not ask the Lord for possessions, wealth, honor, or to take the lives of those who hated him. Instead, Solomon prayed for wisdom and knowledge so that he might rule his people with justice.

And Nathan warned the king of Adonijah's celebrations of his own ascent in the streets of Jerusalem.

With his declaration for Solomon, David relinquished all his possessions, except for Abishag. He burrowed close to her, and soon, having reigned for forty years, he died.

Behold Solomon's litter.
About it are sixty Mighty Men of Israel,
all girt with swords, ready for war.
King Solomon has a palanquin
made from the cedars of Lebanon.
Its posts are silver,
its seats are gold, its lining purple.
All this the daughters of Jerusalem
fashioned and sewed with love.
And the king's mother crowned him
on the day of his wedding to Pharoah's daughter,
the day of his heart's gladness.

Solomon took the throne. He paid little attention to Adonijah's preening, though he killed others who stood in his way. Until, that is, Adonijah asked Bathsheba to request of Solomon that he be given Abishag as his own wife. Solomon knew what this entreaty meant. He put Adonijah to death, for the inheritance of a king's woman was a sign that his brother had not given up his ambition. Nevermind Adonijah's parades through the streets on David's mule. A mule—even a royal mule—could be replaced more easily than a prize concubine. Now only Solomon would determine the fates of the women in his household. And Abishag disappeared, though some said they could hear her voice echoing in the night.

In dreams I seek my love.
I go about the city, the streets, and the markets.
I cannot find the one who occupies my inner being.
I ask the watchmen as I pass by. They are blind to him.
Blind to me.
When I find my love, I will not let him go.
O Daughters of Jerusalem,
by the leaping gazelles,
by the deer in the field,
never awaken love until it is ripe.

Years passed. Solomon, who had not asked the Lord for riches or undue power, acquired them nonetheless. The king, who would be called "the wisest man that ever lived," turned his attention to building palaces and city walls. To expanding his borders as far as the Euphrates. His greatest achievement would be a holy temple to house the Ark of the Covenant, the stone tablets on which the Lord himself had written the commandments for Moses, then contained them in a golden box that was safeguarded by David in a flimsy tent.

These tributes to Solomon's wealth and power required more slave labor, more burden bearers than even his father had conscripted in Israel and Canaan, and more materials than could be found in Israel and Judah. Solomon sent traders and ambassadors far and wide to find exquisite goods with which to construct and furnish his edifices so that they would surpass all else anywhere in the world.

Solomon's traders and ambassadors traveled north, east, and west. Far into the south in Sheba, they begged an audience with the powerful Queen, sometimes thought to rule the whole of Africa. And

while they waited, they explored the city, aghast at the marvels on display in the marketplace. Spices, magnificently woven fabrics, the skins of animals they had never seen fashioned into cloaks and aprons, exotic, elaborate jewelry, baskets made of reed and cane and rope, handsomely constructed clay and metal household goods and tools, as well as sinful icons for worship, such as golden suns and silver moons. There were naked figures of goddesses with horns upholding planets or cornucopias of fruit and grains. There were effigies of animals believed also to be deities.

The traders and ambassadors frowned and stroked their beards in disapproval. They had seen much during their travels, but what they saw in Sheba was far out of the bounds of propriety. Surely the Lord would smite these people as he had annihilated the wicked cities of Sodom and Gomorrah.

"What's this?" the traders and ambassadors asked at one stall stacked high with oddly carved and sewn leather, ivory, and wooden wares laid out alongside their familiar sandals. "Shoes," the merchant replied. "They are called shoes." The envoys wondered first at the word "shoes," and, after the merchant explained, they wondered how feet could fit into such malformed things. "Impossible. Ridiculous," they agreed.

At the proscribed hour, Solomon's traders and ambassadors entered the Queen's throne room. They were seated with other foreign visitors near the royal platform. The room glowed with opulence and was crowded with courtiers, supplicants, and hundreds of servants, many waving large, feathered fans toward the throne against the oppressive heat. Trumpets sounded. The crowd stepped aside and dropped to their knees. The trumpets blew again and there appeared the handsomest woman Solomon's emissaries had ever seen. Her black skin gleamed. Her bejeweled crown enfolded a nest of black coils, while curly tendrils framed her serene face. The gold around her neck, hanging from her ears and wrapped around her wrists were as dazzling as the smile she bestowed on all she passed. She was bare breasted, and her long skirts swayed like silken clouds. Her feet clicked as she mounted the steps to the throne, then turned and lifted her hem to sit. The traders and ambassadors gasped at the steep arc of her feet. Three women arranged her skirt around her ankles. Settled, the Queen raised her arms and the crowd stood. She looked around the room and pointed at Solomon's envoys.

"Tell me why you are here," she asked. "What do you want of us in Sheba?"

"We come from Israel from the court of King Solomon," they announced in chorus, bowing.

"The wisest man in the world?" The Queen chuckled. "Tell me a story of his wisdom. Tell me of a deed that displays his legendary sagacity."

The eldest ambassador stepped forward. "Once there were two women who came before the king with a baby. Each claimed the child was hers and begged the king to decide which should possess it. The king listened to each as they argued and finally declared that the only solution would be to cut the child in half and give half to each woman. One agreed. But the other burst into tears, beating her breast and screaming, begging Solomon to give the child to her rival rather than kill it. That one, the wise king realized, was the babe's true mother and thus the child was awarded to her."

"Oh, emissaries," the Queen yawned. "Every visitor to my lands tells that story to show King Solomon's wisdom. I am so sorry there seem to be no others."

Then, in a loud, sinister tone, she added, "Therefore, now, I will have each of you cut in half for boring me with that worn-out tale." The court burst into laughter and the Queen grinned. The traders and ambassadors grasped one another, reeling in fear and horror.

"Oh no, no, no!" the Queen said as the laughter died down. "The court is amused because they know that in this land, we do not perform such barbaric acts, even on our enemies, and those, we thank the gods, are few. We do not make war, unless we are forced to, unless we are attacked." Her hands fluttered toward a group of servants, who guided the shaken emissaries to a cool, private chamber, where they were offered water, wine, and food enough to feed an army.

"Did you see her feet?" they asked each other as they ate. "It must be true that her mother was a djinn, for those feet are formed like the hooves of goats or deer."

"Some claim her mother was a djinn, but others say that when she was pregnant, her mother laid eyes on a ram and so the Queen was born with cloven hooves."

"It is believed among these pagans that such hooves are the sign of virginity and power." And they all sighed, stuffing their mouths with meats, fish, grapes, honey, and delicate breads.

Hours later, with no announcement, the Queen clicked quickly into the room. The sleepy envoys bent awkwardly over their bulging stomachs.

"Now," said the Queen. "To what do we owe the honor of your visit? What is your request? What do you want or need from our lands?"

The tradesmen spoke of wood, fabrics, carpets, gold, artisans. They described the great palaces and temples King Solomon was building and that he desired to enhance them with the most pleasing objects in the world. "For the Lord loves beauty," the ambassadors added.

"So do I." the Queen said. "Give me an inventory of what you require. Tell the king that in two months I will deliver all the goods he asks for. I will bring them myself. But tell him, too, that I wish to test his wisdom with hard questions. I will send a hoopoe to let him know when I am a week away. They say that Solomon can speak the language of birds." The emissaries tried not to show their surprise. They knew of no such thing, yet their king was renowned for his magic, so they supposed it could be true.

Solomon was sitting by a window when the hoopoe arrived. The bird landed calmly on the sill and looked fearlessly at the king.

There were birds in cages and birds in the sky, but he had never seen a bird so bold. Its cinnamon-gold crown was outstretched to display onyx tips. Its wings were striped and its tail, too, was banded in black and white. Opening its shiny black beak, the bird chirped awhile. Solomon waved his hand to shoo the bird away. Realizing the king didn't understand him, the hoopoe did not move but opened his beak again and, this time, its voice crackling a bit from the long dusty journey, said aloud that the Queen would arrive at Solomon's palace in a week's time. Then off he flew. The king was astonished by a talking bird, but he was not impressed with its message. His spies had already informed him of the Queen's every move. Her retinue, with hundreds of camels and carts and moving tents, was miles long, laden with spices and foodstuffs, carpets, tapestries, precious stones, marble, silks, frankincense, myrrh, and rare algum lumber. Here were goods the tradesmen had discovered in the marketplaces of Sheba and a thousandfold more.

When they returned to Jerusalem, the emissaries reported all they had seen in Sheba and testified that the Queen's feet were indeed cloven hooves. Solomon went to work. He had his floors polished until they glistened, then sheets of glass laid on them. Under the glass he caused water to flow with bright, darting fish, swaying leaves, and flowers of the sea. Each day his servants fed the fish, adjusted the plants, and shined the glass, so that soon Solomon had a rich, aquatic realm beneath the steps rising to his throne.

The Queen's caravan crossed the border of Israel and slowly funneled into the outskirts of Jerusalem. A voice some

might have recognized as Abishag's murmured around the Queen

I am black and comely.
O Daughters of Jerusalem,
do not gaze at me.
I am dark.
The sun has glazed me
and made me beautiful.

When at last they stopped and the hundreds of camels were unloaded, the Queen retreated to her rolling palace, a tent on wheels, attached to another for bathing and still others for cooking, dining, and quartering her servants. Her maids washed her, then dressed her in regal clothing, ready to meet the "wisest man that ever lived."

King Solomon settled on his divan grinning down at his tiny lake. Did the Queen really have hooved feet as his emissaries had reported? He would soon know.

The court watched, enraptured, as the veiled, fully clothed Queen approached. Her gold crown was luminous as a halo. She clicked ceremoniously toward the throne, then stopped suddenly, catching her balance so as not to plunge into the water. The king held his chin in his hands to conceal a smirk. The Queen raised her skirts. One by one she removed her ivory hooves, handed them to a maidservant, then stepped gingerly with bare feet onto the cold glass.

"Shoes!" the traders and ambassadors whispered from their perches among the nobles. Solomon scowled, confused.

It was a trick! Not water after all. The Queen raised her veil, tipped her head at the king, curious and critical. She strode across the aquarium. She stepped onto the stairs leading to the throne. She peered directly at the king, nodded her head but did not lower to her knee. The assemblage growled quietly at her arrogance. Solomon beckoned her to come closer.

She was glorious. A woman the like of whom Solomon had never encountered. Not one of his carefully chosen thousand wives and concubines—even Pharoah's daughter—could match her face, her figure, her bearing. What's more, she was his equal in wealth, lands, and power. He stood. He motioned her to sit beside him on a smaller, but no less elaborate, couch.

"I am told the Queen has some 'hard' questions to ask me," he said to the court. "And I have some for her. You are all dismissed while we exchange our riddles in private." Soldiers guided the disappointed, muttering crowd from the room.

When the room was empty, the king asked, "Is it true you're a virgin, and that—because I have caused your ungodly hooves to be replaced by human feet—I may now have you?"

The Queen wriggled her beringed toes. "I'm afraid not," she laughed, then reminded him, "Wise King Solomon, am I not asking the questions?"

The king sat back and drew a deep breath.

Outside the deserted throne room, all ears that could find a space were pressed against the walls and doors. From holy men to tradesmen and ambassadors, from horse groomers and soldiers to scullery maids, rumors ran wild. What did they hear? A few scholars and scribes hurried to write down what they or others thought they heard. (And so it was that across the ages, earwigged riddles and hard questions were passed down and transformed as the speculations went from person to person, priest to priest, sage to sage.)

The court was finally allowed back into the room. Before they parted each to their rest, Solomon again asked for the Queen's virginity and again she laughed. "I would make a bargain with you," he said. "In exchange for your virginity, you must swear to take nothing from Jerusalem that belongs to me." Thinking little of it, the Queen agreed.

That night a great feast was laid out, with marvelous foods. On her plate, mixed into her meats, were paprika, onion seed, and garlic. Solomon watched as the Queen devoured the meal, then excused herself. She was tired, she said, and must begin to ready herself for the long journey back to Sheba.

Late that night, the Queen awoke, parched with thirst. The paprika, onion seed, and garlic had done their job. She sat straight up, her mouth desperately dry. She reached to the table by her bedside, grabbed the water jug, and gulped and gulped and gulped. As she laid it back down, she saw, too late: "Property of Solomon."

He entered the room. He took her by the hand. "Now you owe me your body," he said, drawing her to his own bed.

Outside, a small, birdlike voice chimed under the moonlight

The king lies beside me.
our fragrance opens the sky,
awakens the stars.
All night he lies between my breasts,
gentle, lingering, tasting my fruit.

Seven days later, the Queen and her miles-long caravan slowly departed Jerusalem, this time laden with gifts from Solomon. Whatever she asked for, he gave her. She did not ask for the babe she was sure stirred in her belly, but she would nevertheless love and teach him. Someday she would send him to meet his father.

She was anxious to be home with her gods and her people. The months it would take to return to Sheba could not pass fast enough. She lay back on her divan, holding her ivory hooves in each hand and clicking them together.

"The wisest man that ever lived?" the Queen said aloud to herself and hooted with laughter. "He is certainly the wiliest trickster that ever lived."

The Shulamite's Lover and her Brothers

If you can't find me,
my fairest of women,
follow the tracks of the flock
and pasture your kids
at the shepherds' dwellings.

You are magnificent as the
Pharoah's mare.
Your cheeks are lovely
framed with hooped earrings
behind your braids.
Your neck is charming
adorned with strings of beads.
I will make you circlets of gold
and spangles of silver.

How beautiful you are, my
beloved.

Your eyes are doves.
Your hair is like a flock of goats
leaping down from Mount Gilead.
Your teeth are white as shorn sheep.
Your lovely lips are threads of scarlet.
Your neck is a splendid tower of
David.
Your breasts are twin fawns.
All of you is beautiful,
my unblemished love.

O my dove, nesting in the clefts of
the rock,
in the covert of the cliff.
Let me see your comely face.
Let me hear your sweet voice.

Winter has passed.

The rains are over.
Wildflowers spring from the earth.
The time of singing has come.
You are a lily among the brambles.
Hurry, my love, and come away.

Before the day breathes
and the shadows flee,
I will visit your mound of myrrh,
your hills of frankincense.
You entice me.
A locked fountain,
a sealed spring.

I come to my garden, my bride.
I gather my myrrh with my spice.
I have eaten my honeycomb.
I have drunk my wine, my milk.
Eat friends! Drink deeply and be drunk with love!

The Brothers

We have a little sister.
She has no breasts.
What shall we do for our sister
on the day she is spoken for?
If she is a wall,
we will build upon her a silver turret.
If she is a door.
Will we confine her with boards of cedar?

excerpts from *The Song of Songs, which is Solomon's*

Shirin and Khusraw

Hormuzd sat on the throne of Persia, and he was called Light of the World's Justice. He named his son Khusraw Parviz, the Victorious One.

Khusraw was a boy of winning eloquence and boundless energies. By the time he was nine, he was schooled in all the learned disciplines. When he was fourteen, he proved himself an expert horseman and consummate hunter. And by the time he was sixteen, he was a wizard in the arts of war, with sword, spear, and arrow.

Shirin's name means "sweet," and so she was and more. She rode ahead of all her maidens in the hunt. She danced like a dragonfly skims the air. She spent her words carefully, yet generously, schooled as she was in the arts of wise rule, for Shirin would one day inherit the throne of Armenia from her aunt, the Great Lady, Mihin Banu.

Khusraw would one day make Persia the glittering mistress of the East. But there were more than a few impediments that caused him to stumble along the path, not least his own arrogance.

I am Shapur. From boyhood, Khusraw and I were each other's second selves. But whereas Khusraw was bound to his father and throne, I traveled. With paints and brushes and an eye that never overlooked nuances, I took myself in every direction.

Our teacher was Bozorg Omid the Sage, who taught us the mysteries of stars and maps, and impressed upon us the subtle ways of man and beast.

One day, Bozorg Omid advised Hormuzd: "What good is it, Magnificence, to guard your own benefit with zeal, if the state of your subjects goes untended? Who will respect a throne when those who uphold it have nothing? The rights of the ruled must always rule."

The king then ordered a fanfare of trumpets and proclaimed new laws,

making strong decrees that promised to protect the people equally. Khusraw Parviz admired his father's uprightness, though he was too young, too much the darling of the court, to realize the importance of Hormuzd's laws.

I only heard the tale later. I was in China, with my friend Farhad, studying the arts of painting and sculpture, drawing and engineering.

The story I heard was this: On a spring day, when the sun sparkled and the game was plentiful, Khusraw rode with his companions to the hunt. At twilight, they came upon a village snug on the lush green plain. Khusraw commandeered the village elder's house to pass the night drinking and carousing with his companions.

The harpist played loud notes of revelry, so that the villagers slept not a wink. Khusraw and his friends got drunker and drunker, rocking the house with raucous laughter, until at last they passed out. The harpist played on, but finally, he, too, collapsed onto his instruments, which protested with such a twang, the village children awoke screaming.

Just before daybreak, Khusraw's servant crept out of the elder's house and reeled hungrily into the vineyards to pick grapes. The horses whinnied and reared with fright at the staggering apparition. They broke loose of their tethers and stampeded into the fields, trampling the newly sprouted crops.

A few hours later, oblivious of the earlier commotion, the huntsmen awoke and blearily meandered home, holding their aching heads and napping under trees along the way. The outraged villagers were already sitting before Hormuzd, voicing their complaints, when Khusraw arrived. The prince dismounted into the embrace of two stem guardsmen who steered him by the elbows to his father's throne.

Hormuzd leaped up snarling at his heir. "No sooner do my decrees go forth than they are trampled by your horses' hooves. Since when are you, my highborn son, to take pleasure at my people's cost?

"Bring forth Khusraw's grape-stealing servant!" the king commanded, and when the trembling creature appeared, Hormuzd gave him as a slave to the village elder whose vineyard he had violated.

"Bring forth that minstrel!" the king demanded. "Cut his fingernails! Unstring his harp!"

Then Hormuzd ordered the hooves of Khusraw's horse to be cut. As much as I adore my paints, Khusraw adored his horses. This ruthless penalty was even harder on him than that his father next presented Khusraw's own throne to the peasant whose crops had been destroyed.

The king stalked out of the chamber. Khusraw sank to his knees before the elders of the court. He pleaded that they pardon the servant and the harpist. He begged them to spare his horse. "Do not punish them for my misdeeds," he wept, writhing on the ground. "Here is my sword and my submissive head. I can bear any sorrow except my father's anger."

Only Bozorg Omid remained aloof. But so much did the elders love Khusraw Parviz, they promised to intercede with the king and offer the boy's apologies. But before they could reach Hormuzd, Khusraw wrapped himself in a shroud and walked barefoot from the city to the Caves of the Ascetics. It is said that Hormuzd watched him go with a tear of approval misting his imperial eye.

Khusraw was always given to sweeping gestures. They elucidated his success … and illustrated his foolishness. He had little of the false pride of kings. But I wondered—throughout our lives—whether he lacked some of his ancestors' judiciousness.

He made his atonement alone. He took no sustenance into the caves. Now and then, someone left a jug of water and a loaf of bread beside the entrance, yet the prince touched nothing. Weeks passed until—unbathed, untrimmed, and in rags—Khusraw walked off the mountain. No one recognized him. In this humble and miserable state, Khusraw Parviz prostrated himself before Hormuzd to beg forgiveness.

Father forgave son and kissed him, returned his princely throne, and sent the relieved peasant back to his village with gold enough to be jolly his life long.

It was on this very night that I arrived home from my studies in China. I had taken my time, divagating as usual, seeking adventures and fresh sights with which to fill my vision and my drawing pages. I'd journeyed back through Armenia, lingering long among mountains and gleaming lakes, rivers that rush over cliffs, honeysuckle, juniper, yellow thistles, and gray sage scenting the clouds and mists. I was anxious now for the cheerful company of my best friend, my second self, to tell him of the fine hunting for wild boar, lynx, and bear in that place of marvels. But Khusraw was not to be disturbed. Dressed again in finery, clean and clipped, he slept soundly in his own soft bed. Dreaming of his grandfather.

Not having Khusraw to drink with, I found others who told me the story of the prince's peccadillos, punishments, and penance.

It is said of me that I can draw pictures on water. When I draw a person's head, it moves. The bird whose wings I draw will fly. When Khusraw finally rubbed the sleep from his eyeballs and joined me for supper, I showed him page after page of drawings from far and wide, a traveler's log in pictures. When I reached the pages that expressed Armenia's beauty, I could not contain my excitement about its splendors, the *khatchkars*—basalt slabs carved so delicately they resemble lace—the exquisite metalwork, the delicacy of weaving and embroidery, the black stone on which mares in heat rub themselves so every foal born to these mares can outrun the rain. I told him of the grandeur of the court and the glorious wealth and property of its queen, Mihin Banu, who had no use for husbands, for she was stronger than any man. At that, the prince laughed aloud.

"Extraordinary, indeed," I agreed, "but the most awesome wonder of Mihin Banu's court is her niece, Shirin." Khusraw's eyes widened.

"Her face," I continued, "is a wild rose, her lips as sweet as her name. Her speech is charming and clever, and she has been chosen as the heir of Queen Mihin Banu. I have never seen a maiden as enchanting as Shirin!"

Khusraw leaned into me like a hungry cat. His bugged eyes searched my pages for an image of the princess, but I had none, for as yet I had not been permitted to draw her or even come that close.

"And," I added, Khusraw's breath buzzing in my ear, "never have I seen a horse as noble, with such lightning hooves, as the queen's black steed, Shabdiz!"

Khusraw nearly toppled into my lap.

He struggled to his feet and shook the wine from his brains while I shook his wet wheeze from my ear. "Did you say, 'Shirin'? Did you say, 'Shabdiz'? The ghostly graybeard spoke true," he shouted.

"What? Maybe you did go mad while I was absent," I said.

"Listen, Shapur, listen! This is not the time for jokes. You can believe me or not, but listen." He sat. He stood. He sat again.

"Last night," he said. "Khusraw Anushirvan, my grandfather, visited my sleep."

Oh yes. That immortal soul. Greatest of all Persian kings, who expanded his lands to the Black Sea and the Indus River and far into the mountains of the Afghan.

"He spoke to me," Khusraw Parviz continued, pacing now as he related the visitation. "He said, 'You have accepted punishment and thus I foresee a happy future. You will have four things that will be worth more than anything you have lost or could lose:

"'You will ride Shabdiz, the world's swiftest steed—he will shake his mane to your glory across a mighty empire bordered by the seas.

"'You will sit on Taqdiz, the throne of thrones.

"'You will have the musician Barbad to play at your bidding—his is the lightest touch and far surpasses the broken notes of your lost harpist.'"

At that, I thought to object, for I favored Barbad's apprentice, Nikisa, but Khusraw held up his hand for silence while he finished.

"'And best of all, my grandson,' the ancient spirit told me, 'you will have Shirin, your destined love, whose sweetness, beauty, loyalty, and fortitude will sustain you all your days.' And having said that, Khusraw Anushirvan vanished and I awoke."

There was a full minute's silence. Then Khusraw begged me to return to Armenia. "Bring Shirin to me at once, dear second self, friend of my life."

"As long as my brushes and paint attend me, my prince, you have nothing to fear," I said. "Failure has no chance against my artistry."

It was spring when I arrived. All the woods and fields were dewy emeralds. Clouds swirled in skirts around the high peak of Mount Arafat, the snowy breast that nurtures the land of Armenia. Rivers rushed through vast, jagged gorges. Peach, apple, and apricot trees blossomed, and the rough ground was carpeted with wild grain. I rode enthralled until I came to a cave, where I tethered my horse. I inched toward it on foot and within I found an aged priest, who welcomed me and gave me shelter. At twilight, he pointed to a meadow, a verdant terrace ringed by oaks and pines, anemones, tulips, and diminutive iris.

"That field," he announced proudly, "it is there the royal party is accustomed to spreading their picnic cloth."

I had reached my destination.

At dawn, I sat on a rock outside the cave and in the glowing orange sunrise, painted a portrait of Khusraw Parviz. Then I stole down to the meadow and hung the picture from a branch. I hid in a mossy crevice between two boulders and waited.

Shirin and her attendants appeared on the shimmer of the morning, cavorting like leaves in a breeze. I peeked from my hiding place and watched as they spread rugs on the grass, sipped wine, and fashioned wreaths of flowers for one another, singing in high harmonies and dancing to the music of lutes. Crammed between the stones, I could not draw this magical scene, nor could I direct my focus on Shirin—and a good thing, too, since I was here on behalf of my friend and not to get my own heart broken.

The women pranced lightly on the grass, hips swaying, arms undulating, golden bracelets catching the dappled light. They twirled round and round, gossamer mantles and red skirts spinning. As they looped and coiled, their voices rose in a column of song that seemed to vibrate the treetops. Suddenly, Shirin stopped and gasped, pointing at my portrait of Khusraw.

Her maidens rushed to her side and held her steady, for she appeared about to faint. One of them guided her to a carpet and sat her down, while another plucked the picture from the branch and brought it to her.

Shirin gawked at the image of Khusraw Parviz with frenzied passion, thrust it to her heart, and embraced it, her face flushed as if with fever.

"What is this hex?" the maidens cried, looking anxiously from one to the other. The princess shivered, clutching the portrait. A pretty young woman snatched it from her. Then the maidens linked arms and circled tightly around Shirin, a dancing fortress of defense, while one of them burned rue to drive the spell away. Khusraw's face pocked and puckered under the little aromatic fire lit on top of it.

At last Shirin came to her senses and her maidens offered her milk. She gulped it gladly, for as I would learn, the princess savored the thick white liquid over all foods. When she had drunk the cupful, the party packed and left that lovely meadow.

With the coast clear, I popped out of my hiding place, rubbing my aching back. In the dwindling light, I painted a second portrait of Khusraw Parviz, exactly like the one before, though perhaps more luminous, for I was working at dusk.

I slept that night stretched out on silky grass and at dawn took up my hiding place again. Just as I hoped, by mid-morning, the princess and her companions returned to their picnicking place. And what did they see? Another portrait of the same man hanging from yet a different branch. Shirin swooned to the ground before her maidens could catch her. In that moment, I saw her soul, like a firefly, soar toward the portrait and alight and settle there as if it had found a home.

When Shirin's eyes fluttered open, though she reached for it, the maidens would not bring the portrait to the princess. Instead, they rolled their carpets and fled the meadow. At least this time they left my portrait unharmed!

On the third morning, I watched as Shirin and her companions rode past the meadow toward another. I followed them and somehow managed undetected to hang the portrait again. Then I squatted behind a tree and waited.

Soon, of course, the princess caught sight of the dazzling man in the branches, but now she said nothing to her maidens. Instead, she seized it with her own hands and covered it with kisses.

Her attendants could not stop her, and when at last she was done with her ardent display, she sent them to search for whoever might explain this mystery. I bit my lip not to laugh at those beauties rummaging through the bushes. While their backs were turned, I stepped from behind the tree and made myself visible to Shirin.

She gave a little shriek and called to her maidens. "Look! There! Go to that stranger!" and the women rushed toward me, demanding I tell them anything I might know. What unique pleasure, I thought, to be accosted like this.

I smiled. "It is a secret I can impart only to the princess herself," I said. "Alone."

This was almost too much for them. Although Shirin dismissed them, the maidens hovered nearby, holding hands, alert to any dangers as the princess summoned me to her and bade me sit beside her.

"The one you love," I said, "is Prince Khusraw Parviz. He has dreamed of you, his destined love, and sent me here to find you."

Shirin clutched the portrait to her heart. "Indeed, it is destined. This man is my fate. What can I do?"

I was installed in the palace as an honored guest. I ate and slept well, while Shirin pleaded with Queen Mihin Banu to let her ride Shabdiz the next day on the hunt.

"He is too high-spirited," the queen replied, but Shirin cajoled until her aunt reluctantly gave in.

How charming were these young women all readied for the hunt, for their custom was to dress in manly garb. Shirin, wearing an indigo and gold cloak with blue pantaloons, swung atop Shabdiz and sat the saddle with assurance. The hand that firmly held the reins wore the seal ring of the crown prince of Persia.

"It might be that you'll meet Khusraw himself," I had told her. "And if so, you'll know him, for he'll be wearing crimson from head to foot, and his horse's hooves will be shod in red gold."

Shirin winked at me as she set forth at a gallop from the palace. Shabdiz soon left the other horses in his dust. Her companions tried vainly to keep up, but when they arrived at the hunting plain, there was no sign of the princess. They waited. They searched high and low, fruitlessly, all day. They returned to give the queen the doleful news that her dearest Shirin had disappeared.

I sat quietly among the courtiers and watched as Mihin Banu's face turned pale and tears sprang from her eyes. They say she wept and mourned all night. Yet in the morning, to our surprise, she looked calm and happy, as if nothing had happened.

"Near the break of day," she told the assembled courtiers, "I had a dream that my beloved falcon had flown away, and in the dream I grieved as I had been grieving for Shirin. But as I grieved, dreaming, the bird returned.

"This is a fortunate omen," the queen said. "There is no need to search for my dearest niece."

Shirin and Shabdiz galloped for four days and four nights toward Persia. On the fifth day, they came upon a pool, clear and clean, delicious, and refreshing. Shirin was weary and dusty. She satisfied herself that no one was about, tethered Shabdiz, undressed and hung her robes and hunting gear on a tree, and loosened her braids. I have often imagined her sliding into the pool, the whiteness of her skin like silver, iridescent against the cerulean water, her face like the reflected moon. She washed her hair; she lay on her back and floated. She dreamed of Khusraw Parviz.

She floated and dreamed with no idea that on the very day Khusraw had sent me to Armenia, his enemies began circulating coins they had struck in the prince's name. It was not long before Hormuzd held a handful of these counterfeits and despaired. Could his son, his pride and joy, be plotting against him to capture the throne? What else could this mean? The greatest rulers are ruled by suspicion, and everyone is suspect, even their dearest sons.

Fearful and alarmed, Hormuzd ordered Khusraw to be cast into prison. Only the sage Bozorg Omid was unwilling to entertain such deceptions, and he urged his pupil to flee.

Khusraw told his servants he would be hunting for a fortnight and if a beautiful woman appeared riding a black stallion, like a peacock on a raven's back, she was to be welcomed as an honored guest. Should she so desire, a new palace was to be built for her, wherever she wanted it. Then, disguising himself in green and brown robes, rather than his customary crimson, Khusraw departed for Armenia. He rode so straight and fast, he covered two days' distance in one.

He reined his horse at a blue pool in a tranquil meadow. He was tired and thirsty. Just as he started to dismount, he saw a vision floating in the pond, dreamy as a lily.

Khusraw's heart caught fire. He stared at her through the reeds on the pond bank, paralyzed with love. The vision glanced his way. Startled by this sudden stranger, Shirin gathered her long black hair around her like a cloak. Thus attired, she emerged on an opposite bank, dressed quickly, mounted Shabdiz, touched her heel to his flank, and galloped into the late afternoon shadows.

Khusraw watched in wonder at Shirin's flight and when she had vanished, he wept for love.

At Moshku, Khusraw's own palace, the princess presented his ring and was greeted with brilliant ceremony. But when Shirin was asked to tell her story, she refused, insisting she would wait for Khusraw's return. Bozorg Omid kept his counsel, saying nothing of Khusraw's flight or the real reason he had left or when or even if he would return.

"The weeks went by like flights of swallows," Shirin told me. "They with a destination, and me lost and lonely in that palace where there were no pleasant views. I stood for hours, gazing out the windows, longing for the majestic mountains of Armenia, but all I saw were dust and crowds of people and the houses of the city piled one upon another."

At last, Bozorg Omid took pity on her and revealed that Khusraw had ordered a new house be built for her if that was her desire. Shirin smiled for the first time in many days and asked that it be constructed on a mountain plain.

And so it was, although the plain that Khusraw's enemies chose was so hot and unhealthy it could turn a child into an old man. There Shirin repaired, as if to a prison, and her misery increased while she waited for her true love.

Meanwhile, Khusraw had arrived in Armenia. Mihin Banu sent a retinue to welcome him, I among them. How glad we were, my second self and I, to reunite. And what festivities and celebrations! Khusraw sat at the foot of the queen's throne while musicians played and dancers whirled about us in bright colors, bells jangling on their delicate ankles. Games were played, and fires burned in every tent, cooking lavish feasts.

"The black steed, the blue robes, that incomparable beauty floating like a lily in that pond? It was no doubt Shirin you spied. On her way to you," I said.

"What bad luck," Khusraw replied. "She is where I was, and I am here. Go quickly, Shapur, I beg you. Return to Persia. Bring Shirin back!"

Mihin Banu gave me her second swiftest horse, Golgun, who like Shabdiz had been sired in the Cave of the Black Stone. I left regretfully, for if there was any place that had subdued my wanderlust, it was Armenia.

I arrived in Persia to find the princess disconsolate in her wretched new palace. She laughed with joy to see me again, for by now she had nearly given up hope of any word from Khusraw. Despite Bozorg Omid's secrecy for the sake of the prince's safety, I revealed the truth. I told her of the false coins and the father's doubts, of the prince's enemies and his flight.

Within the hour, we departed that noxious place. Shirin left Shabdiz in the stables of Khusraw's palace, a gift of love awaiting him.

"I don't think it will be long before he returns to Persia," she said sadly.

We did not know that—two days earlier, in his grand palace overlooking the city, physicians clucking at his bedside—the emperor Hormuzd had passed on, into the arms of his glorious forefathers.

Stars cross and the fates play tricks. As we were dashing toward Armenia, a messenger arrived at Mihin Banu's court to tell Khusraw that his father was dead and that he must hurry home to claim his rightful throne. Even as he sobbed and mourned Hormuzd, loving him in spite of everything—for he understood that monarchs must be vigilantly mistrustful—Khusraw prayed that he would find Shirin. He prayed that he would come across us as he rode back and she rode forth. But there are many winding paths through those jagged mountains, and many tall peaks to hide the traveler.

At the merry court of Mihin Banu, Shirin and I were met with great rejoicing. I reclaimed my paints and brushes and meandered contentedly in the hills, while Shirin hung about the court, downcast.

In his capital city of Mada'in, Khusraw Parviz, king of Persia, found himself alone. Each day he rode Shabdiz and talked to the stallion as he might have spoken to Shirin. With our teacher Bozorg Omid by his side, he tried to rule with justice, like his father and grandfather. The months passed into a year. The people seemed content with their new king, but it was not to last. His enemies spread gossip that Khusraw had killed his father. "He is a murderer," they whispered, "unfit to rule Persia. He values a gulp of wine more than the blood of a hundred brothers. He will surrender his kingdom for the price of a stallion. He is so distracted by love, he cannot follow the logic of day-to-day leadership."

And so it went, tongues wagging, rumors hissing through every street and alley of Mada'in, and a rebellion was sown. The people turned against their young ruler. They threw stones at his cavalcade when he processed through the streets. They wrote ugly words on walls demanding his downfall.

"You must leave again for a time," Bozorg Omid advised, so Khusraw saddled Shabdiz, riding without rest toward Armenia. He stopped on his journey only once to enjoy the diversion of a hunt.

In the mottled autumn light, Shirin, riding as usual ahead of her attendants, spotted a stranger, the same man who had surprised her while she bathed in that wilderness pool. She reined Golgun and he reined Shabdiz. They gaped at each other, captivated, not daring to move lest the slightest motion break the spell. Was it minutes or hours they were frozen in each other's gaze?

At last, Khusraw dismounted and extended his hand to Shirin, who slipped from her horse as a petal drifts from a rose.

And so, it would seem, ends this tale of love, happily, after mishaps and missed connections, with the long-awaited encounter and the first kiss.

I was overjoyed to see my second self, and he to see me. Mihin Banu prepared gifts worthy of an emperor. She scattered his path with jewels, though she withheld her most precious gem.

When all had gone to bed that night, Mihin Banu walked hand in hand with Shirin in the moonlit garden. "I see how you love him and he loves you," the queen said. "Yet although Khusraw is known to have been taught to rule with justice, you, as a woman, must guard against deceit."

Shirin bristled. "He will not deceive me," she said.

"He will not mean to," Mihin Banu replied. "But men are easily aroused and quickly distracted. What's more, it is said that in Persia, he possesses a thousand beautiful women." Shirin said nothing, for she knew this to be true.

"My child, you must not satisfy all Khusraw's desires. You must not let him tire of you. Keep your jewel and he will be as addicted to you as to opium. Yield, and you will be a trampled flower before the world. If he is the moon, you are the sun."

So Shirin vowed by the seven heavens that although she hungered for fulfillment with Khusraw, she would not succumb until she was his wife. Mihin Banu allowed Shirin to sit by Khusraw's side, she allowed them to hunt and feast and take all manner of pastimes, but she forbade them to converse privately or to be left alone.

We passed the days in bliss. Never was air so sparkling, sky so blue, grass so thick with blossoms. Rarely did Shirin and Khusraw leave each other's sight.

"O Shapur! She is graceful, yet she is not a fragile gazelle," Khusraw sighed. "She is a lioness, and my heart pursues her eagerly."

"Pursuing Shirin," I asked, "have you forgotten the pursuit of your empire?"

Khusraw shrugged.

Months rolled by and what sumptuous feasts we had. One banquet ended as another began! Music, song, wine, and poetry in praise of love! Every hour, Khusraw pleaded with Shirin to follow him to a secret place where they might talk of love and embrace unseen.

"My love," she rebuked him gently, "we must not so forget ourselves in this enchanted garden that the garden of our future goes untended. Remember that you are a king, and a king deposed. If you would enjoy my bloom, salvage your good name and let your state flower."

Khusraw was finally spurred to action. The very next morning, we set out together, he on Shabdiz, and rode without rest to Constantinople. We went before the emperor, where Khusraw Parviz pledged eternal friendship, asking in exchange for men and arms. We waited as the emperor of Byzantium consulted his astrologers, while those bearded men scanned the skies and squinted at constellations, and finally Khusraw was called before the court.

What counsel, what differing interpretations of the stars might Bozorg Omid have offered had he been there? "The emperor's astrologers tell him that I am on the rise," Khusraw confided to me. "They say a lasting peace with Persia is the benefit and fortune of all."

"Yes. It seems so, indeed."

"The emperor has therefore agreed to give me not only a force of fifty thousand men, but his daughter, Maryam, in marriage, with a pledge that I will take no other wife besides."

I stopped in my tracks. The vision of Shirin, heartbroken, swam before my eyes. Khusraw walked on. "I am sorely trapped," he continued. "To pursue duty is to deny my love and to deny duty is to deny my love as well."

I trotted to catch up. "To have Shirin, you must redeem your crown," I said.

"I want her above all else."

"Is this an unbending condition of the emperor and Maryam?" He nodded. He was crying.

His face revealed no pain when, within the week, he signed the marriage contract and wed Princess Maryam. While Khusraw warmed his marriage bed, then mustered fifty thousand men at arms, Mihin Banu died. While Khusraw Parviz reclaimed Taqdiz, throne of thrones in the city of Mada'in, Shirin was crowned queen of Armenia.

As during the reign of her exalted aunt, it was said that perfect peace prevailed and Shirin's people prospered. That the falcon drank together with the quail and the wolf lay with the lamb. Shirin believed that Khusraw, having regained his throne, had not yet come to claim her, for he was busy securing the realm. She sent gifts to him but heard nothing. She was now so dear to me, a friend of friends after all our journeys and detours, that I could not let her go on deceived. I returned to Armenia with the trading caravans and the news: Khusraw Parviz had married the Byzantine princess, Maryam, and promised her never to take another wife.

Shirin's face remained as placid as if she had been told that we would have mountain trout for supper. She did not betray her despondency. But across the months, her government began to fray, neglected, until she realized she must leave a regent in her place and go to Persia. This road, I thought, as Shirin and I traversed it yet again, is becoming a gully. We followed it straight back to the palace that had been built for her on that wretched, poisoned mountain plain.

Although I went directly to him and told him of our arrival. Khusraw would not visit Shirin for fear of Maryam's wrath and the Byzantine emperor's might. Night after night, he washed his liver with wine, and day after day, he soothed his heart with stronger liquor. I was helpless to stop him, helpless to do anything but sit with him each evening while he sank into angry silence, listening to the minstrel Barbad sing songs about the love between Khusraw and Shirin. When one song ended, Khusraw slurred for another, then another and another.

Until one night, he staggered to his feet and lurched to his wife's quarters. He told Maryam that Shirin had left her own kingdom for his sake and was languishing at her palace.

"Bring her here as your slave," Khusraw Parviz demanded.

Maryam clutched their newborn son to her chest. "I will kill Shirin if I ever see her!"

Who could blame her? And yet Maryam had a mean spirit, imperious and spiteful, so that sympathy for her was hard to come by.

Khusraw wobbled back to his chambers and grabbed me by my shoulder. "Go to her, friend of my life," he pleaded. "Beg Shirin to meet me secretly, under cover of night."

"Beneath Maryam's suspicious eye?" I asked, doubtful. Khusraw laid his head on my lap and looked at me like a hungry dog.

"Tell me, Magnificence, do you really believe that Shirin will submit?" At that, he blubbered and fell unconscious.

I had never heard Shirin raise her voice. Now she shrieked like a magpie.

"Am I beneath the princess Maryam that I must crawl to the king in the dark? Is Queen Shirin not as royal as Maryam and Khusraw? Khusraw has Shabdiz! If he wishes to see me, let him ride the black stallion to me, in broad daylight! Until then, speak no more to me of Khusraw!"

I visited Shirin often, for as I've said, her friendship had become as precious to me as Khusraw's. We spoke no word of the king and occupied ourselves with myriad entertainments. Her days were protracted. Although Khusraw's name was never mentioned, she could not somehow make herself go home and reclaim her throne, but seemed suspended. Longing weighed her down; her radiance was shrouded with sorrow. We played chess, rode, and hunted; we talked long hours while Shirin and her maidens plied the wondrous needlework of Armenia. I even taught her to use my brushes and paint, but while she enjoyed it, she had little talent for it. Yet her mistakes amused her, and it was good to hear her laugh.

It was during one of those lessons that she looked up and said, "Shapur, I crave milk. A drink of milk would bring such comfort. The thick milk of Armenia is like a mother's love." I raised my hand to summon a servant, but she raised hers to stop me.

"It's no use. I cannot pasture cows in the unhealthy fields around this palace. They are overgrown with poisonous weeds."

My old schoolmate, Farhad, sprang to mind. "I have a friend," I told Shirin, "with whom I studied in China, a youth of immense skill and cleverness. He is a scholar who has mastered the works of Euclid and Ptolemy, yet his accomplishments with sculpture are even greater. So deftly does he carve the most obdurate stone, it sings with joy as he chips it with his chisel. Moreover, he is strong as two elephants."

Farhad's arms were massive. He looked as if he were anticipating an embrace as we stood in Shirin's court, waiting to see her. He was patient, for such is the nature of one who carves stone and builds strong, meticulous structures. But when she appeared, he stared slack-jawed like one possessed and barely heard a word of her greeting.

"I have need of milk," she told Farhad. "What is required is a channel from a distant pasture, where flocks can graze safely. Shepherds in that distant pasture will pour milk into the trough and it will flow to me here."

I answered for him. I agreed on Farhad's behalf, for he stood helpless, deafened, and blinded by urgent love. When she left and his mind began to be restored, I explained what the queen wanted. Before I had finished speaking, Farhad picked up his axe and shovel, set to, and within a month, the channel was finished. In the rock by Shirin's door, Farhad dug a pool, which foamed with milk.

I called her to come, and when she saw how milk bubbled at her feet, she gave a delighted little yelp, praised Farhad lavishly, unclasped two pearls that dangled from her ears, and offered them to him. He grasped them, held them to his mouth, then dropped them into the milk pond and ran from the palace, overwhelmed.

I was the fool who told Khusraw that Farhad was smitten with Shirin. Khusraw ordered the engineer to be brought to him from the desert. He showered Farhad with gold, saying, "Your talents are known to me. There is a road I wish to travel, but a grim and towering mountain blocks the route. I want you to cut

through that treacherous mountain and make it passable."

Farhad looked shrewdly at Khusraw. I didn't think he had it in him, but love encourages daring. "I will," he said. "If I succeed, I demand that you give me Shirin as my reward."

I could not believe my ears when Khusraw agreed. But the task seemed impossible, and he was sure Farhad would fail. Jealousy is a slayer of justice.

I rode to the mountain with Farhad and watched in awe as he carved an image of Shirin in that forbidding rock. Then he carved another of Khusraw riding Shabdiz and began his dreadful labor. He kept at it day and night, and it wasn't long before I left, seeing that Farhad was not disposed to distractions and having run out of things to paint in that bleak place. I returned to call on Shirin.

Farhad wielded his axe steadfastly across the weeks, pausing only to stare adoringly upon Shirin's likeness, to kiss its feet and climb to the mountaintop to declare his love. His prowess was becoming legendary, and word of his achievement reached Shirin.

"This is an accomplishment more marvelous than my milk channel. I must see it," she said, so together we visited Farhad at the mountain, where he had almost completed the road.

I called his name, and Farhad turned from his work to glower at whoever was disrupting his rhythm. But seeing Shirin, he so lost his senses, he turned quickly back, beating his chest with one hand while with the other he continued slashing the rock. Shirin sat on Golgun, unable to think of a word to say.

"What help can I offer?" she asked me, and while I strained to find an answer, she dismounted, drew a flask of milk from her saddlebag, and offered it to Farhad. He said nothing but drank it all in one gulp. Whereas milk will calm the blood, in Farhad it only increased his passion. His eyes were wild as he stared at her. She stared back, confused, and then slowly gathering her wits, she made ready to depart.

We mounted, and Shirin, as always, took the lead. Golgun, exhausted by the steep climb up the mountainside, put one hoof forward and stumbled, but Farhad reached for him before he could fall. As if he were lifting an infant, he placed horse and rider on his shoulders and did not set them down until he reached Shirin's palace gate.

I met Farhad on the road. My horse was panting with exertion, while Farhad, cool as water, was striding back toward the mountain, where he worked with such ferocity that the project was almost complete that very afternoon.

In Mada'in, Khusraw's spies told him of Shirin's visit to Farhad and that there was no question now that Farhad would complete the task and succeed in winning Shirin's hand.

Khusraw's messenger found Farhad cleaving the last half-mile of rock. Pretending he was merely a passerby, he hailed Farhad. "Why do you toil your life away like this?" he asked with feigned innocence. "A strong young man like you should wield his chisel on a maiden!"

Farhad scowled at him. "I work for my king and my love."

"Aha! And who might your love be?"

"Queen Shirin. I love Queen Shirin and have no words for her but my labors." Farhad raised his powerful arm and shattered a boulder to gravel. "Nor do I have one more word for you! Begone! I'm busy!"

"Did you say Queen Shirin?" the stranger shouted over the crash of splintering stones. "Have you not heard? Shirin died yesterday, taken by fever. All her palace howls with grief."

The men working for Farhad watched in horror as he sucked his breath and flung his axe so savagely, the blade split. It quivered on a rock with a sound like thunder and sparks like lightning. Farhad groaned. His wide arms flapped, and he threw himself from the mountain. Down and down and down Farhad plunged, whirling through thin air, landing at last in a canyon and smashing like the boulder he'd hewed but a minute before. The axe handle, made of pomegranate wood, fell after him and speared Farhad's heart.

There it took root and sprouted into a tree. To this day, on those tree branches, the red fruit still grows, sweet and juicy within its protective shell.

Shirin stood at her window watching the channel of milk flow toward her door. Her tears cascaded into the pool, and wherever a tear dropped, milk frothed into a little pearl. Every week that passed after Farhad's death seemed more pitiless than the one before. She could not stop crying. He had been faithful, where Khusraw had not. What drives us to love whom we love? Why can we not help ourselves, despite the melancholy and dejection that love inflicts?

When finally her weeping subsided, Shirin ordered me to design and build a beautiful dome over Farhad's grave. It would be a place of pilgrimage for true lovers. Shirin set herself and her maidens to work, composing poems of love, which I would carve in ribbons around the tomb.

Khusraw was tormented by his cruelty, the cowardly jealousy and possessiveness that had provoked him to send the messenger to Farhad and kill him. I knew he felt remorseful and guilty, but I could not bring myself to sit by his side consoling him as he roiled in wine and self-pity. Months went by while I avoided my second self, occupied, I told him, with the construction of Farhad's resting place.

So Khusraw sent a letter to Shirin. She read it again and again, kissing it each time she unrolled it. Soon, between the lines, she guessed that Khusraw had crafted Farhad's death. She put his letter aside and turned away.

I had forgiven, if not forgotten, and had made my peace with Khusraw, when Maryam died. He wore mourning. He withdrew from his court. He pretended sorrow, but his heart rejoiced. The promise that bound him to the emperor of Byzantium was gone. All that remained of Maryam was their son, Shiruyeh, a surly child, a stranger to his father, in whose soul Khusraw had perceived evil from the beginning, a spirit like Maryam's, cold and vindictive.

"It would be best if I killed him," Khusraw said, "and dropped him in his mother's grave."

I shivered at the thought, and yet even I, who cannot read the stars, wondered if this might not save us in the end.

But Bozorg Omid counseled as ever for prudence. "Could it not be, Magnificence, that from bad comes good? Who can know God's will?"

Shirin, too, mourned Maryam. Sincerely, as was her duty. When the proscribed period of mourning was over, she sent a letter to Khusraw.

Again, I became the messenger between them.

"There is good and bad in life," Shirin wrote. "Weddings and deaths. There will be other brides for you when you can overcome your grief."

Grief was never so quickly overcome! I carried a letter back to Shirin the next day, and in it, Khusraw offered to marry her.

And now, it would seem, ends this tale of love, happily, after mishaps and missed connections, with all the obstructions vanquished, all transgressions pardoned, the way clear.

Even as he tried to be a fair and righteous ruler, Khusraw was impulsive, given to satisfying his every whim. I dashed back and forth like a lizard from palace to palace, delivering letters, and while he awaited an answer to his proposal, Khusraw gave way to feasting and enjoyment.

"Tell me," he asked a group of guests one evening. "Where are the most beautiful women on Earth to be found?"

"O Magnificence, this is easy! Isfahan, of course!" they cried. "For Isfahan is the home of Shekar, beauty of beauties." They spent the rest of the night praising

Shekar, vividly describing her charms. The next morning, Khusraw mounted Shabdiz and set out for Isfahan to see for himself.

He returned with Shekar as his bride. "Never, *never* is Khusraw's name to be mentioned in my presence," Shirin ordered her household and all who visited her. She had at first appeared indifferent, but dishonesty was not in her nature. The aloofness she tried to cultivate soon turned to such sharp heartache, she prayed from sundown to sunrise for God to release her from her plight.

I had difficulty disguising my disgust. No longer did Khusraw and I share second selves, I told myself, for this person I had loved from childhood was not one I wished to resemble.

Was it God, answering Shirin's prayers, or was it Khusraw's mercurial character that caused him to tire of his new companion and send her back to Isfahan?

Then Khusraw's heart wrapped itself once more around the memory of Shirin. It was a freezing cold winter morning when Khusraw Parviz set out from his grand palace on a royal hunt. The commander of the armies of Byzantium and an ambassador from China made up the splendid entourage. Before us went youths leading horses, scattering incense. Guards rode elephants. Musicians played drums and pipes. Banners of all colors flapped in the breeze. Falcons rode the leather-gloved wrists of the hunters. Khusraw wore crimson and gold and rode Shabdiz, his bridle also tasseled in crimson and gold. We hunted birds and lions and deer.

With the first day's hunt ended, his guests settled to sleep with their bellies full, in silken tents, under warm, thick quilts of the finest wool and velvety fur. Khusraw left the camp and rode toward Shirin, with me and several other companions, as well as a company of servants. In the frozen night, on the noxious plain outside her palace, Khusraw ordered a fire to be lit from precious scented woods so that in her sleep, Shirin would smell that glorious fragrance and be softened toward him in her dreams. In the morning, he steeled his courage with cups of mulled wine. He sent me ahead to Shirin's court to tell her of his arrival. She thanked me and bade me kindly to wait for the king in the courtyard where she had planted trees and flowers and set with khatchkars reminiscent of Armenia.

Shirin gave each of her attendants a tray filled with gold coins to scatter before the king. Paths were laid of carpets and embroidered cloths. Aloe-wood was made ready to burn. Then Shirin went to the roof of her palace to watch for him.

Billowing snow announced the lover's appearance. First came his companions resplendent in coats of ermine, fox, and bear. Then Khusraw Parviz himself, carrying white narcissus, her favorite flower. Shirin clutched the ramparts to keep from falling, took a deep breath, followed by a long, swooning sigh, and quickly retired to her chamber.

Gold cascaded at the king's feet. Silks were spread; tents were raised and covered with jeweled canopies. And in the largest tent of all stood a golden throne. Khusraw Parviz, the Victorious One, laughed with delight and triumph and rushed with his bouquet to the palace door.

"What's this?" he bellowed. "Does the door not open?"

"No, Magnificence," his companions replied, pushing and pulling and pounding. "It seems to be stuck."

"Or locked," the king muttered, the flush of conquest fading from his face. He turned to Shirin's servants. "Tell the queen that I have come to beg forgiveness at her feet. I will remain here until she shows herself to me, however long that may take."

The servants ran to deliver the message. The king cooled his heels in the courtyard.

At last, when Khusraw's nose had all but snapped off and his beard was stiff, the servants returned. "Queen Shirin will

only speak to you from her roof," they told Khusraw, who looked up to see his beloved in her finest robes, a vision of loveliness, the dream of his youth, looking down upon him. On his knees, he kissed the icy ground. He praised her gifts: the gold, the silks, the throne.

"But is locking the door the way to treat an honored guest, much less a king?" he demanded.

Her heart was torn between anger and desire, hope and hopelessness. In a voice filled with contempt, she listed her grievances, from his marriage to Maryam to his trickery of Farhad to his dalliances with Shekar. "And there is much, much more, O Magnificence," she sneered.

"You come here, merry with wine. Look at you! Bright with liquor and ready for amusement. If you seek love, then leave and return sober to take me as your wife.

"If you seek only pleasure, then return to Shekar or some other, newer plaything, and never show your face to me again, never write to me, never think of me, as I will never again think of you!"

In his wildest dreams, Khusraw had not imagined his sweet and patient Shirin in such a rage. Rarely had he been confronted in this manner, except by his father. Few people are willing to tell a prince or king the stark truth.

Khusraw tried to stutter an apology. Words of repentance and excuses about the excesses of youth stuttered off his tongue, but before they could take shape, Shirin was at him again, her voice from the palace roof carrying across the quiet white plains.

"Youth! You are no longer so young, my king!" she scolded. "And yet you behave like a boy only just coming into his manhood! Perhaps, Magnificence, you should grow up before you grow old!" From there she launched into a recitation of her love and fidelity and her thoughts about Farhad, "a man who would have been faithful to me, a solid man, unlike you, with no cracks and fissures in his heart—and yet you broke him. Oh, would that I had such a man!" She fairly spat upon Khusraw, wide-eyed with shock below her.

"Farhad died for me! It is more than I would ask of any lover. But what have *you* done, Khusraw, to prove *your* love?" Her fury could have melted glaciers. He hung his head, and the frost on his beard dripped pitifully on to his chest.

Spent now, Shirin turned away and left her roof. Khusraw, dazed by the onslaught, left the palace. He had sought adoration without condition and found only righteous bitterness. We rode through cold rain back to the camp. The king ignored his guests and dismissed his companions. All but me, though I was in no mood to hang about in Khusraw's tent comforting him once again.

He paced like a madman, grinding his teeth and drinking.

"Each time I draw a picture," I said, filling his wine cup, "I must tear it up and begin again and again until I have it right. What beauty is won with ease, my king? Does a rose not have thorns? Take heart, Khusraw! Fortune is good and in the end all will be well."

Khusraw drank on, pouting into his goblet. Late in the night, as I waited for him to lose consciousness, I heard the sound of hooves. The guards were drunk and snoring. I stepped out of the tent. In the dark, I recognized Shirin on Golgun. She had followed the tracks of Shabdiz through the woods and found our camp. I helped her dismount.

"I cannot help it, Shapur. My heart cannot stand to be without him. I have left my country and my throne to be near him. For all that he has suffered me to endure, I want him."

I smiled sympathetically. I could not understand it, really, yet I admired her perseverance, her forbearance, her undying devotion.

"What can I do to help you, my queen?"

"First, dear Shapur, hide me in the camp until such time as I decide to show myself to Khusraw."

"Done!" I whispered.

"If Khusraw does not agree to marry me, then, my friend, I beg you to escort me safely back to Armenia."

"That will not be necessary," I said, tethering Golgun. "Fortune is good," I repeated. "In the end all will be well."

I guided Shirin through the blackness to my own tent. Seeing that she was comfortable, I returned to Khusraw.

He dozed fitfully. I leaned over him and shook him. "You sleep badly, my king. Awaken and be more at ease awhile."

Khusraw sputtered. "I have had a dream. I was in a beautiful garden with a beautiful maiden at my side."

What's this? I thought. Another detour from his destined love? More petty distractions? How could I advise him to turn in the right direction?

"You are beset by beauty, my king," I said, stifling a yawn and settling down on a pile of carpets. I was more than ready for bed. "The maiden was surely Shirin and no other. The dream tells you simply that you will soon be reunited. Do you not remember the visitation of your grandfather? See how this is the final pledge coming true. You must celebrate this good omen with festivities."

The next day, as the sun descended the sky, Khusraw called forth his cupbearers. The cooks prepared a feast and we made merry with the guests. When they were satiated, content and nodding off, Khusraw and I repaired to his tent, where he sent for his spellbinding musician, Barbad.

It was Barbad whom the king's grandfather, that ghostly diviner, had promised in the dream long ago. The assurance of a musician, especially such a one, is a gift surpassing all the world's treasures. And now I realized, too, how music would fulfill the happiness that Khusraw Anushirvan had guaranteed Khusraw Parviz.

Barbad appeared in the king's tent. His apprentice, Nikisa, whose musical style I had always favored, meanwhile arrived secretly at my tent, where Shirin was concealed.

"Stand outside and I will whisper instructions from within," she told Nikisa. "Let me direct him to my heart's true measures, while Barbad gives voice to Khusraw."

So it was that the lovers conversed in song. Their music was clear as the crisp night air. Each word shone like a star. Nikisa sang for Shirin: she would not be a slave to Khusraw. To which Barbad replied by pledging Khusraw's eternal love.

Nikisa sang of loneliness: Shirin would rather die than live without Khusraw.

Barbad bewailed Shirin's locked door: let her come to Khusraw and he would make her his queen and never leave her side.

Let it be so, I prayed. Too much time has passed with too many mishaps and missed connections. Too many selfish, careless, boyish betrayals, driven by spoiled intemperance, each duplicity a barb to a heart that was never less than absolutely constant. Moreover, I said to myself, I'm sick of this. It's time to travel, to see new lands and new images. My brushes were stiff, my paints drying out.

Suddenly, Khusraw was yelling over Barbad's song,"Forgive me, my love," once, twice, a hundred times.

Hearing his voice, Shirin cried out over Nikisa's tones. Khusraw, recognizing her sobs, ran into the camp, seeking the source. Shirin stepped out of my tent and rushed to him. He tried to embrace her. She pulled back.

"I will not be yours until I am your wife," she said.

Khusraw roared for his secretary. By now, the whole camp was awake. The Byzantine commander of armies and the Chinese ambassador lurched from their tents rubbing their eyes. Then and there, Khusraw ordered the marriage contracts drafted.

Khusraw could not stop studying Shirin's exquisite, joyful face or admiring aloud the grace of her hands, the

melodiousness of her speech. She stayed in the camp for seven days, and in that time, Khusraw doted on her constantly. In Mada'in, Bozorg Omid, although nearly overtaken by old age and death, scanned the heavens for auspicious omens and fixed a wedding date. Khusraw sent a caravan of camels and horses laden with gifts for Shirin to fetch her from her palace.

His nobles stood at attention to receive and applaud the bride. She did not come riding in a sheltered pavilion upon a white camel. Instead, she sat upon Golgun, unveiled and proud. On her head, she bore a tall, gold crown engraved with suns and eagles, the symbols of Armenia. Her arms were covered in gold bracelets, her earrings were gold, and gold brooches adorned her flowing gown of creamy white, the color of milk she so cherished. Her skirt was embroidered in the custom of her country with tulips, roses, hyacinths, lilies, carnations, and little roosters.

Shiruyeh sat on the throne of the crown prince, next to his father, scowling, ambition and hatred written all over his face. He brightened with ravenous desire at the sight of Shirin.

Shirin and Khusraw exchanged their vows. The blue sky deepened to purple with the coming of night and there was revelry throughout the land. In the court, we feasted and drank, while Barbad and Nikisa played until the early hours of the morning. Then, as light lifted the heavens, Khusraw was carried to the bridal chamber where Shirin had withdrawn, long wearied of the festivities.

We hoisted him seated in our arms to her chamber. His head lolled on my shoulder. In one hand, he waved a wine flask. The other waggled at Shirin, who quickly blew out the candles and slipped out of the room. We set Khusraw on the bed, where he waited, slurring his undying loyalty into the empty pillow beside him. I stood outside the room with

Shirin, holding our fists to our mouths to suppress our laughter, as a wrinkled, hunchbacked old servant entered the queen's bedchamber, leaving the door open. Khusraw took the crone in his eager embrace, mumbling words of love. He opened his bleary eyes. He screamed and cursed. He ordered the ancient woman from the room. And only then did Shirin go to him, for he was sober now and no longer beyond his senses.

As the dawn broke, the lovers were united in ecstasy at last. After all the mishaps and missed connections, the strength of the lion mingled with the sweetness of the rose. That day and night and for days and nights after that, they lingered. Then Khusraw sat again upon Taqdiz, the throne of thrones, and shared his good fortune with his people.

I, who had prayed for the end of this love story and the freedom to travel again, was presented with Shirin's prettiest handmaiden in marriage. A wondrous enough gift, but when Shirin implored me to take the regency of Armenia, I could not refuse and knew my fate was sealed, my feet were bound. Soon, I was traversing the path Shirin and I had trod so often, long ago, headed with my bride to the charming old court of Mihin Banu, the Great Lady, where I would now rule. There, too, I would record this tale, rendering each episode in delicate, luminous pictures.

It was many years before I saw Khusraw and Shirin again. But messengers and travelers always brought me happy news of Khusraw's just, sober, and peaceful rule and the prosperity of his people. The prophesy of Khusraw Anushirvan was satisfied. Khusraw Parviz now possessed the four things promised to him: he had Shabdiz, the world's swiftest steed, who carried him to glory across a mighty empire bordered by the sea; he sat upon Taqdiz, the jewel-encrusted throne of thrones; in his banquet hall, the musician Barbad played with an unsurpassable touch; and at his side was his destined love, Shirin.

And still this love story was not concluded.

Shiruyeh plotted. He schemed. He conspired to seize his father's throne, although someday he would rightfully inherit it. Perhaps he sensed Khusraw's dislike of him and feared that the king would choose another to replace him. He made alliances in secret with Khusraw's enemies and with his grandfather, the emperor of Byzantium.

Stars cross and fate is fickle. Khusraw bowed in prayer one morning, giving thanks to God. His mind upon worship, Khusraw did not hear Shiruyeh enter, flanked by troops. They sneaked behind the king, constrained him with chains, dragged him out of the palace, and cast him into a dungeon.

As the envoy from Persia told me of Shiruyeh's treachery, I remembered the ominous sense I'd had those many years ago, when Maryam died and Khusraw proposed to kill their son. I shuddered. I was not surprised to hear that when Shirin received word of her husband's capture, she followed him to prison.

"Great was Khusraw's grief," the envoy said. "Great was Shirin's comfort. And greater still was her will to protect him, so that while he slept she paced back and forth, trying to stay awake, afraid that harm would come to him if they were both asleep."

Nevertheless, one eerie, moonless night, with no star visible in the sky, Shirin sat beside Khusraw, her arm across his back. No matter how she fought the sleep that weighed upon her eyeballs, her drowsy head lowered and she succumbed.

The assassin crept unheard into the dungeon. He stabbed Khusraw in the liver. Khusraw Parviz awoke to find himself wounded and close to death. He was thirsty, but he would not awaken Shirin, for he knew how weary she was. Blood flowed unstaunched like a waterfall from his wound. Without the slightest motion, moan, or whisper, Khusraw Parviz, friend of my childhood, my second self, breathed his last.

The blood had soaked through his robes and into hers. Shirin awoke, wet and chilly. She sat abruptly, removing her arm from where it rested on Khusraw's back. He did not stir. She shook him. Her heart throbbed with fear, and then it went numb with sorrow.

With that report from the Persian envoy, I called for the fastest mount in Armenia, sired in the Cave of the Black Stone, and I rushed to Shirin.

When the hours of her weeping passed, Shirin asked the jailors for musk and camphor so that she could bathe her husband's body. She walked out of that prison beside the cot that carried her husband's body. She returned to the palace, where a courier from Shiruyeh was waiting.

Finally, he would be king. And he would have his father's widow for a wife. He coveted Shirin, as he coveted Taqdiz.

"The crown prince asks that you marry him," the courier announced. "He promises you a life of luxury and ease."

Without so much as a pause, to the courier's disbelief, Shirin agreed to the proposal.

"I ask only that all of Khusraw's possessions and all of mine be distributed to the poor," she said. Shiruyeh agreed.

Within the hour, Shirin called men to Khusraw's throne room. She ordered them to dismantle Taqdiz, to divide its golden frame into many small pieces and remove the jewels embedded there. She stood upon the palace balcony, having summoned the poor to stand beneath, and watched as her servants allotted the fragmented throne of Persia to the people.

So it would be that Shiruyeh would never sit upon his father's throne of thrones, but would have to construct his own.

Khusraw Parviz was placed upon a golden bier. He was carried through the streets of Mada'in, buoyed along by the wails of his subjects. Shirin processed behind her husband. She was not clothed in mourning, but to the astonishment of all, she wore a gown dyed of cochineal, the scarlet of Armenia. She did not wear her crown. That, she had given to me, with an embrace of deepest friendship.

Our procession reached the vault that housed the royal tombs. The bier was carried inside. Shirin followed. "Leave me, please," she asked. "Let me say farewell alone to Khusraw."

Shiruyeh, exasperated that the throne of thrones he had craved was gone, was nevertheless flushed with glee that his father's beloved would soon be his bride. He would not have all that his father possessed, but he would have the most treasured. Anxious to please her, Shiruyeh readily agreed to let Shirin follow Khusraw into the tomb. She smiled wanly at him and entered the vault, barring the entrance.

Shirin went to Khusraw's side, face wet with tears. She covered him with kisses. She removed a dagger hidden in her generous red robes. She stabbed herself in her liver.

Shirin's blood ran over Khusraw Parviz's body, and he awoke for a moment. The lovers kissed. The stars paused in their celestial course in stark wonder at a love so fine.

Maiden in Distress

On a summer evening,
Mullah Nasruddin strolls past a walled garden.
He is curious. Surely there are irresistible delights within!
Mullah Nasruddin climbs the garden wall.
A beautiful maiden is locked in the embrace of a hideous monster.
A misshapen, green, and drooling ogre!
Mullah Nasruddin, ever chivalrous, leaps into the garden.
With blows and curses, he puts the beast to flight.
He turns to accept the maiden's thanks.
Surely her gratitude will come as kisses and caresses.
Mullah Nasruddin reels backwards,
struck hard in the eye with the maiden's fist.
She calls her servants.
They seize Mullah Nasruddin.
They beat him.
They throw him into the street.
Half insensible, he hears the maiden
crying and wailing for the lover Mullah Nasruddin has frightened away.

"There is no accounting for taste," said Mullah Nasruddin, and went on his way.

Tahmina, Rustam, and Sohrab

Many years ago, Afghanistan was many kingdoms. Two of them were always at war: the Kingdom of Samangan and the Kingdom of Aran, whose capital was Balkh and whose champion was called Rustam. Rustam was known far and wide as a warrior and a wrestler, the strongest, bravest man in the kingdom. He had even slain the white giant of the Mazindaran forest.

One day, Rustam rode his great horse Rakhsh to the borders of Samangan on a hunting foray. After a long chase, he killed his deer and lay down to nap under a conifer tree. When he woke at dusk, his horse was gone, and after searching awhile, he finally set off on foot. At last, he came to the city of Samangan, where he was met at the gates by the king's chamberlain and escorted into the throne room.

"My horse was stolen," Rustam told the king. "If Rakhsh is not returned to me, I will destroy your kingdom."

The king knew Rustam's reputation and was alarmed. He sent men to look for Rakhsh and asked Rustam to be his guest for the night. Rustam was tired and agreed. The king entertained him with a feast, with wine and music and dancing girls. At midnight, Rustam was shown to his room and began preparing for sleep.

As he removed his sword and leathers, he heard rustling at the curtain. Rustam turned to see a beautiful girl standing in the doorway, her head bowed, her chin nestled in a long, thick, blue-black braid flung over her shoulder. A gold ribbon was woven in the braid, and she wore a gauzy robe with golden trim over a sage green gown. She was slender and there were rings on her toes.

Rustam was captivated. He gazed at the girl as if spellbound.

She lifted her lovely head. Her lips were red as pomegranate, her eyes were shaped like almonds. She looked straight at him and said, "I am Tahmina, the king's daughter. It was I who had Rakhsh stolen, and he is safely stabled. I wanted you to come here. I want to marry you."

Rustam was startled and delighted. He took her hand and dragged her along the corridors roaring for a *mobbad* to hear their vows. The king stumbled half asleep from his chambers, and when he was told the reason for this ruckus, he staggered down the corridor after the couple, waving happily and shouting for joy. His kingdom would be saved. He would trade the girl for the horse.

Rustam and Tahmina took their vows and went to bed. At dawn, as Tahmina slept peacefully, a smile on her exquisite face, Rustam woke, climbed the great stupa of the Buddhist monks, and drank and caroused with the king and his men to celebrate his joy and satisfaction. At noon, Rustam rolled off the round structure and returned to the palace, where Tahmina awaited him, still smiling.

Rustam took her in his arms and gave her his signet ring. Sadness passed over the princess's face, for she knew he was leaving to pursue his wars and adventures.

"If you have a girl," he said, "then let her wear my ring in her hair. If you have a boy, let him wear it on his finger."

Then Rustam, son of Zal, the white-haired one, mounted his horse and departed for Aran.

Nine months later, Tahmina gave birth to a little boy she named Sohrab. She put the signet ring around his arm and watched him grow across the years into the image of Rustam. He was tall and magnificently built and the finest swordsman and wrestler in the all the kingdoms. On his fourteenth birthday, Sohrab called on his mother and asked her to tell him of his lineage so that he could prepare to be a champion.

Tahmina was proud of her son. "You will soon be a full-grown man," she said. "And I will miss you, for you will be the king's champion. Your father is none other than Rustam, but he has not been seen since before your birth and I know not where he is."

The boy was excited. "I will try to find him. My father will rule Aran and I will become king of Samangan."

Tahmina trembled at these words, suddenly afraid for her lost lover and her beloved son.

And soon, as happened so often, the king of Samangan, Sohrab's grandfather, declared war on the king of Aran. Sohrab was named the royal champion and sent to fight Rustam. He gave Sohrab a stallion sired by Rakhsh, powerful enough to hold the large young man, heavier still for the armor, shield, and sword he carried.

Tahmina stood on her balcony, fighting her tears and waving at Sohrab as he marched away at the head of the army of Samangan.

After several days' journey, the army reached the border of Aran guarded by a white castle overlooking a high mountain pass. And there, surrounding it, was another army, captained by a tremendous knight, all in black.

The black knight signaled his army and it moved forward, down the hill to the plain where Sohrab and his army waited.

The army of Aran stopped, and its black knight moved forward alone. Sohrab, too, moved to the center of the field, and when the two met, they exchanged the usual courtesies. Then they backed away and charged. Sohrab's lance drove through the black knight's armor and straight through his chest. The knight toppled from his horse. Sohrab's lance broke in half and fell from his hands. Just then, another horseman galloped through the ranks, carrying a bow and shooting arrows at Sohrab. They struck his headpiece, but Sohrab was not hurt. They struck his breastplate but did not wound Sohrab. Sohrab swung his horse in a circle and drew the heavy sword hanging at his side. He held it high in the air, charging

the archer, swinging his blade across the bow, the shield, and the archer's armor. The bow and shield shattered, and the breastplate dented. The horseman plunged to the ground and lay quietly. Sohrab leapt from his animal, pulled his short dagger, and pulled aside the archer's corselet, ready to stab. But to his horror, lying before him was a lovely young woman.

Sohrab was overwhelmed with love. As he knelt beside her, she opened her eyes and saw that he had fallen in love. Miraculously, she was not wounded, so Sohrab escorted her back to the palace, and at the gates, he spoke his love aloud for her.

"No," she said. "I am the daughter of the king of Aran. You and I are enemies. We cannot permit love to grow between us."

Sohrab's heart stung with disappointment as he watched her enter the castle and the gate shut behind her. Inside, she mounted a fresh horse and rode through a secret gate and onto the road to Balkh to tell the king of Aran about the giant young champion who was approaching at the head of the army of Samangan.

The king of Aran knew there was only one man who could meet Sohrab on the battlefield.

Rustam took up his position a few miles from Balkh to await the approaching army. In the morning, under the blue skies, the two armies met and the champions rode to the center of the field. They exchanged the courtesies, but Rustam had never heard Sohrab's name.

The warriors retired to opposite ends of the field. The herald's trumpet blasted, and the two men set their lances, raised their shields, and drove their animals toward each other. Each hit the other in the breastplate. Their lances shattered, but both men held fast. Then each circled back, drew their swords, came at each other again, and this time both fell from the saddle. The fight continued on foot until their shields were split, their armor riven, and their helmets gashed on all sides. They threw their swords aside and grabbed each other to wrestle. On they went, and suddenly Sohrab had Rustam on the ground. He pulled his dagger, but Rustam said quietly, "Surely you do not take advantage of the first fall."

Sohrab drew in his breath and backed away. Rustam arose, and the two retired from each other to catch their breath and begin again. Each man prayed for strength, then ran at the other. Rustam wrapped Sohrab in his arms, threw him to the ground, and, before the young man could turn, Rustam drove his dagger into Sohrab's chest.

"You will repent this day's work," the young man wheezed. "When my father, Rustam, hears of it, he will destroy you."

Rustam gasped. "What token do you have to show you are the son of Rustam?"

Sohrab held out his hand feebly and Rustam saw the signet ring.

"Oh, my son, I have killed you! The one man in the world I would never see harmed."

"Don't weep, my father. You did not know I was your son. Go now and, for my sake, bring peace at last to these two kingdoms."

> So, on the bloody sand, Sohrab lay dead.
> And the great Rustam drew his horseman's cloak
> Down o'er his face and sat by his dead son.

Then Rustam washed the boy's body of its wounds, wrapped it in fine cloth, and carried it to his ancestral home, where he buried Sohrab in his family tomb. Then he set about to bring peace to Samangan and Aran and would fight no more.

When Tahmina heard of Sohrab's death, the light in her life went out. She had loved Rustam, and she had loved the son of Rustam. She gave away her property, dressed in blue, and lived alone in a dark room until her life ebbed away.

The Stone Bride and Stone Groom

On the road from Kabul to Paghman, deep in the mountains among arching rocks, the jagged boulders, and giant gray pillars of stone, is the village of Khaja-Mosafer.

One bright day, a bridal couple celebrated their wedding in the beautiful gardens called the Place of the Holy Pilgrim. All was gaiety, music, dancing, and feasting. The bride was exquisite in a dress embroidered all in silver, with golden jewelry and a gold disk upon her forehead. The groom was resplendent in his crisp white *salwar kameez*, his vest sewn with many mirrors.

Suddenly, a messenger appeared, running and panting so hard he could barely spit out the warning that an enemy was approaching. "They will sack the village and kill us all," the wedding guests cried, and rushed in all directions dragging their children to safety.

The bride stood stiff with terror and prayed aloud: "Oh Allah, rather kill me and my husband now than let us be slaughtered brutally by this enemy." She had barely got the words out when she and the bridegroom were turned to stone, seated on their wedding thrones.

To this day, when good women and men appeal to the Stone Bride she will move ever so softly, and their wishes will come true. But if evil women or men request anything from the Stone Bride or Stone Groom, the couple will fall upon the petitioners and crush them.

Vis and Ramin

Once there lived a king, who ruled with an iron hand.
He enjoyed good fortune, for all stood ready to serve him, whether from fear or ambition.
When he called them forth for a banquet at Nowruz,
all the nobles and every maiden, all the generals, and all the kings came to pay tribute
from Iran to Azerbaijan, Gurgan, Khurasan, Isfahan, Shiraz, Kohistan, and Dehistan.
What a splendid New Year's feast it was!

Shah Moubad wore the crown of world conquerors and rode an elephant adorned with splendid gold and decorations. Mighty warriors marched before him and moonlike maidens strolled beside him. Minstrels praised the ruby wine, and all wore wreaths of tulips. Blossoms showered from the trees. Nightingales sang to the roses. Rivers danced gaily, released from winter frost. Sweet rain brought forth the new grass. Shah Moubad cast coins and jewels to the cheering crowds celebrating the first day of spring.

Of the many beauties at Shah Moubad's Nowruz feast was Shahro, royal princess of Mah. Her eyes were spellbinding, her lips tasted of sugar, her teeth were pearls, and her speech was like warm honey. Ambergris-scented locks fell to her waist in curls linked like chainmail and threaded with silver. Moubad watched her walk like a swaying cypress and called her to his side.

"You who are all beauty and grace, you should be with me, either as wife or lover. As the world waits on my command, I will wait on yours."

"My lord," Shahro replied, "why do you taunt me? I am unworthy to be your lover or your wife. I am in my life's

autumn and time has yellowed the roses in my cheeks. Age has bent my figure. Humiliation is piled upon old people who play at being young!"

If Shahro was this captivating now, Moubad thought, what might she have been in her youth? Aloud he said, "If you will not be mine and fill my days with joy, then give me your daughter."

"Majesty, who better than you as a son-in-law?" Shahro answered. "Though I have several children, I have no daughter. But if I give birth to one, you and you alone will be my son-in-law."

Shahro and Moubad joined hands in token of the bond. They wrote the treaty on silk with rosewater and musk:

"If Shahro gives birth to a girl, the child will rightfully belong to Moubad the king."

Many years passed and the memory of the contract faded. Shahro was thirty and in her old age when at last she gave birth to a daughter, bright and lively as the Sun. All gazed awestruck at the infant's face, and they named her Vis.

As was the custom, as soon as Vis was born, Shahro gave her to a nurse, Bibi Shirin, renowned for her goodness, her talents as a foster mother, and her skills at sorcery.

Bibi Shirin took the child to Khuzan, her home, where she cosseted the girl with tenderness and everything her heart desired.

The nurse also devoted her life to the upbringing of Shah Moubad's younger brother, Ramin, who had been sent to her as a child. He was handsome and skilled as no other with lute and bow and arrow. Vis and Ramin grew up together for ten years until Ramin, on the brink of manhood, was taken back to Marv and to Moubad's glorious castle.

Vis longed for love. She was restless and lonely. Bibi Shirin could no longer care for such a princess. She wrote a letter to Shahro:

"Vis has grown up with a thousand charms. I have taught her to read and to write and taught her all the household duties and religious rights that are proper for a girl of her stature.

"I can no longer look after a princess who has reached marriageable age. Decide soon what must be done with the daughter you have not seen these many years."

Shahro sent for Vis, and when she saw her gorgeous face and form, she rejoiced. "You are all excellence and glory. Earth and Heaven are decorated by you!" Shahro exclaimed. "I do not know of a husband in all the world who is more worthy of you than your brother Viru. Be his mate and make our family glorious and my days happy by this union."

Vis had never seen her brother. Viru was handsome and virile. Passion welled in Vis's young and yearning heart.

Shahro called for the astrologers to find an auspicious date for the union. She took her children's hands, praising the angels and offering up prayers.

"May you enjoy each other, and may your years be happy," she said, joining their hands and blessing them. "Be true lovers to one another. Be eternally steadfast, shining together."

Bibi Shirin shook her head. "This affair will have an ill-omened end," she said, but no one heard.

An ashy cloud rose from the sea, and in its wake, a rider appeared on a black horse. His trappings and clothing were all of royal blue.

General Zard, half-brother to Shah Moubad, rode straight into Viru's audience hall without dismounting. His brow was furrowed in anger, his eyes bloodshot from the long journey.

In dread silence, he handed Shahro a letter sealed by the king:

"We made a bond in friendship. We took an oath. Do not now forget our treaty. You promised your daughter. You will send Vis to me in Marv, where I will keep her in luxury, give her the keys to my treasury, devote my

heart to her, and be pleased with whatever is her pleasure.

"And I will send you enough treasure to fill a whole city with gold. Mah will be prosperous. I shall hold Viru as my own son and make a marriage for him in my own family."

The color drained from Shahro's face.

Vis rushed to her side. "Mother! What has happened?"

Shahro handed Vis the letter.

"Mother! You lapsed far from sanity to give an unborn girl in marriage!"

Vis then turned to Zard. "Is it customary in Marv for two men to take the same wife? Why seek a woman who already has a husband? Have you not noticed the celebration around you? Return to Marv. Don't come back to frighten us with more empty letters.

"And take this message to the king from me," Vis said. 'Your mind is addled; your time has passed. Viru is my husband, and my heart is glad. Why should I reject a fruitful youth for a dry and barren old man?'"

Zard turned his black horse. "How self-obsessed you are in Mah, you devotees of an odious faith who would marry sister to brother and blithely break a solemn oath," he said, and rode back to Shah Moubad.

That night when Vis and Viru retired to their wedding chamber, her monthly blood came on, so there could be no fulfillment. Shah Moubad sweated so profusely it was as if his whole body was melting from rage. He threatened vengeance upon the land of Mah, upon Viru and Shahro, swearing that blood would boil in the streets and souls would scorch with the hellfires of war. He summoned his forces. He marched upon Mah.

Viru, too, gathered an army. Many died; among them was Qaran, father of Vis and Viru.

Shah Moubad watched the battle from a hilltop. Then secretly, he rode to Shahro's palace, where he sent a message to Vis. With his army encamped outside, she was a bird in a snare.

"Oh Nurse," she wept, falling into Bibi Shirin's embrace. "Viru is far away on the field of battle. Our father is dead. To whom can I appeal to seek redress for this injustice? What greater evil can now engulf me than to fall into Moubad's hands? I have no helper. I shall be far from friends and at the mercy of enemies."

His spies had told Moubad that the blood had come upon Vis on her wedding night. When such a thing happens, the bridegroom must always abstain from his wife lest ill fortune visit him all his life. The king rejoiced and summoned his half-brother Zard and his womb-brother Ramin to ask their advice.

Ramin spoke to Moubad with kindness and wisdom: "Your Majesty, do not suffer distress on account of Vis and her beauty or much woe will befall you. Vis will never be your lover or deal with you righteously. How can you seek love and support from a child whose father you have killed and who was given to you like chattel even before she was born? When you have an enemy as your companion, it is as if you had a snake in your sleeve."

Ramin's advice only goaded Moubad. In private, he said to General Zard, "See what can be done so that I can have my way and save my reputation. If I give up, I will be disgraced."

"Your Majesty, offer much wealth to Shahro. Subvert her with coin," Zard advised. "Foster in her the hope of favor, then inspire in her the fear of God."

So it was that Shahro surrendered Vis to Moubad. The preening king entered the castle and took the delicate young hand of Vis, while hapless Viru's heart wept. The king traveled happily toward Marv with Vis in a litter. She felt as if she were locked in a casket. She sat stalwart and cold as a corpse.

Breezes blew and her sweet perfume drifted into the nostrils of the guards riding alongside. And among those was Ramin. Suddenly, a fresh spring gust arose, stirring the litter curtains. Vis's face was revealed from behind the veil. At one glance, Ramin's heart became his slave and he fell from his horse.

The procession halted. Cavalry and foot soldiers stood around Ramin, sure that he had died or that some epilepsy had blown him down. But at last consciousness crept back and he mounted his horse again, only to ride on, vacant as a madman, his eyes fixed on the curtains enclosing Vis.

In the palace at Marv, settled in her seraglio, Vis wept day and night, lamenting for Viru. She spoke to no one; she answered none who addressed her. At the sight of Moubad, she screamed and tore at her body. She would not show him her face but turned toward the wall and wailed. Moubad had no joy of Vis.

Ramin, overcome by the burden of a love he could not possess, grew more desperate each day. He sought out lonely places to sit. He could not eat. He did not sleep.

In Mah, in the palace of Shahro, nurse Bibi Shirin spoke to the Moon: "What Fate is this that Vis should suffer? Her mouth is not yet cleansed of mother's milk. Her breasts are not fully swollen. She is innocent of treachery, but her mother and brother have betrayed her."

Bibi Shirin prepared thirty camels for the road, loaded with all her foster daughter might need. In a week she arrived in Marv. She found Vis sitting in dust and rubbing ashes into her filthy curls. Her head hung low and she was skinny as a heron's neck. Her nails scored her cheeks, as if from a rusty sword.

"Light of my life!" Bibi Shirin exclaimed. "Don't be so fierce! Nothing will come of it but lifelong misery. You possess youth, beauty, and majesty. You have no choice. You must resign yourself with goodwill and some cheer to this Fate."

Vis tore again at her cheeks, wailing against destiny and keening for Viru.

"Mourn if you like, my light," Bibi

Shirin said. "Viru was both your brother and sweetheart, but you knew no joy of each other. It is over! That time is gone! Stop indulging in this fury. Here you are and here you must stay."

At last Vis rose from the dust and bathed. Bibi Shirin dressed her face and hair. Vis looked at her reflection and the tears welled again. Yet she obeyed her nurse and sat upon the throne.

Shah Moubad drank wine and celebrated for a week when Vis agreed to enter his bed, but she trembled with fear and revulsion.

"What choice do I have but to take my own life? I cannot bear to sleep with Moubad," she sobbed. "O Mother Nurse, please find a potion with which I may flee from the terrors of oncoming night."

"This I will not do!" Bibi Shirin cried.

"Please," Vis persisted, "contrive some enchantment. Perhaps you could cast a spell to render him impotent with me. After a year, you could release it and perhaps by then something will have happened to spare me from my ill fortune. If you do not, I know of no escape but to kill myself!"

"Light of my eyes, your heart is rotting from so much suffering," Bibi Shirin replied. "But since you are so unreasonable, I will cast a spell on the king to protect you from the demon that has entered you."

The nurse brought brass and copper and described two talismans in the likenesses of Moubad and Vis, then tied them together with iron and sealed it with a spell. So long as the iron clasp was fastened, a man would remain spellbound and impotent. But should anyone break the clasp, there and then the spellbound male would be released.

She took the clasped talisman into the open country. She buried it by the bank of a river.

"I have done as you wanted, though it distresses me," Bibi Shirin told Vis. "I have added to the spell that when a month has passed, your bad luck will come to an end and you will become content, the wrath in your heart will be gone. Then I will unearth the hidden talisman and lay it on the fire, burn it, and inflame your heart with happiness.

"As long as the thing is in water and moisture, the king's fetters will hold. Water has in essence a cold nature; manly strength is cut off by cold. The moment fire burns the clasp of the talisman, the candle of manhood burns again."

"O Nurse," Vis exclaimed, "thank you with all my heart. But I still cannot bear to enter his bed this night."

At the wedding feast, Ramin sang sorrowful songs of love and longing.

That night, Moubad was drunk on wine and could not summon his manhood.

Before the month of Bibi Shirin's spell was up, the sea rose, and the waters of the Marv River so swelled that half the city was destroyed. The flood carried away the nurse's talisman of the king.

Shah Moubad was now bound joylessly forever. His member had died; his skin felt like a prison.

Vis had experienced two husbands, but she remained intact. And alone.

Ramin, too, was alone, seeking secret places to dream and sing of Vis. The lute was his constant and best friend. He meandered lovesick through the garden below Vis's balcony, ever afraid to look up.

That was where Bibi Shirin found him, and for the first time since love had overtaken him, Ramin felt happy. She had been his foster mother, too, and now she spent her days with Vis, a privilege for which the prince would have given everything.

"You are the face of everlasting fortune!" Ramin cried. "I have missed you all these years."

They took hands and walked in a meadow of wild lilies. They reminisced about Ramin's childhood with laughter and affection. At last, Ramin confessed his love for Vis.

"From the moment I saw her, my heart was taken prisoner in hell. The breeze that unveiled her face was a cataclysm."

The nurse sighed. "I wish I could cure you of this malady as I did when you were small."

"Mother Nurse," Ramin said, looking hard into her eyes. "Have mercy on your helpless child! I implore your help. Save me from this burning fire! Take a message to Vis. Tell her, 'You have stolen my heart, come seek me out, come rescue me.'

"Take her this message, Nurse, and tell her to meet me in this garden, where I await her in my dreams, day and night."

"Ramin!" Bibi Shirin raged. "Detach your heart from that child. Do not recklessly throw yourself into danger.

"Don't ask me, Ramin, to jeopardize Vis by tempting her to betray such a tyrant as Moubad. I would never dare recite your message to her," the nurse said.

"Mother Nurse don't cut off my hope," Ramin pleaded. "How can you sprinkle salt in my wounds? Give this message to Vis, and as long as I live, I will be grateful."

His entreaties continued until Bibi Shirin's tender heart could take no more. "Once every day at this time, pass by this splendid garden," she told Ramin. "I shall bring you news."

Vis lay on her bed, her pillows wet with tears.

"You are not sick," Bibi Shirin scolded. "Arise! I have news. Prince Ramin—an angel on Earth, the boy with whom you played as a small child—has fallen headlong in love with you. You are made for one another, like an apple cut in half."

Vis hung her head. "Don't tease me. Ramin may be the ornament of Marv, but he is no Viru!"

"My daughter," Bibi Shirin replied. "You will never be with Viru again."

Vis turned from her nurse in disgust. She stood on her balcony and stared angrily into the garden, where Ramin, unseen, lurked and waited.

"Bibi Shirin! What news?" he begged that evening when the nurse sought him.

"I gave her your message, dear Ram, but she gave no answer and was angry with me," the nurse replied.

"Tell her this," Ramin pleaded. "Not all men are faithless and shameless. I should not be counted as one of them. Tell her I swear a hundred oaths that as long as I live, I will keep the contract of love for her."

With those words, Vis at last agreed to see Ramin, and, at first glance, it was as if she beheld her own dear soul.

Ramin encircled Vis in his embrace. Their bed was set with rose petals and green grass, with mint and hyssop, with jasmine and aloes. They pressed lip on lip, face upon face and exchanged a thousand kisses before joy exploded in their bodies and they became as one. He pierced her soft pearl, and when he drew the arrow from the wound, target and arrow alike were covered in blood.

Vis gave Ramin a nosegay of violets, saying, "Keep this always in memory of me. Whenever you see violets freshly blooming, remember me."

And the lovers swore their loyalty until the end of time. They swore to the Lord of the World, by bright Moon and shining Sun, by propitious Jupiter and pure Venus, by bread and salt, by Fire and Spirit. And by day and night, as the heavens turned, they adored each other.

Word reached Shah Moubad that his younger brother, who had been so ill with a sickness none could name, was now well. He sent Ramin a letter inviting him to join a great hunt to celebrate the king's recent victories. Viru would come and Moubad sent, too, for Vis. But as he cheerfully prepared for the hunt, word came to the king that enemies were reaching the gates of Marv.

Although he had tried and tried, Moubad could have no bliss with Vis. Still, he slept nightly with his arms tight around her. So Vis lay, when Bibi Shirin entered the king's bedchamber and whispered to Vis that Ramin was preparing to depart for the battlefield that very morning with Moubad and Viru.

"Rise up," the nurse whispered. "If you wish to see Ramin's face, slip to the roof and look for him there."

Shah Moubad leapt from the bed, wild with fury.

"Filthy, low creature," he screamed at Bibi Shirin. "Dog! Rancorous whore! Subversive hag!"

He turned to Vis. "Self-willed as you are, you have forsaken honor, shame, and your oath. You have deserted religion and the righteous path. And so long as this nurse guides you, destruction will dwell with you!"

Then he sent for Viru. "Discipline your sister!" Moubad ordered. "And do not spare Bibi Shirin, for if I must do it, I will harm them beyond all bounds. I will burn Vis's eyes with fire, and then impale the nurse on the stake. I will banish Ramin from this city and never mention his name again. I will cleanse my soul from the shame of all three!"

Before her brother could speak, Vis hissed into Moubad's face. "Puissant king! Why do you frighten us with retribution? All you have said is true. Kill me. Banish me. Gouge out my eyes. Manacle me forever in chains. Drive me naked into the bazaar.

"Ramin is my choice, soul of my body, my very life. He is the light of my eyes, my heart's ease, my lord, lover, sweetheart, and friend. Now you know my secret. Do what you please. I will lay down my life for Ramin."

Viru grabbed her by the arm and led his raging sister out of the room. "Why have you spoken like that to the king in my presence and ruined both your own reputation and mine? Are you not ashamed to brag aloud that you prefer to consort with Ramin and not Moubad? I leave you with God and your husband!"

"And good riddance, Viru! You and our mother have betrayed and deserted me," Vis said, returning to the room, where Moubad opened his arms to her.

He addressed her softly. "I have given you everything…"

"Your Majesty," Vis replied. "I have stationed my heart here against my will. If I had not found peace in Ramin, I would not be alive today. As long as I see his face early and late, what does your 'everything' mean to me? I obey you for Ramin's sake."

Moubad's eyes turned red. He roared, "May Viru's house and home be annihilated. May Shahro's womb dry and shrivel, for none but heretics are born of that mother! She has had more than thirteen children, each as putrid as she. Each suckled by a sorceress nurse."

He pointed at the door. "Out you go!" he screamed. "Take whichever road you choose. May your companion be hardship and may disaster be your guide, the wind behind you, a pit in front, your road bereft of water and bread. May the plain you travel be covered in snow, snakes, poison plants, and mud. May there be no ferry for you across water, no bridge for you over rivers. May ghouls be your only companions at night."

Vis grinned with delight. "Majesty, live forever," she said. "I wish you blessings and prosperity. Marry a new wife who suits you. May you be endowed with greatness and beneficence without me. May I have health and happiness without you! May we quickly forget one another."

She freed her slaves and returned the treasury keys to Moubad. "Fortune has at last awakened from her sleep," Vis told Bibi Shirin as they departed the kingdom of Marv. "God has delivered me."

"May Ramin disappear from the world!" Moubad cursed. And soon Ramin, too, was on his way, reeling like a drunken man deliriously out of the gates of Marv on the road to Mah.

Then Vis and Ramin lived happily for seven months in Vis's seraglio in Mah and left not a morsel of ecstasy unsavored. Shah Moubad visited his mother's chambers and sat at her feet.

"I will kill him," he said. "I shall lay Ramin so low that you will drown in your own tears. My face will be cleansed of shame only when I wash it in his blood."

Moubad's mother rested her hand on her older son's head. "No clever man cuts off his own hands," she said. "Do not kill Ramin, for he is your brother. You have no other womb-brother. Without Ramin, you will be friendless. Spare him so that your house may survive.

"It is from Viru," she continued, "that your destruction threatens. And evil-natured Vis gives herself every day to new lovers."

The blame had shifted. Moubad's mother had saved her younger son. The king set off to Mah the next morning with the blare of trumpets ahead of an army that moved like the sea.

Viru, watching the oncoming death, hearing the storm of hooves on the trembling earth, sent a messenger to Moubad. His letter offered conciliation and the return of Vis to the king's bed. Once again, her brother had let her down. Again, Vis was trapped in the arms of Moubad. The king gazed at her triumphantly.

"Can you swear an oath that Ramin has had no sinful connection with you," he asked. "That you have had no unrighteous intercourse?"

"I swear a thousand oaths on this nonexistent connection," Vis replied, and marveled at how vanity and desire could blur the truth. But true love is never sinful; it is always righteous.

"Yes! An oath," Moubad said. "I will light a fire with musk and aloe wood. There, before the priests, you will again swear this oath. Then you will walk through the fire and your soul will be cleansed of sin and you will escape suspicion. Afterward, I will hold you dear as my life. When purity is made manifest in you, I shall confer all sovereignty on you."

"Go light the fire," Vis said. "You will find me of pure faith."

Moubad summoned his nobles. He summoned Ramin and his loyal general, his half-brother, Zard. He presented innumerable gifts to the Temple of the Sun. He took embers from the temple and heaped up a fire that grew into a high golden dome, leaping and roaring.

Vis sent a secret message to Ramin. "He means to burn us both. He tricked me yesterday with oaths. He means to demonstrate my guilt or innocence in the presence of the whole city by sending me through the fire. He knows that as I walk through the flames, you will rush to save me, and we will both be consumed. This is the moment for flight."

That evening, Bibi Shirin gathered chadors and led the lovers to the baths, where there was a way through the furnace room into the garden. Ramin scaled the garden wall and hauled Vis and the nurse to the top, letting them drop to the other side. Then they shrouded themselves head to toe and went off, Ramin disguised as a woman.

They reached the gardener's hut. Ramin sent the man to summon his squire to bring horses, food, arms, and hunting gear. Then Vis and Ramin rode across the desert.

They lived in pleasure and ease in the desert for a hundred days, while Ramin sang to his darling songs of such sweeping love and devotion, the Sun and Moon wept with delight.

Moubad sought Vis to meet the fire, but when he could not find her, he handed the kingship to General Zard and went off alone with only his sword to seek her. He searched far and wide. He slept on the ground and wandered for six months, and yet she, in her desert nest, protected by true love, eluded him. At last, Moubad gave up and returned to Marv.

Their mother's tears were bitter, for Moubad and Ramin had severed themselves from their brotherhood and cut themselves off from her. Until a letter arrived secretly from Ramin:

"Venerated and dearest Mother, I am safe and sound, resting in the arms of Vis. In Marv,

I was like a deer in the claws of a cheetah. Why did he presume to burn me in fire? He is not God, who metes out fire and deals out retribution.

"I will wander the world until the king's throne is empty and sets me upon it. But should he live long, I will collect an army to drag him off his throne and sit there myself with my sweetheart.

"Keep my words in your heart, dear Mother, no one is wiser than you. Accept the greetings, too, of Vis, who is food for the soul, sweeter far than the scent of the rose at dawn."

The king returned to Marv and was lonely. Night after night he sat at his mother's feet and sighed mournfully.

"O Mother," he said. "My heart feuds against me. I cannot rest a moment without Vis. My soul is suffering. If I see her face again, I shall give her my crown and signet. I shall never turn aside from her command. I shall draw the veil over past sin and never confront her with it. I wish Ramin, too, nothing but good. Let him be my brother. Let him return safely and stay."

His mother took his hand. "Moubad, my darling elder son, swear an oath on these words, that you will not shed the blood of Vis or Ramin. Swear it, and I will give you news of them."

The king swore by the Spirit of Wisdom, by the ancestors, and by pure Water, Earth, Fire, and Air.

"Henceforth, Mother, I shall not seek to wrong Ramin. I wish no harm to his body or soul. I shall show him only love. Vis will be my queen. I shall ignore her past sins."

Thereupon his mother sent a letter to Ramin recounting all that had passed:

"Remember that a mother's command is absolute. When you read this letter, make haste. Come home with Vis in safety."

Was it for the sake of forgiveness that Vis agreed again to enter her husband's bed? The lost talisman's magic was still at work, and Moubad could do nothing but hold her, basking in her beauty until snores and dreams overtook him.

Vis lay quietly, thinking of Ramin, while Ramin tossed and turned. It had been for the sake of peace between the brothers that Vis gently acquiesced. Yet as time went on without Vis, Ramin's mind grew gradually more tortured.

At supper, he took up his lute and sang to her of how he missed her. She hid her smile, while wine clouded Moubad's brain.

Ramin sang on, and the king sang along in drunken revelry. He gazed at Vis, his eyelids bulky with sleep, his clumsy hands caressing her stiff body. Only the smile behind her hand was yielding, directed in secret to Ramin.

At last, the king's head lolled, and he ordered Ramin to pass round more wine. Ramin put down his lute and poured the liquid into tulip goblets. He handed a goblet to Vis.

"You are ever in my thoughts," she whispered.

For his mother's sake, Moubad pretended not to hear and kept his temper in control. He muttered for more wine and song, and when the dawn was rising, went into the seraglio with Vis, while Ramin went to his empty bed.

Alone in the seraglio, the king turned on Vis. "I have seen many flippant and shameless women, but never one like you! Never have I seen a woman as disgraceful as you. Yet you are my pride and I give you all I have."

She could not bear his ownership of her, the entitlement that had begun even before her birth, but with those words Vis was filled for the first time with pity for the desperate king.

"Noble lord, the past is past. Henceforth I shall give you enjoyment and keep you content."

Moubad gazed at Vis in amazement at the words she had never uttered. With his hope renewed, he slipped into sleep.

Vis lay awake, weighed down with pain, thinking now of Ramin, now of Moubad.

She was staring into the darkness, when she heard a movement on the roof and saw Ramin's face at the window. He peered into the seraglio, frozen tears coating his beard and hair and shoulders.

Vis crept from the bed and out the door to her nurse. She awakened Bibi Shirin and sent her into the bed with Moubad. Delirious with love, Vis slipped onto the balcony. Ramin jumped from the roof into her arms. She drew the fur vest off his breast, then stripped the garments from her body. They twined like snakes, so close not a hair could part them.

The king woke in the blind dark and stroked the limbs of his bedfellow. But in place of the supple flesh of his young beloved, the papery skin of an old woman crinkled to his touch. He leapt from sleep like a tiger.

"What demon are you, clasped in my embrace?" he thundered. "Who threw you into my arms?" He shouted for candles and lamps, shrieking at Bibi Shirin, "Who are you? What thing are you? What is your name?"

Bibi Shirin gave no answer and no one in the palace heard the king howling. None except Ramin, lying in his lover's arms holding her as she slept.

"Arise, my love! Disaster is upon us! I cannot bear this deception any longer. I will sever Moubad's head from his body and free the world once and for all of that wretch!"

Vis opened her eyes and placed a hand over his mouth. "Do not be overhasty. Your desire will be obtained on the appointed day." Kissing him, she rushed into the seraglio, went to the king's bedside, and sat down.

"You have hurt my hand from clutching it and pressing it so," she said. "Take the other one for a time."

Moubad let fall the nurse's hand. Released, Bibi Shirin sneaked out of the room.

"Why were you silent so long?" Moubad asked. "Why did you not answer

when I called you? How could you be so frivolous with my heart?"

"Why am I always to blame?" Vis cried. "I wish a jealous husband on no woman, for a jealous husband is ever on the lookout for trouble! I do no more than lie in bed with my husband, who enjoyed his every desire, and he blackens my name with disgrace!"

Moubad craved humble pardon. "I was only drunk. You served me overmuch wine at the banquet. I beg your forgiveness."

Vis was struck with guilt and shame. She determined to be reconciled with him. She held him tightly.

Ramin could bear no more. Once again, he knocked upon the seraglio window, and with the king asleep, Vis crept outside to see him.

The creak of the door awoke Moubad. He sat on the bed and watched as Vis tiptoed back into the seraglio, her hands frosty from cold, her cheeks flushed. He watched her figure illumined by the moonlight and knew he had been fooled.

He grabbed her wrist. He took hold of her hair. He twisted her arms and grasped her hands. He whipped her fiercely on the back, haunches, breast, and thighs. Bruised and bleeding, she called Ramin's name, but he could not hear her, for he had reached the stables and summoned his horse to be saddled.

Bibi Shirin heard, and ran into the room, gasping with fear for her beloved foster daughter. Moubad put out a foot and tripped her, then struck her savagely as if to beat her to death. Vis and the nurse crumpled. Moubad flung them into a chamber, shouting, "Here you will die, you two witches!" He locked the chamber door fast and rode away from Marv to make another war.

It was his half-brother, General Zard, who let Vis and Bibi Shirin out of the chamber. He sent for a physician to bring them back to health.

Vis moaned. She struggled to stand and inched, now walking, now crawling, into the frozen garden, calling for Ramin. She heard only the frosty echo of her own voice. She struck stones against the wall. She threw her shoes over the top of the wall, then tied her chador into a cranny, gripped it and tried to jump onto the wall. The hem of her gown caught in the bricks and tore into pieces. The loop of her girdle snapped from her waist and the trousers were ripped from her thighs. She dropped naked and barefoot on the thorny rose plot. She writhed there, beating her breast with her fists.

Bibi Shirin pleaded with her to come indoors, but Vis fought as if she were trapped in a dragon's jaw. At last, Zard came with three stalwart guards and carried her into the seraglio.

"It is no use," Zard told Vis. "Ramin has left Marv, with no destination but to wander. Nor has he said if he will ever return."

Again, Vis retreated to the ashes and covered herself in dust like a ghoul. Months went by. Ramin was weary of suffering and distress, of wandering here and there, day and night, for his loved one's sake. He sent a message to the king:

"I go to the land of Gurab. Pain strangles my body. Maybe the climate will restore me. I beg Shah Moubad to appoint me governor of that land."

Moubad, pleased that Ramin was gone, granted his brother's wish and instructed him to mete out as strict a justice to the people as he had done. Then Moubad visited Vis in the seraglio and told her the news. She stared at the king with blank eyes, but when he left, she arose and bade Bibi Shirin to bathe and dress her in her finest clothing. Then she sought Moubad in his throne room.

"Ramin will not overcome me," she told the king. "If he were a sorcerer, he could not enchant me. I swear to you and to God that I will never break this promise. Henceforth, you will belong to me and I to you. Reconcile your heart to me this once more. If you smell my mouth, you will detect the truth of my words."

Moubad kissed her eyes and face. She had at last said what he craved.

Without Vis, Ramin was a like a fish without water. He traveled the lands he now governed and visited every city, town, and village. He toppled evil noblemen and his people were free from fear. In Gurab, one day upon the road, he encountered a beauty, smiling at him from her carriage.

"The land is made bright by your presence," she said. "Stay with my family tonight. Accept entertainment from us. We will keep you in comfort."

"Moonlike maiden," Ramin replied, "tell me your name and lineage. Could you desire me as a husband? What dowry would your mother require? Even if the price were life itself, it would be cheap."

The maiden was amused at this flood of words and desire. "My parents are distinguished throughout the land and my brother is the knightly ruler of Azerbaijan. My mother bore me under a sweet-smelling rose tree and named me after it—Gul."

She averted her face. "Why do you speak of suitors and husbands?" she asked. "You are Ramin, the king's brother, whose love for Vis is so precious everyone knows you cannot become attached to another lover."

"Do not blame the victim of disaster," Ramin said, silently cursing his desperation. "Rather pray for my deliverance. Bear with me, become my true companion, my confidante. Be mine with all your heart and I shall be yours with all of mine. I'll take in my embrace no lover but you and forget all others."

Then Gul extracted an oath from Ramin that he would give up his love for Vis and never contact her. For a month, Ramin and Gul reveled in love. "You are the antidote of my sorrow," Ramin told her, "for you are very like charming Vis."

Gul retorted angrily. "How dare you compare me to the witch Vis?"

She turned her back on him, tears streaming down her cheeks. Instantly,

Ramin regretted the wound he had inflicted. He took up parchment and pen and wrote a letter:

"Vis, since our anguished separation this time, I have planted a fragrant rose in my heart. Gul is as precious to me as soul and sight. She will be my wife for all eternity. I have sworn an oath to her by the Word and the Wise Spirit, by Moon and Sun, by Faith, Fire, Wisdom, and Hope that, as long as I live, I shall be faithful to her."

Desperate for a life of love, Ramin tried to wash away Vis and thus redirect his passion.

Ramin's messenger rode like the wind and reached the royal palace at Marv in two weeks. Moubad first read the letter and was amazed by his brother's words. He took it straight to Vis. "Ramin has taken a wife in Gurab," he announced.

A blaze of anguish overtook Vis as she read the letter, but she hid her feelings. "Perhaps now Your Majesty will no longer address odious words to me," she said, "or blame me constantly. I shall present gifts to the poor to celebrate this joy and take many jewels to the Fire Temple. Ramin has escaped from grief and so have I. Now I have no care in the world, for I no longer have to fear your cruelty. Now I shall be happy in my youth and spend my life in ease."

Still smirking, the king withdrew. Vis, clutching the letter, lay on the ground weeping.

Bibi Shirin stroked her hair. "Reconcile yourself. Ramin was left lonely and forlorn and can be forgiven for taking a wife."

Vis sobbed. "I have wasted my youth. Women have husbands and lovers besides. Such husband as I have has imprisoned me, and my lover is gone.

She begged Bibi Shirin to take a message to Ramin:

"Well done, ill-willed, disloyal youth! If love for Vis has altogether departed from your memory, may you be ashamed. You have forgotten how you convinced her to be yours and

to suffer all that has happened since for faith in you. But since you have taken a new lover, let it be. May you have everything you desire in the world."

The next morning, the nurse took the road to Gurab, but when at last she encountered Ramin, he turned his back on her. "Filthy hag!" he shouted. "You have deceived me with your spells, robbed me of good sense and propriety. Now you have come again, suddenly, like a demon, to cause me to lose my way. Leave now!"

Bibi Shirin's report of Ramin's behavior sent Vis into a swoon of desperation like never before. Astrologers, sages, soothsayers, and physicians came from every city. "The evil eye has wounded her." "Some magician has the queen in his spell." "Her complaint arises from black bile." "All her pain arises from yellow bile." "This is the influence of the Moon in Libra." "This is the influence of Saturn in Cancer."

Three moons waxed and waned before Vis could rise from her bed, all her tears spent, to compose ten letters of love.

The first letter spoke of Longing and the Pain of Separation.

The second letter spoke of Remembrance of the Lover and his Vision in Dreams.

The third letter spoke of Seeking a Substitute.

The fourth letter spoke of Fastening Hope upon a Reunion.

The fifth letter spoke of Suffering Cruelty from the Lover.

The sixth letter spoke of Calling Back the Departed Lover.

The seventh letter spoke of Weeping in Separation and Bemoaning Loneliness.

The eighth letter spoke of Asking for News of the Lover.

The ninth letter spoke of Writing a Letter to the Lover.

The tenth letter spoke of Supplication and Craving the Sight of the Lover:

"O come, release my soul from grief. Soften your heart and fill it with sweet affection. How long shall I weep and mourn? I shall say no more in these letters but leave it up to you to make your peace."

Vis sealed her ten letters, wrapped them in her shredded bloodstained garment, and sent them to the Land of Gurab in the care of Azin, her swiftest messenger.

While Azin tore across mountains and plains, Ramin sat as stagnant water beside his wife. He had tired of her company. Love for Gul had been like wine, and he had drunk too much, too quickly, too enthusiastically, too desperately. Now the wine seemed laced with poison and his desire had died.

To cheer him, Gul brought Ramin a nosegay of violets. The prince stared at the bouquet and recalled the day he made a compact with Vis and how she handed him those same flowers, saying, "Keep this in remembrance of me. Every time you see fresh violets, remember this compact and oath."

Ramin gasped and raced away from Gul to weep alone. "I am a crazed, confused creature, careless as Majnun," he said to himself. "I know neither good from bad nor right from wrong."

Ramin dressed in mourning. He called for his fastest horse. He spurred it so hard it seemed to sprout wings. He sped out of the gate of Gurab and headed straight to Marv.

As he hastened along, he spied a man galloping toward him. The messenger Azin advanced with beaming smiles and handed Ramin the letters wrapped in bloodstained cloth. Ramin dismounted with weak legs and sat on the ground. He read each one, and as he did so, his soul found peace.

Azin stood patiently by as Ramin composed a reply:

"My moon, my crown jewel, my graceful cypress, my spring garden, my wine, my radiant pearl. I know no life without you. Let us not look back. We will be happy. I have written this reply by the roadside and been brief for I come speeding after the letter and no bonds will restrain me."

Azin took the letter and departed from Ramin straight as an arrow. Ramin doubled back to take his leave of Gul, then followed in the messenger's tracks.

Day and night, Vis watched the road by which Azin was to come, and when at last he appeared, she could not contain her delight, and planted a thousand kisses on the letter.

It was night when Ramin arrived at the castle of Marv. The watch caught sight of him and sent word to Bibi Shirin. She ran to Vis. "The antidote for your pain has come!" she whispered.

Vis gasped. "O Mother Nurse, devise some strategy whereby Moubad will remain asleep and not discover our secret!"

Nimbly, Bibi Shirin pronounced a spell over Moubad so that he slept like the dead.

Vis sat at the aperture of the window and gazed on Ramin's face below. Then she turned her face away and addressed his horse. "Why did you cut me off? Alas for all the trouble I have experienced on your account!"

"I am guilty, guilty, guilty!" Ramin exclaimed. "I am repentant. I am so sorry! You are my lady and queen over me. I beg for your generosity and mercy. Do not reject me!"

"I have had my fill of your slights," Vis replied. "I shall not seek separation from Moubad or be disloyal to him. Only he suits me, for he loves me, faults and all. He has taken no lover besides me, not like you, fickle and oath-breaking! Go back to Gul!"

Vis slammed the window and turned away. The prince sat all night in the rain, sobbing at Vis's rejection, while she lay awake in her seraglio, her heart cramped and aching with anger. At first light, she rushed to the window, and seeing that Ramin was still there, she called, "I cannot abide your suffering. Many are the nights you slept in comfort, amid silk and fur, not like me, desperate and covered in ashes."

And so it went. She, admonishing him for his infidelity with Gul and for heaping humiliation upon Bibi Shirin. He, begging her forgiveness. Vis could not let go of her resentment: she who had been given before birth to an old man she could not love; been rejected by her mother; been loved by her brother, then betrayed by him. Finally, Ramin, for whom she had taken beatings from her husband, then made her peace with Moubad in order that their lives be spared, so they might go on loving, even in secret. Vis ranted on and on, raving with colorful words she could not stop.

But Ramin, too, was spirited and had resentments of his own. After pleading and cajoling, at last he retorted in harsh tones, though always with a promise of fidelity. Standing under her balcony in the driving rain, he shouted, "Why should I die in vain in the cold? You do not desire me! Well, you are certainly under no compulsion! As for me, I have no lack of sweethearts. Let Moubad be in your embrace and may he have good Fortune of it.

"Now I'm going! Farewell. You are Moubad's lover and he yours."

"So be it!" Vis rejoined. "A thousand blessings on you. At last, I am rid of you!"

Vis shut her doors on Ramin, and he mounted his horse. But as soon as Vis entered her room, she repented and began to weep.

"Stop!" Bibi Shirin ordered her. "Do not go on being your own enemy. You are cutting your throat with your own hand!"

Vis looked up at Bibi Shirin in tears. "Hold him, Mother Nurse. Stop him from leaving until I come."

Bibi Shirin ran to Ramin, who was moving down the road, cold and slow with dejection. Vis rushed through the snow, into his arms. While Moubad snored in his own chambers, oblivious that his bed was empty of his queen, Vis and Ramin entered her seraglio and lay down, one body with two souls. Face lay on face, hair upon hair, they warmed each other and rekindled their love.

For a month they healed their hurt with kisses, while Moubad sat on his golden throne, unaware that Ramin lay day and night in his palace with his darling.

At the end of the month, Ramin appeared before Moubad, as if he had just returned from Gurab. He told his brother about his governance, and Moubad said, "You have been righteous and heroic. The sight of you delights me. When spring comes, I shall go with you to Gurab to hunt. Go remove your travel apparel, repair to the baths, and order clean garments."

Throughout the winter, Ramin saw Vis, and the king had no inkling.

When Nowruz had passed, Moubad sent scouts to track the boar and the wolf. He called forth his nobles and companions to join the hunt. Ramin was also to go. Vis watched him depart and asked her nurse for a remedy against missing him.

As always, the king left his half-brother, General Zard, to guard the queen and the treasury.

The hunt was long, and Ramin's yearning for Vis grew so strong that one night he mounted his horse and left Moubad's hunting camp.

He rode to within a day of his destination, then stopped in a village and sent an envoy.

"Give Queen Vis tidings of me in secret," Ramin told the courier. "Speak only to the queen and the nurse. Give this message to Vis:

"Tomorrow night keep watch in the castle. When half the night has passed, listen for me. Keep this matter concealed until my arrival, for I shall soon end our travail."

Every day, Vis held a banquet for the wives of the nobles. Outside the castle of Marv, the messenger put on a chador and approached the queen on muleback along with the women who were her guests. In this way he gained entry and gave her Ramin's message. Vis quickly sent a servant to Zard with a letter:

"Fortune warned me in a dream last night that my brother Viru was stricken by illness, but that now his health has been restored. I shall go to the Fire Temple to celebrate the happy turn of events."

Then Vis set out with her friends to the Temple of the Sun. She spilled the blood of many sheep, whose meat she presented to the poor with garments and coins. When night spread its shadow, the messenger brought Ramin.

At dark, her friends departed the temple, but Vis's guard stayed with Ramin, mounting their steeds, forty brave heroes, with chadors pulled over their faces like women. They passed through the gate and from the Fire Temple took the road to the citadel, entered, and shut the doors behind them.

The men drew their arms and set about putting the entire garrison to the sword. Ramin stole into the general's chamber. Lionhearted Zard sprang from sleep ready to fight.

"Put up your sword," Ramin demanded. "No harm will come to you from me. I am your half brother, brother of the same father. Throw aside your weapon and surrender."

Zard struck Ramin in his face. Ramin raised his shield and smote Zard's head with such force his brains and blood spilled onto the bed and the floor.

Ramin dropped to his knees, cradling Zard's corpse, but there was little time to lament, for the battle was upon him.

Fighters raged into the palace. There were corpses heaped everywhere. But with Zard dead, his troops soon came under Ramin's mercy. They proclaimed him king. He quickly gathered all the camels and mules in Marv. He loaded all Moubad's treasure, set Vis in a golden litter, and took the desert road to Mah. Word spread as they rode, and kings from every quarter sent armies to Ramin. When they arrived at Viru's castle, Ramin made Vis's brother his chief general.

None of Shah Moubad's nobles dared to tell him that his brother had taken his treasure and his wife. They hid the news for fear that the king's brutal temper would harm them all.

Yet word from his spies did at last reach Moubad that his younger brother had the upper hand.

"If I retreat, I shall become a laughingstock," he told his nobles and generals. And to himself he said, "I am cornered. My army rebels against me. They will choose Ramin as king. He is young and his stars are ascendant. Why did my mother cast me into this calamity by reconciling me to Ramin?"

Then Shah Moubad set off for the Plain of Amul, where he pitched his camp, caroused, and drank with his nobles all night. While he slept in his wine-soaked stupor, a boar sprang out of the marsh, as if it were a manifestation of Moubad's own nightmares. The cries of his army awakened him. A crowd shouted at the beast and rushed after it in pursuit. Maddened by the clamor and attack, the boar stormed straight into the camp.

Moubad stumbled out of his pavilion, rubbing the sleep from his eyes. When he saw the cause of this commotion, he mounted his horse and grabbed the black-feathered javelin that had sent many an enemy to the grave. He charged the boar. He hurled his spinning lance. He missed.

The furious boar threw itself under the legs of Moubad's horse, and with a jab of its tusks, ripped open the horse's belly. Horse and king fell together. Moubad hit the ground. The boar lowered its head and speared the king, tearing him from heart to groin. The days of Shah Moubad were ended.

Tidings reached Ramin that his brother was dead. He thanked the Creator of the World in secret that Moubad had died this way, that Ramin had not had to kill him, and that war had not been necessary.

Ramin packed up his armies, placed Vis in the golden litter and entered Moubad's camp. The nobles kneeled before him, calling him King of Kings.

In Marv, Vis and Ramin were greeted with rejoicing. For many years, people had suffered at the harsh hand of Moubad and now they looked forward to kinder times.

Ramin was a good king. He built much for the benefit of the people. He judged with fairness and an even hand. Learning and culture were precious in his eyes.

Shah Ramin made silvery-framed Vis his sovereign and gave her many lands to rule. They had two sons, fair as their mother, brave as their father, fostered by Bibi Shirin, who loved them as her own. Vis and Ramin lived to see their children's children's children. They lived together for eighty-one years. When death snatched Vis away, Ramin ordered the construction of an exquisite *dakhmeh,* a tower of silence so tall the Pleiades embraced her body.

Then he summoned his older son Khurshid and, before the nobles, declared him monarch. He set the crown on his son's head, he descended from the royal throne and walked barefooted to the dakhmeh, the throne of the next world, where Vis's body lay exposed and mingling with the spheres.

Ramin took up his abode in the Fire Temple, detaching his heart and body from ordinary desire. For three years, he showed his face to no one. Sometimes he sat on the dakhmeh and wept for Vis. He was one hundred and ten years old when the strength left his body. His was a soul washed clean.

Ramin's body was carried to Vis, and the two illustrious remains were laid side by side. In Heaven, they were once more joined as bride and groom.

I have told the tale of Vis and Ramin.
May your Fortune be ever young.
May your night be day, your day Nowruz.
May you be triumphant, and the cords of
your life tied to the Day of Resurrection.

Selected Sagacities from "Vis and Ramin"

This is how you should enjoy the world:
bestow largesse and live!
Since neither the mean nor the generous survive,
you might as well be munificent and merry!

Monarchs fall into fabulous snares
of their own design.
Desire's twin is self-deception.
But old age will do what no enemy can.

Demons can become angels.
In forgiveness there is fulfillment and hope.
There is no torment worse than grief.
In sadness we wage war with the soul.

Old Saturn cowers before Jupiter's hidden secret.
The stars do not change directions.
Destiny stays its course.
But there is success when Fortune attends a formidable task.

What is the revolution of time?
The countless tricks it plays upon our souls.
The world is asleep.
We are but a dream.

- Fakhruddin As'ad Gurgani, eleventh century

I skip like a gazelle with a passionate heart
To see my secluded love.
My darling is there!
But she is with mother, father, brothers, sisters.
Faced with all her kin, I grimly shrink away,
Blasé, pretending she doesn't matter.
Then I fear I've lost my love,
And mourn her
Like a mother mourning her newborn.

- Isaac Ibn Khalfon, ca. ninth century

Miqdad and Mayasa

Whether Mayasa was beautiful is not recounted among the Banu Kinda, and she could not have cared less. She was strong and athletic, the favorite daughter of Jabir, chief of the Kinda people. She stood firm on two muscular legs, was sure and quick and agile with a sword, and could outride and outshoot any man.

Miqdad was a lowly camel driver, shepherd, and horse groom for a rich merchant. His father had died when Miqdad was a baby. Thus, he was poor, for so it is when Fate requires a child to provide for his mother.

Mayasa vowed she would only marry the man who could defeat her in single combat on horseback. So far, she had thrown every one of her suitors from the saddle.

How could Miqdad resist Mayasa's challenge? He, too, was strong and athletic, although he'd never had the chance to prove himself. He'd practiced wrestling and jousting and fencing with sticks among the other herders and the slaves, and he had beaten them all, yet he knew nothing of the arts of weaponry and warfare. Mayasa was an expert.

Miqdad went to his aunt to borrow a black horse and rode to Jabir's compound, where he stood outside the women's tents and drove a spear into the ground. Mayasa strode from her quarters, grinning at Miqdad with menace in her eyes. She swung onto her horse still smiling. Only moments before, she had thrown the latest of her suitors out of the saddle and she bristled with energy and victory.

Mayasa spit for luck on the wrapped point of her lance. Miqdad, unsure whether this was a proper warrior custom or not, spit on his lance as well. Then they trotted to opposite sides of the tournament field.

The crowd, which was meandering home after Mayasa's last combat, shuffled back to their places, bored and quite sure that Miqdad would bite the sand like all the others. So sure, in fact, they did not even bother to ask his name. Jabir had not left his divan and pipe but had lounged in his tent through the last ten suitors. He certainly had no intention of rousing himself for a mere camel driver.

Mayasa's horse stomped the ground. Miqdad's horse stamped in response. Then they were off, galloping full speed at each other. Chins lowered, eyes squinted, lances leveled, closer and closer they came. So close they could see and smell the other's breath. They hurtled past each other, circled, and attacked again.

This time, Miqdad's spear hooked Mayasa's armor. She rose from the saddle, gasping with surprise, and flew high into the air. Miqdad leaped from his horse and ran to the place where she would land, in time to catch her in his arms. Still cradling her, Miqdad entered Jabir's tent and claimed Mayasa as his bride.

"Ridiculous!" Jabir sneered, dismissing the camel driver with a wave of his hand and returning to his pipe. Miqdad stood speechless and helpless, with no idea what to do or say next.

Mayasa jumped from Miqdad's arms. Fists on her hips, she faced her father, demanding to be allowed to marry Miqdad, who had won her fair and square in accordance with her vow. Miqdad alone was the man for her, and that, she insisted, was that.

Jabir rubbed his chin and glowered at the camel driver. All right, Miqdad could have his daughter, and Jabir named a bride price of gold and silver and pearls and white camels and sheep and mares. All of it must be delivered, *all of it*, in exactly ten days.

Miqdad was a brave, intrepid boy. From the time he was very small, he had driven the animals to graze on green slopes in summer and river valleys in winter, and he had returned them to their folds without losing a one. But although

Miqdad could retrieve a lamb lost in a sandstorm, he had not a clue how to find such a fortune as Jabir named. He had never seen or even imagined such an amount. Still, how difficult could it be? He smiled at Jabir.

Mayasa knew better about treasure and was filled with trepidation. Yet she had faith in the boy who had unhorsed her, the one who had conquered the unconquerable girl. She had fallen in love with him in midair and sealed her love as she landed in his arms. She swore, then and there, in front of her father and all the shaykhs and warriors gathered round him, that she would be faithful to her Miqdad. And Miqdad swore to Mayasa in kind.

But before he could go in search of any bride price, Miqdad had, of course, to bid farewell to his widowed mother, for she had reared him alone and he was her pride, her joy, and her support.

He returned the black horse to his aunt, said goodbye to his fellow drivers and shepherds, and took off on foot across the short span of desert to where his mother lived in her patched tent away from the village folk.

As Miqdad walked there approached a caravan, headed by three sons of Abd al-Muttalib, uncles of the Prophet Muhammad—peace be upon him. Abbas, Hamza, and Shaiba offered to share a meal with the boy, and when they learned of the exorbitant bride price Jabir demanded from poor Miqdad, they were indignant. They offered to share the profits of their caravan journey with him, but it was not nearly enough. Later, their nephew would determine that all bride prices must be reasonable.

But later was not now.

Miqdad's mother boiled the last bone of an old goat and served up a thin slab of bread. They ate together while Miqdad told his mother of the day's events. His mother understood that Jabir had set her son an almost impossible task—"almost," for she believed that no accomplishment was impossible for her Miqdad. She sighed, ever so slightly, but not so perceptively that he'd be discouraged. Then she stood and pulled aside the curtains that hid her tiny sleeping place and bid Miqdad to enter. She gestured toward an ancient iron chest.

"Open it," she said, and he did so with difficulty, for the hinges were stiff with age. She told him to look within and bring out each item he found. One by one he removed from the trunk a sword of finest steel, a shield of thick leather, a curved dagger with a gold-studded sheath, a saddle, a bridle and saddlecloth, spear blades, and arrowheads.

Miqdad was astonished. Where had all this come from? Tears came to his mother's eyes as she caressed the leather shield and told him how, on that wretched day when his father was carried into their tent—oh yes, they had once had a spacious tent of finest goat hair—only to be carried out again wrapped in his burial shroud, she had cleaned the blood from his weapons and placed them in this trunk. One day her son would follow in his father's footsteps and win battles against his enemies. She reached deep into a corner of the trunk. She handed Miqdad a bag of gold. The companions who brought Miqdad's father home that fateful day had not touched it, and she had saved it so that when his time came, Miqdad could buy a horse suitable for a boy whose blood was the blood of fine Arab warriors.

When Miqdad recovered from this surprise, he thanked his mother with all his heart. In the morning he went straight to a town where there was a market where the finest horses were displayed.

Miqdad chose the best mare he could find. Truly she was the finest horse in that market.

Miqdad named his horse Rishan and rode her home bareback. His mother helped him with the saddle and bridle and all the other necessities of a well-outfitted Arab warrior. Miqdad girded his father's sword. Wherever he went from now on, his mother said, if people asked who he was, he must answer fearlessly that he was Miqdad, son of Thamir, son of Daghaythar, son of Mansur, son of Miqdad, son of Qais, son of Hamid—brave fighters, forefathers to be proud of, famous ancestors whose names rang clear.

He kissed his mother goodbye. She wished him luck, that Allah keep him and permit no stain upon his name. She wept as he rode off across the desert.

Rishan's pace was so rapid, she could overtake rushing gazelle and when Miqdad threw his spear forward, he could catch up with it and snatch it in midair.

And doing so reminded him of Mayasa, which spurred him on, though where he was headed, he had no idea. Mayasa, meanwhile, awaited her lover by practicing spear-throwing and trick riding and archery and sewing her bridal clothes and choosing her bridal jewels from among those of her mother and grandmother.

Miqdad on Rishan cantered toward the shimmering horizon, along the white and tawny dunes. The landscape turned from soft to hard, gray, and sinister, until Miqdad's path was flanked by towering rocks. In one of those rocks, across a stream, he saw a cave.

Miqdad dismounted and left Rishan to feed on a patch of grass near the river. He waded through the water and entered the cave. Two strides in and Miqdad was stopped cold by a spiderweb, with threads as thick as ropes. No one larger than a mouse could penetrate this cave.

Miqdad peered through the web into the dark. Deep inside there was a fire, enough light to illuminate a figure chained with heavy irons against the cave wall. Miqdad shouted to the prisoner, wishing him peace and announcing that he, Miqdad, had come to release the ill-fortuned captive.

As his eyes grew used to the dark, Miqdad perceived that the prisoner was merely a boy of thirteen, no more. The boy thanked him for his good intention, but begged Miqdad to hurry away lest he too become prey to the evil afoot in that cave.

Such talk only hardened Miqdad's resolve. How could he, who had cared for his widowed mother all these years, whose father had perished bravely in battle, leave this youth to languish? Miqdad chopped at the web with his father's sword as if it were an axe and he, Miqdad, was not a warrior but a woodcutter. Lo and alas, each rope-thick thread came alive and slithered like snakes, wrapping Miqdad's arms and legs and pinning him to the cave ceiling.

Again the boy called to him, thanking him for his generosity. But take heed, he warned, the would-be savior had just made himself a sacrifice for the giant, Zoro, who would return at dusk, ask his name, and wring his neck, then pierce his body with a skewer and cook it. Human meat, the boy added, was the only food that Zoro would eat.

Miqdad cringed. His first adventure—to find a bride price, no less!—and already he was to be fed to an evil giant. All this trouble for love! But he would never lose courage, for where else but in love does adventure begin?

Listen, the boy called excitedly, for he had thought of a temporary solution: Miqdad must tell Zoro that his name was Miqdad, for the giant owned a Book of Knowledge which had told him that nothing and no one could kill him except a man called Miqdad. It was this simple: if Miqdad were to say he was named Miqdad, then Zoro would not eat him for fear that he was the poison that would kill him. He would merely keep Miqdad prisoner...

...until he starved to death chained to the ceiling.

All this the boy knew, he said, for his name was Miqdad, and when he had told it to Zoro, the giant shook with fear, shackled him to the wall, and went off to find a safer meal.

What auspicious coincidence! For Miqdad's name was Miqdad, too. It must be Allah's will, he told Miqdad, which brought the two Miqdads together to destroy the godless giant.

"The sun is going down," Miqdad on the ceiling told Miqdad on the wall, where he could see outside. And indeed, exactly then, they heard clumping footsteps approaching, then smelled the stench of corpses. Standing before them was a creature behemoth as a mountain, covered entirely with green, slimy hair, eyes red as beacons. In one hand he gripped a whip of twisted snakeskins, and in the other he held two dead children by their hair.

He sniffed the air. His molten eyes scanned the floor. The eyes looked right. The eyes looked left. The molten eyes rolled up and spotted Miqdad. Zoro roared. He squeezed Miqdad's calf like a butcher tests a goat's haunch. He poked Miqdad in the arm and in a low, terrifying growl demanded to know his name.

Miqdad straightened as far as the web would permit and answered proudly:

"I am Miqdad, son of Thamir, son of Daghaythar, son of Mansur, son of Miqdad, son of Qais, son of Hamid!"

"And I am Miqdad, son of Ahriman," the boy reminded the giant.

Zoro bared his long sharp teeth and shuddered. He plucked Miqdad from the web like a ripe grape and fastened him securely to the wall with a chain. Then he roasted the two children until their flesh crackled and sat down to eat his dinner.

When he had consumed every last infant morsel, Zoro rubbed his belly, belched, and reached to a shelf on the cave wall where there was a big Book. He slammed the Book onto the table where he sat. He could not read, so he did not open it, but commanded it aloud:

"By the power I have over you, magic Book, tell me truly when I am going to die."

The Book drew breath and answered with a woman's voice.

"Great Zoro, if I must tell you the truth, know that you will die tomorrow."

The giant hammered the Book with his fist.

"Tell me now what will cause my death."

"Master, please don't hurt me," the Book sobbed. "None but Allah can change destiny. You will not die by sword or spear. You will not be killed by club or dagger. You will not die by steel and iron. Wood and stone cannot kill you.

"A man will cause your death. A man who is in your cave. He is Miqdad the Arab warrior. As for the manner of your death, I am not allowed to reveal that to you. Only Allah and his Death Angel know that."

The giant howled and again pounded the Book. Then, perhaps hoping that his demise would not come as the Book predicted, he demanded to know where he would find food the next day.

In muffled, pained tones, the Book told him to cross the river and follow a valley and cross the mountains and there, outside a great city, he would come upon the remains of a battle between Arabs and Persians. There he would find enough bodies to keep him for a lifetime—never mind that only a day remained of Zoro's lifetime. But hurry, the Book warned, for in the morning, the dead would be buried.

At once, the giant snatched up a sack and ran out of the cave into the night. Minutes that seemed like hours passed before the ground stopped shaking and the sound of footsteps faded.

The Book glowed blue and spoke again.

"Miqdad ibn Thamir and Miqdad ibn Ahriman, to you I will reveal what Allah has written. For you have come here as His instruments for the destruction of Zoro. The monster is not immortal, but only fire can kill him. Tonight, when he is asleep, you must take me and lay me on his chest. Then stand well back, for it will be dangerous to be near the dying giant."

How would they accomplish this still chained to the wall?

"Your chain has already broken by the will of Allah but reveal nothing until I give you a sign to act. You will see my light shining in your direction," said the Book.

Sure enough in a few hours, Zoro returned carrying a dead man in his sack. The two Miqdads could hardly breathe for the fumes of the cooking cadaver, but they dared not move. The giant ate, belched, lay down on greasy animal skins, and was soon asleep and snoring so loudly the cave walls rumbled.

A beam of blue light shone into the eye of Miqdad ibn Thamir. He rose carefully so as not to shake his shackles. He tiptoed to the Book. He lifted it with effort, for it was weighty. He carried it to the giant, laid it gently on his chest, and stepped back.

Flames shot from the Book in all directions. It sunk deep into the giant's chest. Zoro smoldered like an ember. Clouds of acrid smoke curled from his body until he was reduced to a pile of evil-smelling ashes.

The Book had disappeared. The two Miqdads glanced warily at each other, then blinked in delighted bewilderment as a beautiful young woman stepped out of the cinders, lighting the dark as she spoke:

"My name is Fatima. Zoro imprisoned me in this book to obey his wishes until such time as I should be liberated by a generous and courageous warrior. Command me now, you two Miqdads. I give you each three wishes."

She pointed a sparkling finger at Miqdad ibn Ahriman, who wished first for a horse to carry him away from this wicked place, second for a swift return to his family, and finally to someday find a loving and lovely wife.

Fatima smiled and nodded. "Your horse is right outside the cave," she said. "Farewell and thank you." She waved her hand, and the web that blocked the cave entrance evaporated.

Miqdad ibn Ahriman wished them luck as he hurried off.

Fatima pointed at Miqdad ibn Thamir.

"Command me," she said.

"I wish to go free on my horse Rishan. I wish to accomplish my quest for a bride price to meet Jabir's demands, and I wish that I may meet my father."

"Wisely chosen, Miqdad ibn Thamir! You will meet your father tonight by following the direction of the North Star. As for the horse Rishan, she is waiting unharmed in the meadow where you left her."

"But first, look into this chest," she said. "Here are clothes and weapons and gold and silver and pearls enough to pay your bride price and make you rich for life. And here is a stone that when you rub it will produce all the white camels, sheep, and mares demanded by Jabir."

Fatima twinkled at Miqdad with something more than admiration. "Yet before you marry, will you come with me to my palace in the Land of the Djinns and make merry with me awhile?" she asked.

But Miqdad yearned for Mayasa and, after all, had made a solemn vow to her. He thanked Fatima and refused.

"If ever you need me," Fatima said, "you have only to whisper my name at night. Now farewell, Miqdad ibn Thamir."

Miqdad found his horse Rishan. He mounted and headed north. He rode through stony gorges and along thin mountain trails. By evening he had reached a barren plain where he saw a lamp at the entrance of a tent. In the tent, a bearded man in full armor sat on a rug, waiting.

"Welcome, Miqdad, my son. I am Thamir, your father. You have found me at last. I have come from the Land of the Dead for a few hours to give you the privilege of your father's company, which you have never enjoyed, and to teach you the art of warfare, the profession of your father and grandfathers."

Miqdad entered the tent. He embraced his father. He learned the details of weaponry, to use the sword, the dagger, the spear, the mace, the bow and arrow.

An hour before dawn Thamir said to his son, "We must part. I return to the Land of the Dead. I will see you in Paradise when your term on Earth is up." He folded his tent, loaded his camel, and embraced his son. "Be brave," he said. "Never fear. Allah will keep you."

Thamir mounted his camel and rode up the steep path to Heaven. Miqdad mounted his faithful Rishan and rode to Mayasa.

And what had Mayasa been doing all this time?

Mayasa was getting married.

Miqdad watched the curved path of stars until he could no longer see his father's figure. Then he whispered in Rishan's ear, and they hurried forward as fast as possible considering the heavy trunk he was carrying. Nine days had passed with only one day remaining before Jabir's demands must be met. A mist appeared along the desert horizon, a mist that revealed itself to be a caravan with an escort of armed horsemen, a camel with a closed litter, and a train of camels loaded with goods.

They stopped, and a man called Shadham greeted Miqdad, who asked to hear the news. Shadham gave the gorgeously outfitted warrior a conspiratorial smirk. He was coming from the estate of Jabir, chief of the Banu Kinda, whose daughter had been betrothed to a poor camel driver named Miqdad. Naturally, Jabir was unhappy with the affair. Shadham laughed and slapped his thighs. Can you imagine? The boy had actually set forth to find a bride price for Mayasa, probably by robbery. How else could he find such wealth? Of course, he never returned. Therefore, Jabir was marrying Mayasa off to Shadham's brother Malik. This was the wedding party laden with presents from Jabir, returning to Shadham's home, where the marriage would be consummated that very night.

Miqdad could barely contain himself. Doubts dashed through his mind: had

Mayasa not fought this marriage? Was she unfaithful to him though he had been true to her? How could Jabir break his promise? There was still one day before time was up. Never mind, he would fight to the death to reclaim her.

No one, he said aloud to Shadham, would marry Mayasa bint Jabir, but Miqdad ibn Thamir. He drew his sword. Shadham drew his weapon and signaled his men.

From inside the litter, Mayasa heard war whoops and the clash and clank of swords. She peeked out of the curtains. Round and round, men battled below her, metal on metal, blood staining the dust. Mayasa could not tell who Shadham and his men were fighting.

Until, that is, Miqdad plummeted from his horse, dazed and gazing up at her. At once, Mayasa tied her skirts between her legs. She swung out of the camel litter and onto Miqdad's horse. He scrambled to his feet, for Shadham's men were suddenly distracted by this female apparition and crying out that they were met by a djinn. Miqdad guffawed—for he knew djinns! He tossed Mayasa his sword, then cut on, using his curved dagger, side by side with his bride. Soon all Shadham's horsemen were defeated.

They counted the bodies. There was Shadham. There were the armed horsemen. Malik the would-be bridegroom had escaped.

Miqdad was mortally wounded, a hard jab to the gut that would not stop bleeding. They set up camp right there on the desert and Mayasa tended Miqdad as best she could, weeping all the while, for she could tell that her true love was breathing his last. The stars were bright, the moon was full. Mayasa wrapped the wound with fine cloths from her bridal gifts and left Miqdad to fetch water for his parched lips.

No sooner was she out of sight than Miqdad called "Fatima," in a voice so weak he doubted she could hear.

"Fatima," he repeated, but before her name could float fully from his swollen tongue into the ethers, there was a flutter of wings and the beautiful djinn appeared before him, sparkling, and holding a flask. Silently, she opened the flask and silently she applied soft ointment to Miqdad's wounds.

Mayasa could not understand it. She laughed with joy and begged to know how her man had healed in the short moments that she'd been gone. Love, it is said, needs no explaining, and neither do miracles.

Then they packed their goods and were on their way to Jabir's homestead when they met Ali, cousin and son-in-law of the Prophet—peace be upon him. Ali told Miqdad he would help the couple in any way he could. Miqdad told Ali of the friendly meeting he had with Abbas, Hamza, and Shaiba, and Ali persuaded Miqdad and Mayasa to become Muslims, which they did on the spot.

Meanwhile, Malik had dashed out of the fray and galloped to Jabir's homestead to tell him what had happened. There was nowhere else for Mayasa and Miqdad to go, and so they appeared in front of Jabir, who pretended to be happy to see them. Jabir offered Miqdad wine and Mayasa retired to her chamber. But the wine was drugged, and when Miqdad was fast asleep, Malik sewed him into a bull's hide and prepared to carry him away, to spit him and roast him over a fire.

Mayasa watched it all. This time, with her father ready to defend Malik, she could not readily go to Miqdad's defense.

Instead, she ran from the house, and leaped on her horse and made straight for the patched tent of Miqdad's mother. She begged her to go find Ali at once. The old woman started out immediately for Mecca. Mayasa streaked back to her bedroom and hopped into bed as if she had never left. She lay on her pillows planning a way to save Miqdad when a figure appeared in the moonlight in her window.

Mayasa shut her eyes, pretending to be asleep. Malik climbed into her bed.

Mayasa turned slowly, as if to greet him with an embrace. She put her arms around his shoulders and lovingly wrapped her big hands around his throat. She clutched her muscular legs around his waist and squeezed. He tried to scream as she choked him. His back cracked like a cooked chicken bone. He beat at Mayasa. She dragged him to his feet by the neck and pushed him hard into the wall. She slammed him again and again into the wall, knocking the wind from him—wham! whack! She pushed Malik again and again until it seemed he would slump dead onto the floor.

He wheezed, gathered strength, and was suddenly upright and upon her again.

When Allah—all-merciful and compassionate—saw Miqdad's old mother trudging quick as she could along the sand, it pleased Him to transport her through the air to Mecca to the Prophet Muhammad—peace be upon him. The Prophet listened carefully to her story. He sent Ali to help, and when Ali arrived at Jabir's home, he commanded Jabir to profess Islam, which he refused. Ali killed him at once and liberated Miqdad.

Free from the skin of the bull, Miqdad stormed into Mayasa's bedroom, where he found her still fighting Malik tooth and nail, knee and heel, wrestling on the floor. He waited for his moment, then lunged at Malik with his sword, graceful and nimble as his father Thamir had taught him only two nights before. He killed Malik with one neat stroke.

Mayasa and Miqdad were married by Ali. The contents of the trunk and the magic stone provided them and Miqdad's widowed mother with everything they needed or could desire. They had twelve sons and Mayasa taught them all how to ride and joust and use the sword, the dagger, the spear, the mace, and the bow and arrow.

Did they live happily ever after? Whenever Mayasa and Miqdad disagreed, they settled their disputes in fair combat.

Miqdad and Mayasa called their eldest son Thamir. Miqdad became shaykh of the tribe of the Qais. Thamir was strong as his mother, handsome as his father, and impatient to become a leader of men. He managed the affairs of the tribe as well as the family fortune whenever Miqdad went on expedition against the heathens in the mountains. Years passed, and one day when Miqdad was thus absent, Mayasa grew ill and died, leaving her other children in Thamir's care.

In the mountains, Miqdad found himself surrounded by enemies. After fighting valiantly for many hours, he fell, wounded in many places. The heathens turned toward home, leaving him there to die while the sun set. In the darkness, Miqdad called softly, "Fatima!"

Immediately he heard a flutter of wings and there appeared the exquisite djinn, holding a little flask. She opened the flask and carefully applied the soft ointment to Miqdad's wounds, which healed at once. Then Fatima took the feverish, dying hero in her arms and flew him to the kingdom of her father, the wise djinn-king. There they lived together for many years in happiness, though Miqdad missed his Mayasa always.

Oh she—she wanted the union, but I
stayed away from her, not wishing to obey the Devil!
Then she came at night, shrouded by darkness,
covered only with a diaphanous veil.
With every glance she cast,
she beckoned me, stirring temptation.
Wisdom, like wet sand, settled on my desire,
and I lay with her all night like a thirsty baby.
But I was strictly weaned
and kept from sucking her breast.
For one like me there can be nothing
in a flower garden beyond gazing and sniffing.
I don't use the garden as a pasture,
like stupid grazing cattle.

—Ibn Farag al-Gayyani, Al-Andalus (d. 970 CE)

Go, eat your bread with pleasure,
drink your wine with joy
for God has approved what you do.

Let your clothes be freshly washed.
Always anoint your head with oil.

Enjoy happiness with your wife whom you love,
all the fleeting days of your life.
This is the portion God has given you.
These alone are what your life and toil will bring.

Whatever is in your power to do,
do it with all your might.
For there is no action, no reasoning,
no learning, no wisdom in Sheol.

—Ecclesiastes 9:7–10

Antar and Abla

When you hear the lion roar, you hear the fighting voice of mighty Antar.
When you see the night sky, you see the radiant blackness of that great hero.
Traveler in the darkness.

This is the story of Antar ibn Shaddad and his love for his cousin Abla. Antar carried his love always in his heart, on his flesh, and in his dreams, sweet and deep as the spring of Zamzam. The vision of Abla brought victory to Antar.

And many times, that vision tormented him, for when the enemies of Antar were upon him, Abla cried out in his dream. In the dreams he dreamed of his enemies, that Abla was stolen from him, taken in lust and violence.

When Antar awoke, he knew to dress himself in armor and javelin and sword, and ready himself for battle.

Abla in Antar's dreams gave warning and she gave love. She was more than a dream and no less than a dream. Abla was hard won as water. Abla was a mirage yet an oasis.

Know this, listeners! Zuhair ibn Jadhima was shaykh of the Banu Abs, chief of the Firebrands, the Knights of Fate. He took in marriage Tumadir, the most beautiful woman in Arabia.

Tumadir bore Zuhair ten sons, and two of these were Shas and Qays, who became enemies of Antar. But among Tumadir's sons was also Khalil the Gentle.

Zuhair and his nobles passed their time in plundering and killing until all Arabia was awed by their power, and all the dwellers of the desert feared them.

Listeners! It happened that the ten sons of Tumadir went raiding with Shaddad ibn Qurad. They crossed the plains, the sands, and the rivers into Ham, seeking horses and camels. Among the treasures they captured was a black woman called Zabiba and her son, Shaibub.

Zabiba was uncommonly elegant. Well-shaped. Delicate. Graceful. The ten sons of Tumadir vied for her with Shaddad, but Shaddad won. He took her as his share of the booty. He carried her home to the camp of the Banu Abs. He gave her a separate tent and let her do whatever she wanted.

Zabiba bore Shaddad a son and called him Antar. Traveler in the darkness. His infant cry was the roar of the lion.

And Shaddad's wife, Semeah, burned with jealousy.

Antar grew quickly, robust, fearless, and solid. He beat the other boys at their games. He thrashed those who taunted him, for he was a slave whose father would not claim him.

They called him lesser. They called him weak of mind on account of the color of his skin. And Shaddad ibn Qurad despised his black son.

Antar tended Shaddad's herds. He walked behind the goats and sheep and camels and horses to the grazing grounds.

Shaibub, his womb-brother, bold and hardy, could outrun any man or deer. He was Antar's only companion. Together they practiced the arts of war, out of sight of others who would scorn and forbid them.

They learned to ride, to leap upon horses and fly with them. To bring the camels to their knees and mount them, then gallop across the desert, faster and faster, balanced on their humps like birds. They whittled branches and learned to fling the lance. They cut the curved whips of river willow and made bows. Their minds, too, were sharpened by their courage and persistence.

Listeners! More than once Antar killed a hungry lion or wolf with his bare hands when they came to feed on the flocks. The Banu Abs did not see this feat. Shaibub was Antar's only witness. They were silent partners, who kept their secrets safe all their lives long.

On his cot at night and against a rock half asleep at noon, Antar the shepherd, Antar the slave dreamed of a maiden whose hair, scented with myrrh, rippled in waves to her knees, whose almond eyes were gray as shadows. The love of Antar for Abla began as a reverie vague as riders on the horizon, a faraway shape undulating in the dust.

Abla paid no mind to any man, though many sought her hand. She was aloof and preferred the horses, for they were truer and stronger than the men she knew and those who courted her.

Listeners! There is nothing strange in Abla's disregard for men, for her father, Malik ibn Qurad, brother of Shaddad, was puny and perfidious. And her brother, Amr ibn Malik, was a treacherous and sullen boy.

Each day, when she had finished helping the women sew the tents or weave the bright-colored fringes for bridles, Abla tightened her veil across her face and wandered out of sight to visit the horses. She let her veil drop and clucked and chucked and talked to the animals until evening began to fall.

Her mother did not chastise her. Here was a daughter whose spirit could not be contained.

It was with the horses at evening that Antar first spied Abla.

While he brushed the shiny coat of Shaddad's mount, he spied be-ringed feet scuffing the sand, dancing beside a mare white as blossoms.

Antar stood. He peered over the mare at the maiden. Her eyes were full of magic. She whispered to the mare. She laced her fingers through its mane. Here was the maiden of whom Antar dreamed.

Abla, seeing Antar watching her, pulled her veil tight across her mouth. She ran, bangles and coins jingling and jangling, back to her mother's tent. Abla spoke no words to her mother about the black slave. She had seen him in the camps of the Abs all her life, but this day it was as if he was a stranger. The glint of longing, the black curly head cocked like a curious crow, terrified her. She lay on her pillows and shuddered with revulsion at his blackness. Even as she closed her eyes to shut him out, to summon the sleep that would cleanse her of fright, the traveler in the darkness would not disappear.

And Abla consumed Antar's thoughts day and night. Still, he performed his duties and secretly practiced the art of war with Shaibub. But now, for the first time, poems sprang to his tongue. He spoke his verses to camels and sheep and horses. He recited them to desert marigolds and to Shaibub, who laughed. "This love disease eats my entrails," Antar told Shaibub.

Antar watched Abla at work or playing with the other girls. She would not smile at him, nor did she any longer go near the horses at dusk.

Listeners! One day, as Antar returned Shaddad's flocks from pasture, two old women staggered to the well. With creaking knees and stiff elbows, they tried to fill a vessel and raise the bucket to water their miserable herds. Daji stood before them. A great bully. The favorite slave of Zuhair's son Shas.

Antar waited his turn at the well with his father's flocks. Daji grabbed the old women's water vessels for his master's cattle. The old women reeled from thirst. Dust coated their ragged robes.

"Be so good, master Daji, to let my cattle drink. They are all I possess, and I live by their milk. Have compassion," cried the more withered of the two.

Daji shoved her aside.

"O master Daji, I am a poor, weak old woman," her companion pleaded. "Time has aimed its arrows at me and destroyed all my men. I have lost my children. These sheep are all I have. Let them drink for I live on their milk. Pity me. Be kind."

Daji struck her in the stomach. He ripped away her veil and she was shamed before the others.

Antar rushed at Daji. He roared his lion's roar. Daji struck Antar a blow in the face. Antar reeled, then ran again at Daji. He seized Daji's leg and pitched him onto his back. He grasped Daji's neck and raised him, then dashed him to the ground. He leaped upon his chest.

Daji lay silent and dead.

"You have slain the favorite slave of Prince Shas!" the other slaves exclaimed. "Who can protect you now?" Antar helped the old women draw water and helped them with their flocks.

At this moment, Khalil ibn Zuhair was returning to the camp after the hunt. "Away!" he yelled at the attacking slaves, "or I will destroy you with this sword."

He took Antar to his tent. He dressed Antar's wounds. When his brother Shas came upon the scene, Khalil spoke in soothing terms, with words of admiration for Antar, so young, a slave, and yet so noble.

And Prince Khalil swore from that day forth to protect Antar against his enemies.

Shaykh Zuhair spoke to the chieftains gathered about him. "This valiant man has defended the honor of women. One day, Antar will shine as a noble warrior and destroy his opponents."

He turned to Shaddad. "Your son's conduct reflects credit on you. His behavior will remain as a memorial to all generations. He has loathed oppression and followed the path of propriety and virtue."

Shaddad ibn Qurad was shamed and angry. He swore never to claim Antar as his son.

He vowed never to free him. Shas became the first of Antar's enemies.

The women and girls collected around Antar. Abla stood on the edge of the crowd. "You acted properly," she smiled. Bells and disks and jewels jangled as she walked away.

And Abla's father, Malik ibn Qurad, became the next of Antar's enemies.

Listeners! It came to pass that Antar was called upon to wait on the women of the Qurad family, to bring them camel's milk to break their morning fast.

He milked the she-camels and cooled the milk in the wind. He properly served first Semeah, the wife of his father, Shaddad, then walked into the women's tent, where Abla's mother combed her daughter's hair.

Abla was dressed only in her gauze chemise. She gasped and ran from the tent, hiding her face with her sable hair.

That evening, when Antar returned with the flocks, he saw Abla playing with the children. Her countenance was brilliant and blooming.

"O Abla," Antar sobbed. "I despair of love for you."

She pretended not to hear.

A slave named Zajir visited Shaddad.

"Your son Antar is so distracted by his love for Abla," Zajir said, "the herds are growing thin and thirsty under his care." Shaddad took up his whip. He seized hold of his son. He tied him with ropes. He beat him until Antar's skin began to flap.

Zabiba watched, her tears flowing. She did not dare say a word, until at last Shaddad left Antar and she approached with balm to sooth his wounds. "O my son, do not cast your eyes upon Abla, for she will be your ruin."

Antar roared his lion's roar. He burst the cords that bound him. He sought the slave Zajir and killed him.

Zajir's master, Rebia ibn Ziyad, became the next of Antar's enemies.

Abla visited Antar's dream. He kissed her three times beneath her veil. Her spirit bid him farewell. A hand stretched out. It snatched Abla away.

Antar awoke and knew there was a danger to his life.

Listeners! While Antar dreamed, Shaddad sat in his tent with his brother Malik, and their friend Rebia ibn Ziyad, scheming to kill Shaddad's son.

"Tomorrow he may destroy someone of rank and power. Then our blood will be demanded, and we will have to pay the forfeit."

Shaddad, Malik, and Rebia planned to waylay Antar in the pasture with the cattle, to destroy him in a secret spot. They followed his steps as he rode the wide plains, reciting verses of praise for Abla and seeing her in every cloud and flower.

Shaddad, Malik, and Rebia followed Antar and the flocks into the lush green Plain of Lions, where no other shepherds dared to go. There they heard him hiss like a serpent and saw him fall upon a lion with his bare hands and kill him.

They trembled. They vowed to find another way to murder Antar.

One day, Shaykh Zuhair demanded the presence of all his men to attack the Banu Temim.

Semeah, the wife of Shaddad, looked round at the camp empty of men. She thought to give a magnificent entertainment at the luxuriant lake of Zatul Irsad with the other women and the children.

Sheep were slaughtered. Wine flowed. The land glittered with spring. Birds sang in the bushes. The girls all brought their instruments. Antar stood among the attendants.

Abla floated and weaved through the dancers. Antar watched and fought with himself against violating her honor.

A cloud of dust appeared. A vast clamor interrupted the songs of the merry makers. Seventy horses and riders, armed with cuirasses, coats of mail, and helmets seized the women and maidens, threw them upon their horses and sped away.

Antar possessed no horse. He had no armor. He ran, and his feet overtook the horseman who had seized Abla. He sprang upon the warrior. He hurled him from his mount and broke his neck. He placed Abla gently on the ground. He took possession of the armor and steed. He pursued the raiders. He rushed down upon them like a torrent. He slew twenty, thirty, fifty. The rest fled in disorder, abandoning the women and maidens of the Banu Abs.

Semeah begged the other women not to disclose this occurrence to anyone, lest their husbands blame them. And to Antar she said, "keep this a secret." And Semeah's hatred for Antar changed to love and tenderness. He became dearer to her than sleep.

Antar gathered the horses and weapons of the dead enemy. He hid the arms in his mother's tent.

The men of the Banu Abs returned, laden with booty. Shaddad went to inspect his flocks. He found among them strange horses and Antar riding the black mare of the chief of the raiders.

"I found the horses strayed from their owners," he told Shaddad.

"Wicked black liar!" Shaddad shouted. He tied Antar with a rope and lashed him. "Evil and abomination are rooted in you. You will breed dissension among the Arab tribes and make us a laughingstock."

Semeah threw herself on Antar's breast. "Sooner beat me, Shaddad. He does not deserve such ill treatment."

Shaddad pushed her back. She cast herself again at Antar.

"What has happened to this wretch that you feel such affection and tenderness after so much anger and indignation?" her husband demanded.

"Loose his bonds. Then I will tell you the whole story."

Shaddad could not believe his ears. Yet he rejoiced that Antar had honorably kept this a secret and allowed himself to be bound and beaten. He asked Antar's pardon. He took him that night to a feast prepared by Shaykh Zuhair for all the valiant heroes of the Banu Abs.

Shaddad praised Antar among the warriors. Zuhair gave Antar a handsome robe. All present thanked him. Khalil called Antar friend.

And Antar's heart soared with happiness. Now he had hopes of winning Abla.

Listeners! In this time of plunder and marauding, Antar's deeds grew and grew. Shaddad became rich. But Prince Shas,

Rebia ibn Ziyad, and Abla's brother Amr ibn Malik ambushed Antar at every opportunity, though again and again he drove them off single-handedly.

And his deeds became the hero tales told round the camp of the Banu Abs and in the camps of other clans.

Antar made many friends. But still he had jealous enemies. Prince Shas hated him, and with Rebia ibn Ziyad still plotted his destruction. Abla's father, Malik ibn Qurad, and her brother Amr determined to do away with him. The amorous verses that Antar spoke for Abla reached their ears and offended them.

"He is a slave. What right has he to do more than menial tasks?" They set Antar to collecting dung for their fires.

The talk reached Abla's mother. She ordered Antar into her presence.

"So, you love my daughter and make verses upon her and cannot conceal your feelings," she said. Abla stood behind her mother and smiled.

"O mistress," said Antar, "my life and death are in her hands. My only wish is to be near her. Her form is ever before me. Her name is ever in my soul. I exalt her beauty."

With this, Abla's heart began to soften toward Antar.

"If you are in earnest," said her mother, "let us hear some of your verses in praise of my daughter's charms." Antar bowed his head and spoke.

"I love you, Abla, as if I were noble born.
Yet I am content with your phantom dancing through my imagination.
You surround every perfection.
In your forehead, Abla, beats the pulse of truth."

Abla and her mother were astonished. And Abla regarded Antar with affection.

"I had no idea that you could speak with such eloquence," said Abla's mother. "You are endowed with high and splendid qualities. I will speak to my husband tonight, that he may marry you to Khemisa, Abla's servant, who is the prettiest of all the slave girls."

The lion's roar rose in Antar's throat. He pressed it down and spoke softly.

"I will never be united to any woman but Abla."

"May God accomplish your wishes," said Abla. "May he grant you the woman you love and may you live in peace and happiness."

Abla's father, Malik ibn Qurad, and her brother Amr were outraged at the shame of a slave's adoration of Abla. With Prince Shas, Prince Qays, and Rebia ibn Ziyad, they planned another ambush of Antar while Shaykh Zuhair was away on a raiding party. One hundred of their slaves would attack Antar as he escorted a party of women to a wedding. Antar was anxious to escort this caravan, for it included Abla. Her mother laughed at him when she saw how mad he was to gaze upon her daughter's charms, how assiduously he attended her.

Listeners! Before the hundred slaves of Antar's enemies could attack, raiders swept down upon the caravan. The women screamed and wept. Antar turned to Abla. She was bathed in tears. Her mother sobbed in terror.

"Soon we'll be prisoners, scattered across the desert," she cried.

"Mistress," said Antar, "give Abla to me in marriage and I will disperse these raiders. I will annihilate them and give you their horses and armor as a dowry."

"This is no time for merriment!" cried Abla's mother.

"Mistress, by the Merciful Lord of Victory, if you promise to marry Abla to me, I will make over to you these horses and slay their masters."

"Defend my daughter, and she is yours."

Antar called to Shaibub to protect his back. He sped forward roaring his lion's roar. He struck the enemy. He slew the first, second, third, fourth, and fifth. He did not see the sixth coming from behind. The horseman raised his arm and aimed his sword at Antar. An arrow pierced the enemy's heart. The terrible Shaibub had dealt the deadly blow. Antar rode back to the women.

Check your tears, light of my eyes. Fear not, Abla, my body labors under the burden of its love. My sword will find any who would harm you."

The women egged Antar on until the raiders were dispatched. But scarcely had he met victory than the hundred slaves of Shas, Qays, Rebia, Malik, and Amr attacked him. Antar and Shaibub turned upon them with blood streaming from their spears and swords. They quickly fled in terror.

The women thanked and praised Antar.

"You are an ornament of men," Abla told him.

Listeners! When Shaddad ibn Qurad heard all that had occurred, he gave Antar thanks and kissed him between the eyes. At the feast that night, he wished to place Antar among the chiefs, but Antar would not consent. He ate with the slaves. The chiefs were astonished at his modesty. They brought him wine. They stood in awe of him and delighted in his verses. For seven days they celebrated in Antar's honor.

Shaddad gloried in Antar. He had acquired a new luster by Antar's actions. Again he kissed Antar between the eyes, but Antar kissed Shaddad's feet. Then he retired to his mother's tent.

"Mother, tell me, who is my father?"

And Zabiba told him the story of his birth.

"Why does he not call me his son, as everyone else does?" asked Antar.

"He cannot resolve this, for he says you are base-born," she answered. "He is afraid of the disgrace you should incur if he gives you the rank and honors of a son. And the Arabs would never consent to it."

"Whoever brings shame upon Shaddad, I would kill. But if he still denies my right and does not acknowledge me, I will strike off his head Then I will do the same to his brother, my uncle Malik, if he does not give me Abla in marriage.

"And should I perceive that the tribe dare despise me, I will level my scimitar at the whole of them and go to another tribe that might better value me, for how often have I rescued them from danger and liberated them from peril."

"Do nothing of the kind!" cried Zabiba. "For they will only hate you the more and you will gain nothing. The men and women love you on account of your noble deeds. Therefore, proceed to no extremes, unless you wish to nurture their contempt."

"But, Mother," said Antar, "my aunt has promised to give Abla to me in marriage."

"Hush, my son. Talk not of impossibilities. This will never happen. How can a slave, without connection or rank, aspire to marriage with an Arab woman?"

Antar stood. His beauty shone like stars in the dark tent. "O Mother, I'll show you wonders," he said.

Listeners! Word had reached Shaykh Zuhair that plunderers and murderers had attacked his people. He rushed home from his raids. Among the chiefs and nobles, among the women and his wives and from the mouth of his most beloved wife, Tumadir, he heard nothing but exultations of Antar's deeds.

"Were we to give him our lives and property, it would be small return for such noble acts," said Zuhair. He ordered sheep and fat cattle to be slaughtered. A feast was served.

Antar entered the tent. He kissed the ground. He made obeisance to Shaykh Zuhair. He turned to seat himself with the slaves, but Zuhair stopped him. He seated Antar by his side. He talked that night only to Antar. Rebia, Shas, Qays, Malik, and Amr burned with rage.

And still Shaddad would not bless him and rank him as a son, so that Antar's agony knew no bounds. He entered the tent of Prince Khalil. His clothes trailed behind him. The tears flowed down his cheeks.

"How often have I relieved them of their foes, and none but Shaibub has ever assisted me. My father has cut off all my hope. I asked only to be recognized as his son so that I might marry Abla, but he refused. Now all my hopes of having her are destroyed," Antar lamented.

"Had you told me of this earlier, I might have remedied the situation," replied Khalil. "Abla will be concealed from you from this day forward. Shaddad will contrive to kill you for your ambitions. Stay here now, while I go and speak to my father."

But Antar was shamed and dejected. "The only place of rest for me is on the highways, for men such as Rebia and your brother Shas have conspired to destroy me."

At dawn he put on his armor and cuirass. He mounted his horse and left the Banu Abs and joined another band. It was the season for raiding. Abla came to him each night in dreams. He dedicated each victory to her.

And though Antar brought riches to his new raiding companions, none would give him more than a slave's portion of the booty. His loneliness encased him like a cloak. Meanwhile, gentle Khalil appealed to his father. Shaykh Zuhair sent for Shaddad ibn Qurad.

"Why do you not grant Antar's request and call him your son as everyone else does? Think you, Shaddad, that among the tribes there is a more intrepid warrior than your son Antar, or a bolder heart than his?"

Shaddad presented half-truths as his excuses. "O my lord, he is indeed my son, and part of my heart," he said. "But my brother Malik told me that if I acknowledge Antar, I will abandon myself to the Arab tribes. Therefore, on account of my brother Malik, I have renounced him."

But Shaykh Zuhair was determined to bring Antar back to the Banu Abs. He sent Khalil to find him, and the prince rode into the desert searching east, west, north, and south until he came upon Antar.

Antar jumped from his horse and ran to kiss the stirupped feet of his friend, but Khalil would not permit him. He kissed Antar between the eyes. He told Antar of Zuhair's encounter with Shaddad. Antar's heart rejoiced. Now, at last, he thought, he might be raised out of slavery, for Shaykh Zuhair was on his side. Now, at last, he might marry Abla.

And Antar returned to the Banu Abs with Khalil.

Shaykh Zuhair greeted him with joy. "If you belonged to me," he told Antar, "I would admit you to my rank and connections, unafraid of the blame that might be heaped on me."

But Prince Shas could not endure this talk to the black base-born he despised. In anger, he quit his father's presence. Antar drank with the shaykh and Khalil. Zuhair rewarded Antar with a gift of two virgin slaves, jewels, and perfume.

In the women's tents of the Qurad, Abla watched for Antar in expectation and delight.

Listeners! Abla of Dreams, Daughter of Visions, was slimly made. The setting sun demanded that she smile in its absence. The brilliant moon called out to her, "Come forth, Abla, for your face is like me when I am full and in my glory." Her form was like the laurel, graceful in every limb. Roses were scattered on her soft, fresh cheeks. Her lashes were swords, her eyes sharp and penetrating.

In the women's tent of the Qurad, she watched and waited for Antar. When he arrived, the women received him with excitement, for he had stories to tell.

His father's wife, Semeah, who had once despised him, kissed him between the eyes. And as he told all that he had seen and done, Abla began truly to love him.

He divided the perfume Zuhair had given him between Semeah and Abla's mother and all the wives of Shaddad and Malik. He presented Abla with the two virgin slaves and the jewels. Then he departed for the raids with Prince Khalil. Many days passed and Abla's longing for Antar grew. Peering through a crack in the curtains, she saw her father and brother feasting with Umara ibn Ziyad, brother of Rebia ibn Ziyad.

Listeners! When the feast was done, Abla was betrothed to Umara.

Abla looked upon Umara in horror. He was a coxcomb. A dandy whose fondness for perfumes forewarned his arrival. A fob, who preferred to spend his days with women and young girls and who was more particular in his dress than they. He, too, had heard the verses of Antar for Abla, and a violent passion had kindled within him. He had unbraided his hair and let it flow down his back. He had dressed most carefully. He had mounted a white-faced mare and visited Malik ibn Qurad. He had offered himself in marriage.

As she pondered her cruel fate, Abla heard the nickering of horses. She heard the laughter of Khalil and the cavernous tones of Antar. All the warriors of the Abs, the Knights of Fate, rode out to greet his return. All but Malik and his son Amr.

Listeners! Abla's mother, in obedience to her father, scurried the maiden away. "You must not see Antar, nor he you, for this is Malik's command. And it does not befit a betrothed maiden to appear before strangers."

"Antar is not a stranger, Mother," said Abla. "Antar is my cousin."

But Abla's mother would not listen and sent her into a chamber, behind thick carpets. As she stared disconsolate at the walls, Antar entered the harem to visit the women. He presented them with plunder. Abla was nowhere about. Of this he wondered but said nothing. He told the women stories of the raiding. He departed then for his mother's tent.

"Mother, did Abla mention me during my absence?"

"God be with you, my son," said Zabiba. "Wake up now! Umara ibn Ziyad has been betrothed to her. Everything is completed but the ceremony itself."

"Tomorrow," Antar told his mother, "I will find and slay Umara."

Early in the morning, he entered the tent of Prince Khalil and told him what Malik had done, how he had betrothed Abla to Umara.

"My lord, I must indeed kill him. Then I will quit this land and country."

"Why must you leave? I am a foe to your foes and a friend to your friends," said Khalil. "Have patience and I will speak to your father and urge him to acknowledge you as his son. Then take Abla from her father, and if he does not consent, I will put my name on her and keep off any suitor until you are in possession of your wife."

Assured, Antar visited the horses. He saw the be-ringed toes in the sand. Veiled, concealed, Abla caressed her favorite mare. She pretended not to see or know Antar, but whispered as she turned away, "O traveler in the darkness, how long will you be rejected?"

And Khalil begged Shaddad ibn Qurad not to deny his son, but to be proud of having fathered such a warrior.

Again, Shaddad refused. "Do you wish that it should be said of me that I was captivated with a Negro woman, even desired to marry her, and that she bore me a son, whom I acknowledged just because he became a great warrior and destroying hero?"

Listeners! Once again position was withheld from Antar. The next day, he mounted his horse to quit that country. And as he passed along the road, he met Umara. The dandy quaked, then plucked up his courage.

"Son of Shaddad," he said, "where were you last night? Your masters were seeking you. Having heard of your eloquence, it was my intention to give you a robe."

"I am not worthy of receiving a present from you," Antar replied. "But when you enter into my mistress Abla, the daughter of Malik, verily, vile wretch, I will wrench your neck off your shoulders."

Then he seized Umara by the waist. He heaved him above his head. He dashed him on the ground and almost smashed his bones. Umara cried for help and fainted with fright.

Abla ran from her tent. Prince Khalil galloped at full speed, afraid of the fate that would befall his friend. At last, Shaddad arrived.

"Wicked slave," he said. "Return now to the care of the sheep and the camels. Never again raise a sword!"

Abla turned away. She visited Zabiba in her tent. "Soothe the heart of my cousin Antar," she cried. "Tell him from me that even if my father kills me, none but him do I desire. None but him will I choose."

Zabiba told her son of Abla's words. Antar rejoiced.

Sent back to shepherding, Antar and his brother Shaibub drove the camels and sheep east to green pasture, while from the west, warriors of the Qahtani rode toward the tents of the Banu Abs. Shaykh Zuhair gathered his forces, who rode to intercept the enemy.

But the winds rose, and whirling sand blinded the Banu Abs so that the two armies bypassed each other. The Qahtani entered the camp of the Abs, where Shaddad and Malik saw quickly that they were outnumbered. Antar and Shaibub, returning with the flocks, watched the conflagration. Man against man. The ground was stained scarlet. The women shrieked. Antar and Shaibub sat upon a hill, contemplating the battle and the defeat of the Abs.

"O my brother," said Malik to Shaddad, "where is your son? Let him liberate us from death and misery."

Shaddad ran uphill toward Antar.

"How can you, in such an hour, sit so still among the sheep and camels?" Shaddad demanded. "Behold! The enemy has plundered our property and slain our horsemen and threatened to capture our women and families."

Shaibub grinned insolently at him.

"What do you want me to do?" Antar

asked. "I am indeed grieved at your distress and wish I could rescue you from destruction and defeat. But I am a slave, not worthy of your consideration. I conduct cattle and camels to pastures. I am employed in milking and gathering wood. I am contemptible and despised." So saying, he walked away.

"What do you mean with this indifference toward us?" Shaddad shouted.

"What do you want of me? Have you ever heard of anyone asking protection and countenance from a slave?"

Shaddad pleaded. "Mount, descend, and destroy the enemy, Antar, and I will grant you all your wishes and hopes. I will raise you to the rank and honor of an Arab. I will recognize you as my son and as a part of my heart."

Malik, father of Abla, also begged, "O my nephew, descend and drive away the enemy from us and I will acknowledge you of our family."

"If I mount this instant, Malik, and destroy this party, will you give Abla to me in marriage?"

"I will," Malik declared. "If you liberate Abla, she will be your wife forever."

"And I will no longer deny you," said Shaddad, "even if the foe tears my body to pieces."

Listeners! Abla's wailing was dreadful. For while Shaddad and Malik made promises to Antar, the Qahtani seized her and all the Banu Abs women. Their dwellings were thrown down. The Qahtani loaded them and all their goods on horses. They left the camp a barren wasteland.

Antar charged impetuously from the hill. He roared his lion's roar. "Ignoble bastards! I am Antar ibn Shaddad! My sword is my father, my spear is my brother!"

The mountains and valleys shook. He sought the horseman who captured Abla. He pierced him in his side lest a frontal blow kill Abla, too.

O Listeners! Whatever their hopes for joy, the fates of Antar and Abla rose and fell.

Abla's father had lied and would not allow Antar and Abla to wed. After

Umara fled in fear, there was Waqid ibn Mas'ara, who heard of Abla's beauty and longed for her. Then there was Tariq al-Azaman, the brigand, and then Mufarrij ibn Hammam. All sought to win Abla. All tried to destroy Antar's happiness. All were brought down by Antar, whose arm was war and whose heart was love.

"Enough!" Shaykh Zuhair at last declared. "The time has come for Antar and Abla to marry and for the divisiveness within our clan to end."

And Antar rejoiced. "Again and again, I plunged myself into the sea of deaths for the sake of my Abla. O my liege lord, truly you are my friend, for you have brought joy and contentment at last to my heart."

And Shaykh Zuhair declared further that the wedding would take place on the next day.

A feast was served in Zuhair's tent. Sheep and fat cattle were slaughtered. The horsemen presented themselves. Antar was summoned to sit next to the shaykh. Then Rebia ibn Ziyad, Shaddad ibn Qurad, Malik ibn Qurad, Amr ibn Malik, and the ten sons of Zuhair arrived. Each sat according to his rank.

In the women's tents, Abla, Semeah, and all the wives of Shaddad and Malik and Amr rejoiced. They took up their cymbals and tambourines. Coins and bangles and chains, bells and disks jingled and shimmied as they danced.

None heard the voice of Umara speaking to the slaves, who carried food and wine to the guests in Zuhair's tent.

Even as Antar ate the poisoned fruit and felt a tearing fire in his belly, listeners, he did not move from his place beside the shaykh, nor let his smile down.

When the night was nearly morning. Antar staggered from the tent, and those who watched him thought he had consumed too much wine, as a bridegroom might. Umara watched furtively. Antar lurched to the tent of his mother and fell into his brother's arms.

"Poison!" said Zabiba. She sent

Shaibub for water. She dug among her trunks and found a vial of herbs she had brought with her from Ham long ago.

"You will not die, my son," said Zabiba. "You will marry Abla tomorrow."

"I will seek who did this and kill him," Antar moaned.

"Never mind, my son, for this is not the moment for revenge, but the time of celebration."

Zabiba administered herbs to her son, and he slept the sleep of health.

In the tents of the women of the Qurad, Abla's mother oiled and scented her hair.

"Sleep sound now, my son," whispered Antar's mother.

"Sleep sound now, my daughter," murmured Abla's mother.

Never was there such a celebration in the camp of Banu Abs. The friends of Antar sent gifts and poems of praise. All were happy. They danced and feasted.

Antar's heart rose into his throat as Abla arrived on the finest Asafir camel. He walked to meet her, to bring her down from the wedding howdah and carry her into the wedding tent.

Abla was hard-won as water. Abla was mirage. Yet Abla was an oasis. And Antar drank deep from the well.

Listeners! The time came when Shaykh Zuhair and Prince Shas drank the cup of death, and Prince Qays became lord of the Banu Abs.

Then came the murder of Antar's dearest friend, Prince Khalil. On his wedding night, an assassin entered his tent and killed Khalil and his bride. Thus was the favorite of Tumadir's ten sons snatched away.

Antar's revenge was swift, but it was not sweet, for no blood for blood would return Khalil to life or end Antar's sorrow.

Then the wars became so intense, tribe against tribe, that Antar and Shaykh Qays moved the camps of the Abs to more peaceful lands in Yemen. When Qays and Antar quarreled, the one believing the other a troublemaker, the other believing the one a weak chieftain, Antar took his Qurad clan to other lands.

Antar fought on into old age, his flesh puckered like crumpled velvet, the battle scars furrowed like veins along his arms and legs and back and chest.

Still, he led the raids and protected his people, and still he was summoned by great kings to win their battles. He carried his love for Abla wherever he went, always in his heart, on his flesh, and in his dreams. Many times, the vision of Abla brought victory to Antar. And many times, that vision tormented him. When his enemies were upon him, Abla cried out in his dreams: a warning.

When Antar awoke, he knew to dress himself in armor and javelin and sword, and ready himself for battle. He rode to meet the danger.

Listeners! It so happened that once in a battle, Antar had blinded an enemy called Wizr ibn Jabit

Sightless, strengthened by anger and revenge, Wizr learned to shoot arrows by sound. He practiced for twenty years.

And Wizr ibn Jabir was the last of Antar's enemies.

Wizr stood upon a hill with his sighted companions. Listening, he saw more than those with the sharpest eyes. A thicket of entangled bushes surrounded the tents of the Qurad pitched at the edge of the Euphrates. Birds dashed through green bushes and sang in chorus with the trickling streams. Wizr heard the joyful festivities of the Qurad. Pluck of stringed instruments, chants of midwives and mothers, slaves, and free women. The talk of the Knights of Fate, the Firebrands, as they feasted.

Wizr's companions guided his steps from the hill to the edge of a thicket on the bank of the river, across from the tent of Antar ibn Shaddad. Alone, Wizr awaited the turn of destiny, listening in stillness and readiness for opportunity.

"If I hit Antar with a shot truly aimed," he said, "I do not wish to linger after he is dead. Not an hour's life do I covet." Listeners! Late at night, the dogs began to bark. Antar slept beside Abla. The howls grew loud and spread around the camp, echoing into the desert. Antar arose and called to his brother, Shaibub. "Let us investigate why the dogs are barking so far into the night in the direction of those thickets."

It was a night of deep blackness. "Brother," Shaibub said, "this darkness is so intense, I cannot see into it, yet I hear the barking comes from the direction of the river." They took up their swords to patrol the bank.

Along the way, Antar stopped, for he felt the pressing need to pass water. He faced the thickets where Wizr lay waiting. When Antar urinated, the sound was like the great rush of a waterfall.

Wizr drew an arrow from his quiver. He lifted it to his bow and pulled hard. He discharged the arrow soaked with death and it flew across the river. It pierced Antar's scrotum, then penetrated deep into his bowels.

Antar did not stir. He made no move. Shaibub at a distance had seen nothing and did not know the harm that had befallen his brother. Quietly, Antar pulled the arrow from between his legs.

Traveler in the darkness. He did not roar his lion's roar. In silence, streaming blood along the ground and into the water, Antar found Wizr and with one blow took his head. The blind eyes fluttered as the head dropped onto the ground. It rolled into the river and floated until it lodged against a rock, staring into the starless, moonless night.

Blood stained the earth. Antar turned to walk across the river and back to the camp of the Qurad.

He walked to his tent leaning on his sword. Shaibub walked ahead of him not knowing. Antar entered his tent. He lay upon the bed. He gently woke Abla. He told her all that had happened. She wept and sighed as she bound his wound.

In the morning, word of Antar's misfortune spread through the camp. Fearful men and women hastened to his presence. Sweetly he spoke to them, words of comfort, but not of reassurance.

"O Antar, how can you be redeemed and spared for us," the people cried.

"Perdition has come upon me," Antar said. "There is no more life for me."

He did not sleep that night. Outside the tent, where he could not see, Abla wept. She beat her cheeks and chewed the flesh of her wrists. She wailed and keened.

Antar heard Abla and sighed. He struggled from the bed. He stumbled outside to join her.

"My Abla, this arrow was poisoned, and it has done its work. I am about to die."

And Abla was filled with terrors.

Then Antar prepared to depart this life, dividing his herds and camels and treasure among his wives and sons and slaves and his brother, Shaibub.

"You must leave this place," Antar said. "I will lead you back to the Banu Abs, back to safety, for with me gone, Shaykh Qays will accept you and enfold you into the tribe again."

"Brother of the same womb," Shaibub said. "We cannot impose this task on you. Remain here until you are free of your anguish, while I convey Abla and the Qurad to the Abs."

Antar rose with a heart harder than stone, though his body was bent with pain. "Let it not be said that Antar ibn Shaddad died irresolute, cringing away from Abla and the clan he has always protected."

In the dream that is death, Abla dressed as Antar in hauberk and sword. She took up his javelin and mounted his horse. She led the people of Abs to safety, across plains and mountains, until they reached the Pass of Gazelles, which is thin as the needle's eye.

In the dream that is death, Antar drifted in the gauze and willow orb of Abla's howdah.

"O Abla," he whispered, "mourn at my tomb. May no evil befall you. May nothing harm you as long as you live."
In the dream that is death, the enemy came upon the caravan and watched as

it lurched toward the pass. "The steed is Antar's steed," their leader observed. "The weapons are his. As for the rider, he is not Antar. He is too small in height. His head is not large enough. Antar must have died. This must be Abla bint Malik who rides. Let us attack them and take their herds and women and children."

Listeners! Abla saw the enemy approach and cried out a warning to Antar. He raised the curtains of Abla's howdah and showed his head and stared at them. He roared his lion's roar. It echoed and re-echoed in the wilderness and mountains.

And the enemy fled.

The Qurad journeyed on until they arrived at the Pass of Gazelles. Abla dismounted and divested herself of Antar's hauberk, sword, and spear. Shaibub lifted Antar from the howdah. He dressed his womb-brother in armor and weapons and set him upon his horse.

And one by one, the people, weeping and wailing, bade Antar thanks and farewell.

Abla's sorrow was deep as the spring of Zamzam. Silent as rock walls in canyons. She mounted her howdah, where the scent of Antar's death lingered. She held aside the curtains and watched him as her camel ambled behind the caravan.

Antar gazed at Abla with the tears streaming from his eyes.

Listeners! Antar's hands rested on his spear supporting his powerful person. When Abla had disappeared from his sight, he cried a great sob of death and with one mighty breath his spirit left his body. His steed stood motionless beneath him.

Abla grieved while the fierce wind rose and scattered Antar's bones across the desert.

This then, listeners, is the story of Antar ibn Shaddad and his love for his cousin Abla.

NOTES

"Yusuf and Zulaykha" (pp. 25–23) is collaged from the Old Testament's Genesis (37–50), Surah 12 of the Qur'an, *Haft Awrang* (Seven Thrones), by the Persian poet Nūr ad-Dīn 'Abd ar-Rahmān Jāmī (1414 to 1492 CE), and Jan Knappert's 1985 translation of the Swahili epic *Islamic Legends: Histories of Heroes, Saints and Prophets of Islam*.

There are many similarities between Joseph in the Bible and Yusuf in the Qur'an. It is a story of deceit, loyalty, and divine knowledge, though their presentations differ. As Samuel M. Taylor writes in "Joseph and Yusuf: Comparing Narratives of Genesis and the Quran"—an article for *Through the Needle's Eye: Religion, Politics and Society*—while in both versions the seductress accuses Joseph of attempting to have her, and in both versions, Joseph is ultimately imprisoned, "the Qur'anic telling," Taylor writes, "describes a subsequent plot in which the master's wife presents Joseph to her female friends who (in their amazement) cut their hands, proclaiming this is none other than a noble angel."

Based on this episode, Muslim mystics use the expression "to cut one's hand" to refer to the tremendous confusion that overtakes one in the face of divine beauty.

"While Genesis adequately notes God's favoritism toward Joseph," Taylor writes, "the Qur'an demonstrates the ubiquity of God's will in the events that prove Joseph's loyalty to Him..."

Joseph's story is among the most popular among Jews, Christians, and Muslims. The seductress is not named in Genesis or the Qur'an, but Islamic poets expanded and embroidered the tale—as poets do with dancing divagations—calling her Zulaykha. John Renard writes, in *Islam and the Heroic Image,* that "Zulaykha's story tells how the lover's total attachment to the beloved can transform

age into youth, lust into devotion, selfish attachment into salutary bewilderment."

"A Flight to Egypt," by Punjabi poet Shiri (d. 1586 CE) was translated by John Charles Bowen in *The Golden Pomegranate: A Selection from the Poetry of the Mogul Empire in India 1526–1858*, and speaks to Zulaykha's long, circular, aching journey to at last embrace the man she loves.

With this excerpt (Drink water from your own cistern…) from The Book of Proverbs 5:15, I integrated stanzas from the Christian and Hebrew scriptures. As Chana Bloch writes in the introduction to *The Song of Songs: A New Translation*, coedited with Ariel Bloch, the mention of sexuality in the Christian Bible is more or less anathema, but The Book of Proverbs in Hebrew Holy Scripture "recommends erotic pleasure as a remedy against temptation, a way of keeping a good man out of trouble." The warning against temptation to share well water can be read as a metaphor against promiscuity, "springs scattered abroad/streams of water in the streets."

***

"Khan Turali and Saljan" (pp. 35–45) is an ancient comic love story from *The Book of Dede Korkut*, an epic of the Oghuz, one of the major branches of the Turkic peoples (they acquired the name Turkoman after their conversion to Islam). The book's authorship is attributed to Dede Korkut, a legendary storyteller, bard, wise old, very old, man, and religious leader. There is evidence that Dede Korkut was an historical figure ("Dede" is an honorific meaning "grandfather").

In Mihri Khatun's untitled poem (I woke, opened my eyes…), she refers to her lover Yskander, or Alexander, and plays with images of the Greek conqueror/god. Mihri Khatun (d. 1506 CE) has been called the Sappho of Turkish poetry. She never married and wrote hundreds of *gazel*s to her many lovers of both sexes. (A gazel—the archaic form of *ghazal*—is a Turkish poetic style somewhat resembling a sonnet.)

Abraham Ibn Ezra (If I made shrouds...) was a distinguished philosopher, biblical commentator, and translator. He was an astrologer and revered poet of the Golden Age of Moorish Spain, who also translated and published many scientific works into Hebrew, continuing what he considered to be his mission of spreading to Jewish communities wherever he journeyed the knowledge he had gained in Spain. He published extensive works pertaining to the use of the astrolabe, an ancient instrument used to make astronomical measurements.

***

"Layla and Majnun" (pp. 47–59) is quite possibly the most popular romance in the Islamic world and the most familiar to Western readers. A centuries-old Arab folktale, the story appears in poetry, prose, and song in almost every language.

Majnun is traditionally identified with a seventh-century poet of the Najd Desert known as Qays ibn al-Mulawwah. *Majnun* is a poet's djinn-possessed madness—and inspiration. The Prophet Muhammad feared he might be majnun when the Revelations came upon him, and he could not, at first, feel confident that they were real or that he had not lost his mind.

The madness that drives Majnun into the desert recalls later Arthurian motifs of the unhappy lover Lancelot, who wanders the forests, befriends animals, and becomes a wild man, touched by the divine. The archetypal themes of forced separation, tribal enmity, and souls joining at last after death are also reminiscent of *Romeo and Juliet.*

"Do not think," Nizami wrote in his *Khamseh*, "that such pain [as Majnun's] is to be deplored, for it rewards the person by relieving him of himself. Having killed the self, the lover becomes identified with the beloved."

Layla's complexities and her life run far quieter than Majnun's. Although she is the more interior of the two, and her position and freedom to move about are highly restricted, her love is just as passionate and plagued as Majnun's. She is doubly vulnerable because of her restraint. Yet she is strong, implacable, and unafraid, especially when she refuses to allow her husband to touch her.

Layla and Majnun is an exquisite story, but—for all its apparent simplicity—difficult and exasperating. Why does Majnun behave as he does? Is he simply insane? Merely self-centered and self-absorbed? He gets at least one opportunity to have Layla, if he'll just straighten up, but he does not. Is he in love with love rather than Layla as a breathing entity, a woman? The story has had hundreds of interpretations and versions. In this one, I wanted to strip Layla and Majnun of all but the spare pain of love.

Nizami, commissioned by a Caucasian ruler of Iranian origin to retell the story, was not impressed by its homely origins, and is often credited for making it an allegory, in the Sufi mode, of a man seeking to reach the Beloved. Majnun lives among animals, which come to him to shape a peaceable kingdom and seem to symbolize that there is resolution and tranquility in Nature.

Of the two poems that follow this story, "Song of Majnun" appears in Nizami's *Khamseh* version of *Layla and Majnun*, as the lovers are reunited at a distance among the palm trees after Majnun recovers from fainting. It was translated from the Persian into German and edited and published in 1963 by R. Gelpke, then published in English in 1966. I have somewhat refashioned it.

From the first, the story of Layla and Majnun has been a touchstone. It is even immortalized in two tunes by Eric Clapton, "Layla" and "I Am Yours."

The second poem (Yes, I am Layla…) is by Princess Zeb-un-Nissa (1638 to

1702 CE) and is thought to be a lyric to her lover Agil Khan, whom she met often at her own gardens in Lahore. Her mother was a famous Persian beauty, and Zeb-un-Nissa wrote in Persian under the name Makhfi'. She was the eldest daughter of Mogul Indian emperor Aurangzeb, who imprisoned her on an island for the last twenty-one years of her life for the crime of corresponding with her brother Akbar, who had—as did most of his siblings—rebelled against their reactionary, spendthrift father.

***

"The Seven Princesses" (pp. 61–89) is layered with stories within a story that is in itself rather thin but moves the action along. In them, the poet Nizami typically does not make strong distinctions between the erotic and the mystical, rather, as Peter Chelkowski writes in *Mirror of the Invisible World,* "he uses one as an illustration of another."

Islamic cosmology, much of it inherited from Zoroastrian thinkers, places the Earth at the center of the seven planets—the Moon, Mercury, Venus, the Sun, Mars, Jupiter, and Saturn—which are considered agents of God. The number seven is the pillar of wisdom and that which brings all things into being. In Islam, as in other beliefs, seven plays an important role "because of its Semitic roots on the one hand," Annemarie Schimmel writes in *The Mystery of Numbers,* "and because of ancient Persian traditions on the other [the cult of Mithras and ancient Zoroastrianism]."

Throughout the Torah, the number seven is profoundly significant. The creation of the world in seven days; the holiday of Shavuot, or Feast of Weeks, marking the harvest. Seven in Judaism is vital and powerful, symbolizing completion.

Christianity holds that there are seven cardinal sins—envy, lust, greed, wrath, sloth, gluttony, and pride—and seven cardinal virtues—faith, justice, prudence,

hope, temperance, fortitude, and charity. These actually originated in ancient Greece and are attributed to the philosopher Plato and to the Greek monk Evagrius Ponticus. Japanese samurai followed the seven-point chivalric code of *Bushido*, thought to have come down from Neo-Confucianism, Shinto, and Zen Buddhism.

In Judeo-Christian tradition, God created the world in six days and rested on the seventh, the crucial Sabbath. The Qur'an states that God created Heaven and Earth in seven layers. Seven is called "the first perfect number," expressed as a triangle and a square: three plus four.

Chelkowski writes that "the seven stories told by the seven princesses can be interpreted as the seven stages of human life of the seven aspects of human destiny, or the seven stages of the mystic way."

Nizami, Chelkowski notes, believed that "the unity of the world could be perceived through the arithmetical, geometrical, and musical relations. Numbers were the key to one interconnected universe; for through numbers, multiplicity becomes unity and discordance, harmony."

For this version, I added colors and objects in the descriptions of the pavilions that are associated with each astrological sign and its numerical correspondence.

My thanks to Nan De Grove for her knowledgeable counsel about Zoroastrian astrology.

Rabbi Moses Ibn Ezra's untitled poem (Caress a lovely woman's breast…) seems to illustrate Bahram Gur's lusty, delighted appetite. Ibn Ezra was a Spanish-Jewish linguist, philosopher, and poet known as Ha-Sallah. His writings had great influence among the Arab literati and he is considered one of Spain's greatest poets.

Ashra bint Ahmad's ferocious poem (I am a lioness…) presents a respite from all those amiable princesses and is addressed to a poet she did not like, who proposed marriage to her. This tenth-century Arab Andalusian was considered a "wonder" of her era. She never married, and during her time it was said that no other woman could equal her in knowledge or poetic style. In addition to her literary talent, she was a skilled calligrapher.

***

This version of **"Bahram Gur and Fitnah"** (pp. 91–95) comes, again, primarily from Nizami—from *The Haft Paikar,* translated by C.E. Wilson—though I have added elements from two other literary works, Firdawzi's *Shahnameh* and Indo-Persian Sufi singer/poet Amir Khusrow's *Eight Paradises,* which each develops the story slightly differently and gives the harpist slave girl different names.

As well as "disturbance," the Arabic word *fitnah* is translated as "rebellion," and, in *The Oxford Dictionary of Islam,* John Esposito defines fitnah as "trial or testing, temptation; by extension, treachery, persecution, seduction, enchantment, or disorder resulting from these things. A *Hadith* [sayings of the Prophet Muhammad] states that the greatest fitnah for men is women. Though the term fitnah is generally negative, a girl may be named Fatin or Fitnah in the hope she will not be a seductress and in recognition of her beauty."

The poem (Bahram Gur rode into the desert…) following this short tale, is adapted from Nizami's *Seven Princesses* in Chelkowski's *Mirror of the Invisible World.* It ends the amorous adventures—and indeed the life—of Bahram Gur.

***

"Solomon and the Queen" (pp. 97–109) is found in Jewish, Christian, and Muslim holy books and has, across the millennia, spun into many literary and religious interpretations. I began my own liberal retelling (perhaps the most presumptuous in this collection) when I fell in love with Abishag the Shulamite, who, despite her

silence, brought the story of King Solomon and the Queen of Sheba to life for me. This young woman is recruited to warm and nurse Solomon's father, King David, impotent from old age and illness. Abishag also "reflects his political impotence," according to the *Shalvi/Hyman Encyclopedia of Jewish Women*, which states that she, "unspeaking … is more a tool to move the plot along than a developed character: she marks first the inability of David to continue his rule and, later, the inability of Adonijah [Solomon's half-brother] to assume that power."

I am not the only one to find her inspiring. Abishag has long been a favorite of poets, such as Rainer Maria Rilke, Louise Gluck, Itzik Manger, Jacob Glatstein, Yehuda Amicha, and Shirley Kaufman, among others.

In *The Song of Songs: A Theological Exposition of Sacred Scripture*, Christopher W. Mitchell claims Abishag may have been the *Song*'s female protagonist. If so, she certainly does have a voice, and a lusty one at that. I have shamelessly tweaked several versions of *The Song of Songs*, also known as *Song of Solomon*, giving Abishag the power of speech and allowing some of her words to overlay what I imagine could also have been the Queen of Sheba's thoughts. After all, many scholars have speculated that Solomon wrote *The Song of Songs* about the Queen. I have amalgamated a few of its stanzas from the King James Bible, Scott B. Noegel and Gary A. Rendsburg's *Solomon's Vineyard: Literary and Linguistic Studies in The Song of Songs*, and Ariel and Chana Block's exquisite work, *The Song of Songs: A New Translation*. My embellishment of the *Song* and of the story of King Solomon and the Queen of Sheba is merely one among hundreds.

The Queen of Sheba is not given a name in the Hebrew or Christian bibles or in the Qur'an, but in later adaptions she has been called simply Sheba by Christian writers (after her lands), Bilqis by Muslim writers (from *balmaqa*, or moon worshipper), and Makeda in Ethiopian Coptic legends. In my story, she is merely called the Queen—uppercase. She may have ruled what are now Ethiopia and/or Yemen, even, some have said, the whole of Africa, though that continent seems a bit vast for one leader to handle, regardless of gender. Many scholars seem to agree that the Queen was from Yemen, but where borders were located in antiquity is pretty much anyone's guess. Ethiopia and Yemen, today, are little more than 500 miles apart. A number of formidable women, pre- and post-Islam—for instance, the Ismai'li queens Asma bint Shihab and Arwa bint Ahmed al-Sulayhiyya (ca. 1028 CE to 1137 CE)—have ruled Yemen with aptitude and justice. Perhaps the Queen of Sheba was one of their formidable predecessors.

In each of the sacred Abrahamic texts, she is converted by Solomon (Shelomo in Hebrew, Suleiman in Arabic) to Judaism or Islam, although a few rabbinic traditions deny her conversion and allow her to return home to her own deities. She was also said to have married Solomon (his one-thousand-and-first wife?). Ethiopian legend tells of their son, Menelik, who visited his father in Israel and either stole or was given custody by Solomon of the Ark of the Covenant, which he took back to Ethiopia, where it remains hidden today. Menelik became the first Solomonic Emperor of Ethiopia, from whom all other kings of Ethiopia, including Haile Selassie, claim descent.

Never a dull moment for millennia! The Queen is depicted as admirably pious, or she is cruelly vilified. In some Jewish legends, she is identified with Lilith, queen of the demons. In a Yemeni folktale, she is connected with a donkey. And on and on. In her excellent article, "Echoes of a Legendary Queen: Contemporary women writers revisit and recreate Sheba/Bilqis," Wafaa Abdulaali writes, "The story of Bilqis's jinni mother was also used to demonize her," with

assertions of cloven hooves or webbed feet. The Queen "was said to have used the help of the jinn to build her great dam, including the Ma'rib Dam [in Yemen]. Sheba has also been described as a lesbian with hundreds of women among her entourage, though Arab historians have distinguished this Bilqis from the queen mentioned in the Qur'an."

The tales and speculations about Solomon and the Queen twist and tangle in scholarly and religious analyses, in Midrash and Aggadah and in poetry, plays, and novels. Interested readers would do well to try to sort things out themselves. It is all fascinating.

A final word about Abishag: Joseph Benson's 1897 *Commentary of the Old and New Testaments, 1 Kings 2:17,* describes the warmth of Abishag's body as "natural, fresh and wholesome, not impaired by the bearing or breeding of children." Although I paraphrased it, since such stuff and nonsense continue to be credited, I nevertheless find it supremely dreary. Various rabbinic and other sources say Abishag was twelve to David's seventy. In Hebrew she is *Na'arah*, a classical ancient reference to girls no older than twelve. Fresh, indeed.

Nipping, tucking, cutting, pasting, tugging, and yanking are the nature of retelling. In "The Shulamite's Lover and Her Brothers," I lifted passages from *The Song of Songs* in which the Lover and the Brothers speak, then modified and played with the literal translations I found in the King James Bible and in the translation from the Hebrew in S. Levanon's article "The Song of Songs: Translation and Notes."

Levanon describes the references by the lovers to myrrh "as a sachet … and a cluster of henna lodging between her breasts. This imagery, of course, reflects the well-known practice of women wearing sachets of spices between their breasts." The lover's "spices" ardently encounter her myrrh.

In *A Miniature Anthology of Medieval Hebrew Love Poems*, Raymond P. Scheindlin notes that, during the Golden Age of Moorish Spain, the "love poets' practice of referring to the beloved by stock pet names such as 'fawn' or 'gazelle' arose out of the need to protect the beloved from the social harm that exposure of the affair might bring upon her..." He adds that "various words for deer are used in *The Song of Songs* and Proverbs as figures of speech connected with lovers … are very common in Arabic poetry, and … found in Greek and medieval Latin."

In a time and place when shepherding, farming, hunting, and close observation of the natural world were dominant, it seems quite natural, too, that comparisons of the beloved's attributes would be made to goats or sheep or wild animals, as well fruits or wildflowers.

In the biblical *Song of Songs*, the voice of the Lover is heard in lines 1:8 9–11, 2:2 14, 4:12 16, 5:1, 6:4 5–9 and 8:13. The lines spoken by the Brothers are found in 8:8 9.

***

"Shirin and Khusraw" (pp. 111–145) is based on the stormy romance of the last significant Persian Sasanian monarch, Khusraw II (590 to 628 CE) and Shirin, likely fictional. Yet according to literary tradition, the first Persian love poems were engraved on the walls of Shirin's palace.

The engineer Farhad, the musicians Barbad and Nikisa, and even Khusraw's superb horse Shabdiz, have historical basis. Shapur is presumably imaginary. Because Nizami's lovely, elastic account lends itself readily to any sort of reshaping, I made Shapur a central character and the narrator.

In less than a century after Khusraw II's death, an Arab poet first wrote of the affair. Since then, right into modern times, Khusraw and Shirin (and the sub-story of Farhad and Shirin) have been the subjects of numerous works of Persian and Turkish literature, stage and shadow puppet dramas, and even a magnificent film, *Shirin*, created in 2008 by Iranian filmmaker Abbas Kiarostami, comprised entirely of close-up shots of women's faces as they watch a movie of the Khusraw and Shirin love story, overlaid with narrative and dialogue. I thank Ashraf Zahedi for introducing me to the film, which I loved and have watched numerous times.

Ferdowsi chronicles Shirin in the *Shahnameh* as the king's commoner mistress. I have followed Nizami, who portrays her as a crown princess of Armenia, although she has also been claimed by Syria and Khuzestan (situated in southwest Iran and sometimes called the Land of Palms). Nizami is said to have modeled Shirin after his Armenian wife, Afaq. He wrote the tale to express his happiness at their marriage, thus making this a love story within a love story.

In *Scheherazade Goes West,* Fatema Mernissi reminds us that, like so many of the heroines portrayed in *The Jewel and the Ember,* Shirin is no shrinking violet, waiting passively behind her veil for her man to appear. Instead, she gets on her horse and rides after him all alone into unknown territory.

But why does she tolerate Khusraw's weak character and bad behavior? (It's common knowledge that women throughout the ages have fallen in love with and tried to save "bad boys.") The Russian scholar E.E. Bertels suggests that Shirin's strength is manifested in her absolute conviction that he will come through, he will measure up to the man she has imagined.

And he does. She succeeds. Despite disappointments, one aggravation after another, and a "bare bodkin" finale, "Khusraw and Shirin" is not a tragedy but a story of love's triumph.

"Maiden in Distress" is a classic Mullah Nasruddin ditty.

Mullah Nasruddin, sometimes called the Khoja, is a trickster character known throughout the Muslim world. All cultures have tricksters who are alternately trouble- and peacemakers, whose antics attack institutions and offer insight into human behavior. The mullah is a Muslim cleric, and like Roman Catholic jokes about priests and nuns or Jewish jokes about the rabbi, stories of Mullah Nasruddin provide a humorous outlet for the community from the sternness of religion.

***

"Tahmina, Rustam, and Sohrab" (pp. 147–153), and the brief romance of Rustam and Tahmina that initiates the unwitting filicide, comes from *The Epic of Kings,* the *Shanameh* of Ferdawsi. It is an archetypal legend, reminiscent of, among others, the tale of Cú Chulainn, the Irish hero known as the Hound of Ulster, who meets Conla, the son he does not know, on the battlefield and kills him.

The English poet Matthew Arnold (1822–1888) told the story in his 1853 "Sohrab and Rustum" and I have interjected three lines from that poem into this version. I also added elements from *A Collection of Afghan Legends*, published in Kabul in 1970 and 1972 (before the 1979 Soviet invasion) by Barrett Parker and Ahmad Javid.

Tales of Rustam are placed throughout ancient Zoroastrian Persia and Central Asia, even occasionally in Arabia. The Takht-i-Rustam, or Rustam's Throne, in northern Afghanistan's Samangan province is said to be where the hero celebrated his marriage to Tahmina. During the Kushan Empire (first century CE), Buddhism was practiced throughout much of the land. Takht-i-Rustam is a stupa-monastery complex, caves carved from bedrock. A stupa is a mound-like structure, where Buddhists hold sacred relics. The monastery at Takht-i-Rustam consists of five chambers, including a sanctuary with a domed ceiling featuring an elaborate lotus leaf carving. The stupa on which Rustam and his companions must have balanced precariously, drunk or sober, sits on an adjacent hill.

"The Stone Bride and Stone Groom" is not a poem, but a short, poetic folktale from Afghanistan. It takes its imagery and action from the country's rough and rugged mountains. It is said that the Imam Ali, son-in-law of the Prophet Muhammad, rode across the terrain and that the striations of the Afghan hills and its deep valleys are the footsteps of his horse. Alas, I chose this story in part to honor the many brides and grooms whose weddings have been destroyed and lives taken by bombs during the years of foreign occupation from 1979 to 2021.

***

"Vis and Ramin" (pp. 155–185), composed between 1040 and 1054 CE by the Persian poet Fakhruddin As'ad Gurgani, is set in Zoroastrian Persia, and is one of the world's great love stories. The tale may be grounded in actual events in the pre-Islamic Persian Parthian dynasty (247 to 22 BCE) and may be one of the earliest Persian romantic epics.

In retelling this story—and abridging it by hundreds of pages—I tried to preserve elements of Gurgani's ornamental language and some of the "codes" embedded in it: for example, the moon is a metaphor for a beautiful woman and cheeks described as any variation on yellow (saffron, gold) indicate age, ill health, or depression. There are many garden and nature similes. As in "The Seven Princesses," a fate laid out by the stars is unavoidable; astrology is one of the story's guiding forces.

Throughout the ages, *Vis and Ramin* has had huge influence on Persian poets. Today, the couple even has a Facebook page.

Vis and Ramin is thought to be the model for the European tale *Tristan and Isolde,* first put to paper by Gottfried von Strassburg in the early thirteenth century. It may be that the Arab *trobar*s in Moorish Spain passed the tale to French troubadours, who carried it into Christian Europe.

There are undeniable parallels.

Tristan and Ramin are both musicians. Each falls in love with the young bride of an old king, and this love proves to be irresistible, passionate, and destructive. Isolde and Vis each have nurses who are instrumental in helping their fates along with sorcery. Both couples escape for a time to live blissfully in the wilderness. Ramin and Tristan lose faith and briefly betray Vis and Isolde with wives who in some way resemble them.

There are also similarities between "Vis and Ramin" and "Khusraw and Shirin": the old woman who takes the place of the bride in bed with an old, impotent king (Moubad) or who does so to "punish" the wildly inebriated young bridegroom (Khusraw), and the young lovers' infidelities (Khusraw and Ramin) by marrying others while their devoted paramours waited. In both tales, when the couples finally marry, they are united far into old age.

George Morrison notes in his 1972 translation that by marrying Vis to her brother Viru, Gurgani may have been reflecting the belief, apparently spread by the Greek historian Herodotus, that consanguineous marriages were common among ancient Zoroastrian Persians. But according to Jamshid Cawasji Katrak in his defense of old Zoroastrian practices, *Marriage in Ancient Iran,* this is untrue. Certainly today, Zoroastrians practice monogamy.

In Gurgani's version of this tale, the nurse is unnamed. I thank Wahid Omar for kindly loaning me that of his own nurse in Afghanistan, a storyteller named Bibi Shirin.

"Selected Sagacities" is a montage extracted directly from Gurgani's tale of Vis and Ramin.

Isaac Ibn Khalfon (I skip like a gazelle…) was among the earliest of the Jewish poets in Spain (ninth century CE). He was distinguished by the scholastic correctness of his versification.

***

"Miqdad and Mayasa" (pp. 187–203) was gathered from Alice Werner's *The Story of Miqdad and Mayasa from the Swahili-Arabic Text* and Jan Knappert's *Islamic Legends: Histories of the Heroes, Saints and Prophets of Islam.*

"Perhaps no hero represents the Islamization of the pre-Islamic Bedouin ideal better than Miqdad, the Mikidadi of two popular Swahili epics," John Renard writes in *Islam and the Heroic Image*. In stories beyond the one in this book, which is limited to the hero's love affair with Mayasa, "Miqdad," Renard writes, "plays a swashbuckling hybrid of Robin Hood and D'Artagnan, who appears out of nowhere when the last strand of hope seems stretched to the breaking point."

The terrible incident of wrapping Miqdad in an animal skin to roast him recalls an actual fate that befell a brother of Aisha bint Abu Bakr, one of the wives of the Prophet.

By inserting what may appear to be non sequiturs where Miqdad interacts with figures from the pantheon of the Prophet Muhammad's Companions, I have tried to mirror how, as Renard notes, Miqdad "clearly exhibits qualities of the folk hero translated into religious terms. In instances such as this, the Islamization of the hero-type does not occur at the expense of the hero's folk qualities."

The untitled poem (Oh she—she wanted...) by Ibn Farag al-Gayyani has a beautiful, chaste, contemplative yet ironic ambience. Al-Gayyani was a poet of Al-Andalus during the Emirate and Caliphate period of 756 to 1020 CE and was the author of a lost *Kitab al-Hada'iq,* or *Book of the Gardens.* He died in prison in 970 CE, where he was placed by the Andalusian Umayyad ruler al-Hakam II (961–976 CE) for excessive wine drinking. Al-Hakam found alcohol so abhorrent, he proposed to destroy all the vineyards in his realm.

Of Ecclesiastics 7:10 (God, eat your bread with pleasure...), Chana and Ariel Bloch write in *The Song of Songs: A New Translation* that the speaker "sees love as God-given consolation for the dreariness of existence."

***

My telling of **"Antar and Abla"** (pp. 205–228) is a drop—but a vital drop—in the massively popular romance *Sirat Antar*. This triumphant saga of a Black man's rise from slavery is "the closest thing to an Arabian national epic," Renard writes in *Islam and the Heroic Image*. Today, in the Middle East, "glass painted images of Antar and Abla are still popular ... along with printed pictures in comic-book style."

The legends of Antar ibn Shaddad are among the oldest surviving Arabic epics. They are still told in coffeehouses throughout the Middle East, and storytellers inevitably embroider extravagantly. The *Sirat Antar* "includes traditions from at least seven, and possibly as many as twelve, centuries," Renard tells us. "In over thirty volumes, the work came to embrace pre-Islamic Arabian material ... Islamic stories ... Persian features ... Christian material relating to the Crusades, and folkloric themes."

In addition to his physical prowess, Antar was a poet, the author of one of the seven "Golden Odes" of pre-Islamic Arabia. His renown was so great, the Prophet Muhammad said he wished that he could have known Antar and directed parents to tell their children of the Antar traditions.

Antar's love for Abla is an intense focus within the saga from its beginning. She is love as creative force, inspiring Antar to come into his own, reject bigotry, and demand his paternity. But as the long legend continues, Abla appears and recedes like a dream-wraith.

Antar—according to Ben Harris McClary, in his 1981 introduction to Terrick Hamilton's 1819 partial translation of the epic—"was indeed the

true prototype of the Knights errant of [Europe's] own Age of Chivalry." The legendary death scene of the eleventh-century Spanish knight known as El Cid (al-Sayyid) from *The Song of the Cid* (*Poema del Cid* or *Cantar del Mio Cid*), in which his corpse is propped on his horse to lead his men against the Moors, is thought by some to be derivative of the death scene of Antar.

Very little of the *Sirat Antar* has been translated into English. There are partial translations into Danish, French, and Russian. The Antar epic inspired operas, dramas, and even Rimsky-Korsakov's Antar Symphonic Suite in Opus 9. Indeed, *Sirat Antar* was in vogue among Orientalists at the turn of the twentieth century into the 1920s, and again for a while in the 1950s.

Perhaps too busy with his huge *The Book of the Thousand Nights and a Night,* Richard Francis Burton did not translate the *Sirat Antar,* but he admired its "true chivalric spirit."

"And why," he wrote, "does the 'knight of knights' love Abla? Because 'she is blooming as the sun at dawn, with hair black as the midnight shades, with Paradise in her eyes, her bosom an enchantment and a form waving like the tamarisk when the soft wind blows from the hills of Nijd'? Yes! But his chest expands also with the thoughts of her 'faith, purity and affection'—it is her formal as well as her material excellence that makes her the hero's 'hope, and hearing, and sight.' Briefly, in Antar I discern 'a love exalted high, by all the glow of chivalry.'

"The true children of Antar," Burton concluded, "... have *not* 'ceased to be gentlemen.'"

For gentlemen (and ladies), sensual beauty was kept virtuous through faith and purity—these are certainly expressions of European ideals, especially during the Victorian era. Yet Renard points out that Antar is an example of the Bedouin ideal. He triumphs over trial after trial, finally wins the hand of Abla, and overcomes the prejudices against him for his Blackness.

Abla and Antar have no children. She remarries after his death, but the story goes that she spoke so often of Antar and so frequently told her new husband how he did not measure up, he finally killed her.

"Antar and Abla" was, for me, the most difficult retelling in this book; I found its length and detours incredibly daunting. I was driven back to the keyboard—and the "delete" key—more times than I care to remember. I had to leave out fascinating elements of Antar's story. Uncovering Abla as an active Self, peeling away passivity (she is unlike others of Antar's women, who I did not include), could be wearisome, particularly after Antar finally wins her and she disappears for lengthy periods of time.

I worked with Hamilton's *Antar: A Bedoueen Romance* (which takes us at least through the beginning of Antar's legend and his courtship of Abla), H.T. Norris's *The Adventures of Antar*, chronicling Antar's later adventures in Ethiopia, including many of the hero's romantic escapades, and Peter Heath's *The Thirsty Sword: Sirat Antar and the Arab Popular Epic.*

My solution for the "problem" of Abla was to approach her as something of a dream figure. Dreams are customary in popular and courtly romances (for example, the dream of Khusraw Parviz in which his grandfather comes to bestow upon him a woman, a horse, and a throne). Dreams perform several functions, Renard says, "to articulate motives for a new action, to warn in time to avert disaster, or to provide instructions on proper action."

In dream, or *as* dream, Abla can assert her power and manifest the strength and autonomy she is otherwise denied by father, brother, tribal custom, and later, sadly, by the myriad tellers of the legends of Antar.

The true soul, and thus true love, exists, after all, most vividly in dream.

Acknowledgements

The thank-you-deeply portion of a book is always difficult, for there's a chance of forgetting someone without whom life and work would be so much poorer.

I am lucky to have a close cadre of friends, family, and colleagues who stand by me from book to book and project to project, keep me going, keep me steady, keep me inspired and sane (and I hope occasionally I do a little something for them). Friends, family, counselors, and colleagues such as Karen Leggett Abouraya, Reed Bye, Christopher Collom, Felicia Furman, Ellen Geiger, Bernice Hill, Shireen Malik, Clara Redmond, Rickie Solinger, Mary Tuma, Beth Wald, Victoria Watson, Andrew Wille, Ashraf Zahedi.

Massive gratitude to my editors, Michel Moushabeck and David Klein at Interlink. And there are more, who have given me wonderful help, inspiration, and encouragement.

My children and grandchildren. Always and ever. My late husband Jack Collom offered me unwavering support, patience, and love.

I thank my dear friend Nan De Grove for her counsel about Zoroastrian astrology. I thank my dear friend Wahid Omar—to whom, with his wife Soraya, this book is dedicated—for showing me the story of Vis and Ramin and for lending me Bibi Shirin, the name of his own nurse, a storyteller from his childhood in Afghanistan, since the nurse in Gurgani's version is nameless.

I thank Betsy Tobin for the wonderful collaboration that brought some of these tales to life in our 2000 Now or Never Theatre theatrical productions of *There Was and There Was Not: Wonder Tales of the Islamic World.*

How do I express my appreciation for the people whose histories and cultures, arts, and letters have offered me a consuming passion, a mission—and thus a life worth living.

There are others, of course, to whom I owe thanks. I send you my best wishes for prosperity and the hope that in understanding one another, we may all find common ground … love … beauty … and peace.

Bibliography

Abdulaali, Wafaa. "*Echoes of a Legendary Queen: Contemporary women writers revise and recreate Sheba/Bilqis.*" (Cambridge, MA: Harvard Divinity Bulletin, 2012). https://bulletin.hds.harvard.edu/echoes-of-a-legendary-queen/

Ahmad, Aisha and Roger Boase. *Pashtun Tales: From the Pakistan-Afghan Frontier*. (London: Saqi Books, 2003).

Augustine, St. *City of God*. (New York: Penguin Classics, 1984).

Ausubel, Nathan, ed. *A Treasury of Jewish Folklore*. (New York: Bantam Books, 1980)

Bloch, Ariel and Chana Bloch. *The Song of Songs: A New Translation*. (New York: Random House, 1995).

Bournoutian, George A. *A History of the Armenian People, vol. I: Pre-History to 1500 AD.* (Costa Mesa, CA: Mazda Publishers, 1993).

Bowen, John Charles Edward. *The Golden Pomegranate: A Selection from the Poetry of the Mogul Empire in India 1526–1858.* (London: John Baker, 1966).

Burton, Richard Francis, trans. *The Book of the Thousand Nights and a Night: A Plain and Literal Translation of the Arabia Nights Entertainments*, Vol. 1-6. (New York: The Heritage Press, 1962).

Bushnaq, Inea, ed. *Arab Folktales.* (New York: Pantheon Books, 1986).

Camp, Claudia V. "Abishag: Bible," *The Shalvi/Hyman Encyclopedia of Jewish Women*. https://jwa.org/encyclopedia/article/abishag-bible

Capellanus, Andreas, Perry, John Jay, trans. *The Art of Courtly Love.* (New York: Columbia University Press, 1941).

Chandler Leon, Shana. "The Deep Meaning of the Torah's First Great Love Story," *The Jewish News of Northern California*, November 21, 2019. https://www.jweekly.com/2019/11/21/the-deep-meaning-in-the-torahs-first-great-love-story/

Chelkowski, Peter J. *Mirror of the Invisible World: Tales from the Khamseh of Nizami.* (New York: Metropolitan Museum of Art, 1975).

Corrigan, John, Frederick R. Denny, Carlos M.N. Eire, and Martin S. Jaffee. *Jews, Christians, Muslims: A Comparative Introduction to Monotheistic Religions*. (Upper Saddle River, NJ: Prentice Hall, 1994).

De Grove, Nan. *The Beginner's Guide to Astrology.* CD. (Boulder, CO: Sounds True, 2004).

Elmaliki, Menal. "The Queen of Sheba in Pop Culture: Her Origins and Influence." https://www.arabamerica.com/the-queen-of-sheba-in-pop-culture-her-origins-influence/

Esposito, John L. *The Oxford Dictionary of Islam.* (Oxford: Oxford University Press, 2003).

Etheridge, John Wesley. *Jerusalem and Tiberias; Sora and Cordova: A Survey of Religious and Scholastic Learning of the Jews, Designed as an Introduction to the Study of Hebrew Literature*. (London: Forgotten Books, 2018)

Ferdowsi, Abolqasm, Ahmad Sadri, trans. *Shahnameh: The Epic of Persian Kings.* (New York: Liveright Publishing, n.d.)

Franzen, Cola, trans. *The Poems of Arab Andalusia.* (San Francisco: City Lights Books, 1989).

Garnett, Lucy. *The Women of Turkey and Their Folklore, The Jewish and Moslem Women.* Vol. II, (London: David Nutt, 1891).

Gelpke, Rudolf, trans. *The Story of Layla and Majnun, by Nizami,* (New Lebanon, NY: Omega Publications, 1997).

Gibb, Sir Hamilton. *Arabic Literature: An Introduction.* (London: Clarendon Press, 1926).

Handal, Nathalie, ed. *The Poetry of Arab Women: A Contemporary Anthology.* (New York: Interlink Books, 2001).

Hamilton, Terrick. *Antar: A Bedoueen Romance (1819)*, (Delmar, NY: Scholars, Facsimiles & Reprints, 1981).

Heath, Jennifer. *The Scimitar and the Veil: Extraordinary Women of Islam.* (Mahwah, NJ: Paulist Press/ HiddenSpring, 2004).

__________, ed. *The Veil: Women Writers on Its History, Lore, and Politics.* (Berkeley: University of California Press, 2008).

Heath, Peter. *The Thirsty Sword: Sirat Antar and the Arabian Popular Epic.* (Salt Lake City: University of Utah Press, 1996).

Horne, Charles F., ed. *The Sacred Books and Early Literature of the East.* (New York: Parke, Austin & Lipscomb, 1917).

Kabbani, Rana. *Imperial Fictions: Europe's Myths of Orient.* (London: HarperCollins Publishers, 1988).

Kadari, Tamar. "Queen of Sheba: Midrash and Aggadah." *The Shalvi/Hyman Encyclopedia of Jewish Women.* https://jwa.org/encyclopedia/author/kadari-tamar

Katrak, Jamshed Cawasji. *Marriage in Ancient Iran.* (Bombay: Godrej Memorial Printing Press, 1965).

Knappert, Jan. *Islamic Legends: Histories of the Heroes, Saints and Prophets of Islam,* Vols. 1 and 2. (Leiden, The Netherlands: E.J. Brill, 1985).

Levy, Reuben, trans. *The Epic of Kings, Shah-nama, the National Epic of Persia by Ferdowsi.* (Costa Mesa, CA: Mazda Publishers, 1996).

Levanon, S. *The Song of Songs: Translation and Notes.* https://faculty.washington.edu/snoegel/PDFs/articles/Song%20of%20Songs%20Translation.pdf

Lewis, Geoffrey, trans. *The Book of Dede Korkut.* (London: Penguin Classics, 1974).

Lyall, Charles James. *Translations of Ancient Arabian Poetry: chiefly pre-Islamic poetry with introduction and notes.* (Westport, CT: Hyperion Press, 1981).

Mann, Vivian B., et al., eds. *Convivencia: Jews, Muslims, and Christians in Medieval Spain.* (New York: George Braziller, 1992).

Menocal, María Rosa. *Shards of Love: Exile and the Origins of the Lyric.* (Durham, NC: Duke University Press, 1994).

____________. *The Ornament of the World: How Muslims, Jews, and Christians Created a Culture of Tolerance in Medieval Spain.* (New York: Little Brown and Company, 2002).

Mernissi, Fatima. *Dreams of Trespass: Tales of a Harem Girlhood.* (Cambridge: Perseus Books, 1994).

___________. *Scheherazade Goes West: Different Cultures, Different Harems.* (New York: Washington Square Press, 2001).

Minorsky, V. *Iranica,* Vol. 775. (Tehran: University of Tehran Publications, 1994)

Modi, Jivanji. *The Religious Ceremonies and Customs of the Parsees.* (Bombay: privately published,1922).

Morrison, George, trans. *Vis and Ramin: Translated from the Persian of Fakhr ud-Din Gurgani.* (New York: Columbia University Press, 1972).

Norris, H.T., trans. "The Adventures of Antar." *Approaches to Arabic Literature, 3.* (Wilts, England: Ars & Phillips, Ltd., 1980).

Nykl, A.R. *Hispano-Arabic Poetry and Its Relations with the Old Provençal Troubadours.* (Baltimore: no publisher listed, 1946).

O'Grady, Desmond. *The Golden Odes of Love: Al-Muallaqat.* (Cairo: American University in Cairo Press, 1998).

Parker, Barrett and Ahmad Javid. *A Collection of Afghan Legends.* (Kabul, Afghanistan: Afghan Book, 1970).

Renard, John. *Islam and the Heroic Image: Themes in Literature and the Visual Arts.* (Macon, GA: Mercer University Press, 1999).

Richmond, Diana. *'Antar and 'Abla: A Bedouin Romance.* (Boston: Charles River Books, 1978).

Seabrook, William B. *Adventures in Arabia: Among the Bedouins, Druses, Whirling Dervishes & Yezidee Devil Worshippers.* (New York: Harcourt Brace, 1927).

Shaheen, Jack G. *Reel Bad Arabs: How Hollywood Vilifies a People*. (New York: Interlink Publishing, 2001).

Scheindlin, Raymond. *A Miniature Anthology of Medieval Hebrew Love Poems* (Bloomington: Indiana University Press, 1985)

Schjeldahl, Peter. *Columns & Catalogues.* (Great Barrington, MA.: The Figures, 1994).

Schimmel, Annemarie. *The Mystery of Numbers.* (Oxford: Oxford University Press, 1993).

________________. *Deciphering the Signs of God: A Phenomenological Approach to Islam.* (Albany, N.Y., State University of New York Press, 1994).

________________. *My Soul Is a Woman: The Feminine in Islam.* (New York: The Continuum Publishing Co., 1999).

Shah, Idries. *Caravan of Dreams.* (London: The Octagon Press, 1968).

Shulman, Temina Goldberg. "A Love Triangle for the Ages," *The New York Jewish Week*, October 24, 2017. https://jewishweek.timesofisrael.com/a-love-triangle-for-the-ages/

Simpson, Mariana Shreve. *Persian Poetry, Painting and Patronage: Illustrations in a Sixteenth-Century Masterpiece,* Freer Gallery of Art, Smithsonian Institution, (New Haven: Yale University Press, 1998).

Taylor, Samuel M. "Joseph and Yusuf: Comparing Narratives of Genesis and the Quran," *Through the Needle's Eyes: Religion, Politics and Society*. December 17, 2012. https://throughtheneedleseye.wordpress.com/category/islam/

Von Strassbourge, Gottfried, trans., A.T. Hatto. *Tristan.* (London: Penguin, 1960).

Walther, Wiebke. *Women in Islam.* (New York: Markus Wiener Publishing, 1993).

Wilson, C.E. trans. *Nizami: The Haft Paikar (The Seven Beauties): Contains the Life and Adventures of King Bahram Gur and the Seven Stories Told Him by His Seven Queens,* Vol 1., (London: Probsthain & Co., 1924).

Yegenoglu, Meyda. *Colonial Fantasies: Towards a Feminist Reading of Orientalism.* (Cambridge: Cambridge University Press, 1998).